I CAN'T HEAR
THE DRUMS ANYMORE

Fragments from Life

BY
HOWELL HURST
© 2018

I Can't Hear
The Drums Anymore

Published by Howell Hurst
2443 Fillmore, 380-7019
San Francisco, CA 94115
www.howellhurst.com

ISBN NUMBER: 978-0-692-07179-3

All cover design concepts and copy are by Howell Hurst
Digital Graphic Production by Richard O'Brien
Printed in the USA

Also Available by Howell Hurst

Subterfuge
*A novel of crime, espionage,
and political intrigue.*

Preview at www.howellhurst.com
or at Amazon books

Contents

For
Jamie

Beating Toward Monterey

We are on a starboard tack, the water is kicking up over the bow, and I am fretting about whether we will make it into port or have to continue bucking the waves all night. It has been blustery ever since we came out of the Panama Canal into the Pacific Ocean. We've been combating the coastal winds several days now. John and Robert are sleeping and I am at the helm. It is about three in the morning and the moon has poked through a mass of clouds and lighted one broad acre of round, flat ocean like a snow covered back yard. I pulled past it about thirty minutes ago off to starboard. My compass heading is short about ten degrees of magnetic north and Big Sur lies off to the right.

Bob is snoring. John sleeps quietly. I think about Robbie and wonder how she is doing three thousand miles away in Florida. And Kathleen, wherever she is, how she is doing, and what it will be like when my sleepers and I finally sail into Monterey Bay and anchor out for a week to enjoy the town. To port, about thirty degrees off north, a bit forward, about a fifth of the way up into the sky, is a big, bright star blinking. I wonder if it is really a giant mass of burning gases as I hear suns are, or maybe only an electronic satellite. I can't figure out how to tell the difference, so I just look at the blinking until I stop thinking about it.

Aft and starboard, a couple of hundred yards off the Big Sur coast, I earlier heard sea lions barking from rocks where they were resting. Now, they have gotten quiet. It is very quiet out on the ocean except for the splash of the water. The wind is about thirty-five knots in our face, which is a fair blow. Swells are coming in every ten to twelve seconds, and as we plunge through them the salt water splits over the bow, comes down across the deck; some runs out the scuppers, and a good chunk makes its way occasionally into the cockpit with me. I have on my foul weather gear, including a wool stocking cap and my knee length boots. I am dry and warm and comfortable.

It is good being alone in the boat, with Bob and John sleeping: to be able to think about Robbie and Kathleen three thousand miles off. I wonder if I had the chance to do it over again would I have the sense to do it right. I first saw Robbie when I was holding a trombone in junior high school. She walked into the band room in a tight red, white, and blue knit, sleeveless sweater and my heart dropped into my pants. I shouldn't say it that way; it wasn't sexual. It was just that she looked so good and lean and she had such pretty high, taut breasts; and that perky, lean nose; and that sharply outlined mouth, she had it too. No doubt about it. She was the first love of my life.

Now, sitting in the sloop in the Pacific Ocean, beating north against a thirty-five knot wind, it is finally clear she was the last love of my life. Which I guess is to say the only love of my life, actually the best thing I ever did, but blew bad, really bad. That part is the worst thing I ever did. I try to remember the first time we made love together, but I can't. What I can remember is how afraid I always was that I was inadequate for her, not sexually, but in my mind. What I mean to say is that my mind would not be strong enough for her. You see, I couldn't keep up with her when she talked about literature, which was her first love. What *were* metaphors and things like that? How did a second meaning slip into a story of cows that meant the writer was really talking about nature, or religion, or some other complex idea? That kind of thing was always running through my mind when we made love. What would I do when we were through feeling each other's body? How would I react when she talked about a metaphor over coffee in the cafeteria next day after we made love and her lips trembled?

You see, when she would kiss me, her lips trembled as she did it. I wondered what was that? Was something the matter with how I kissed? The trembling was unique. I liked it very much. I'd kissed a lot of women in my life, but none of their lips had ever trembled when kissing me. What could it mean? I think I know now. I think it meant she loved me and that the trembling was her emotions all bunched up together. I think it meant she was yearning for me to love her too and that was enough, she didn't care whether I knew what a metaphor was. If so, why didn't I understand the trembling? I felt in the back of my mind that it was something terribly special that she was offering me, something uniquely hers that she wanted to make mine also. I think she wanted my lips to tremble back. That's what I think now. I didn't know what to think then.

And Kathleen, the daughter we had a year after being married. It was bad the way that happened. We were drunk one night. We'd been to a party at her English professor's house near the fort where I was in infantry boot camp, and I didn't use any caution; neither did she. It was three months after we'd been married, and it was two months after I'd taken the airline stewardess, who'd served us on our flight to Kansas City on our honeymoon, out into the park and made love to her on the grass under the swings. I tried to figure out for a long time why it went that way. I even spent eighteen months in the Veteran Administration's psychological counseling program looking for an answer, and the best they could come up with was I hated my father because he was a mean son of a bitch, and so I slept with other women to show him I was independent, and that hurt Robbie, and it hurt Kathleen, and it hurt me, and I guess sometimes that's just the way things are and it's too late to do anything about it now but accept it. All I remember was that with the stewardess I didn't have to figure out what trembling lips were about, because her lips didn't tremble. She just got into the grass with me and it was all so mindlessly simple.

"Hey, how are things?"

That's John yelling up at me from below.

"Everything's fine."

"What're you doing?"

"Just thinking."

"What about?"

"Just about the water. Go back to sleep."

"You sure?"

"Yeah. I'm sure."

"You don't need any help?"

'No."

"OK."

John is quiet again now, and so is Bob, and so are the seals. I can still hear the wind and feel the waves, though; they're very strong winds and waves. I bet you know what I mean. I'm sure you do. Things that happened to you when you were first young and you didn't know what they were until years later. Those that hurt, mostly, are most important I think. They're the teachers. And I think the questions are more important than the answers, maybe. It's like figuring out what a metaphor is, you know? You can't learn that out of a book. It comes from living one until it gets inside your skin and you don't have to think about it to know what it is.

The moon just picked up another spot off to starboard. This one is also about an acre or two in size, flat and calm. It looks like snow on a back yard too. Strange how the ocean works that way at night. There can be swells coming in, but someplace, for some reason, there'll be a flat piece of water that catches the moon and comes up into your eyes like it had some kind of meaning to it. The stars are that way too. Clouds aren't. They're just there, white and milky, with no meaning. But the stars, the sharp stars coming out of millions of miles and light years out in the heavens down to you, and the moon landing from two hundred and fifty thousand miles away on a little acre patch of flat ocean, and lighting it like snow on a back yard. These have some sort of meaning.

I wish I knew what it was.

Bogart, Where Were You
When I Needed You?

S he looked like Lauren Bacall. Medium long straight hair, lean-lined leathery face, a good looking woman, adult carriage, taut lips like when Lauren sat across from Bogey, inwardly silent, strengthening him for his trip into the next room to knock the socks off some schlumpf. Like Lauren, quietly stood her ground, legs bracing beautifully the deck of the old refurbished tugboat rocking freely in the Caribbean waves. Alive it was on the waves, calypso band jamming, gin and rum and beer pouring free from the bar, the smell of reefer floating over everyone like a benediction; black and white people dancing, their flesh flashing in the moonlight, much rum and gin and beer, cool people real gone, long gone downtown Saturday night local cruise line, *The Bajun Queen,* a giant old ocean tug, with fish smells from having been long gone down to the sea in Barbados.

A well built woman, small to medium stature with firm, high, conservative breasts, legs as beautiful as a race horse's, moreso, more beautiful, no giggles, no silly banter, straight talk, adult, no girl, a grown woman. The first talk, the introduction, the innocent conversation, I liking her immediately, her holding pattern flexible to my words, not belligerent or competitive, the waves rocking us on the boat, and the band blaring. Good music. Good looking woman. The same quiet Bacall voice, head down, looking up at me from downcast

eyes, like looking through Venetian blinds, her hand thrust
through her hair, sexy, knew what she was doing
Refusing to eat with me at first.
"The lines are too long," she said.
This her first line of defense for me to penetrate. Persis-
tent, I countering her talk about "I can't stand to wait in lines."
"Me too," I said, "especially to eat."
We talked some more. She looked around, seeking Mr.
Right, I thought. Leaning in toward me, she said,
"I want another drink."
And she sighed slightly as *the first touch* she leaned
against me. She was Canadian, Toronto business manager of
a video company, cool, contained, crisp, with the touch of a
smile coming on as she talked of editing and creating, and how
difficult artists are. She kept her corporate side muted all the
while with her entanglingly deadly smile and her reef teeth,
while we glided gracefully to the bar and ordered, and I met
her friends. A tour group, thirty in a hotel, but not her, instead
sharing a cottage with two men, her own room, independent;
and the toss of her lean smile, me all the while for the thou-
sandth time falling prey. Damned fool. When will I ever learn?
Once more the kind of woman I'd be proud to love. A strong
woman with her own career, no way for me to treat her like a
parrot in a cage. Too strong for that. I imagined not having to
eat suppers all alone, but with her, the old sharing thing. Dumb,
I suppose after so many years, seeking that simple, elusive
companion love.

Why? I wondering at the bar, this woman so pleasing me
with no exceptions, relaxing with me, loosening to me, letting me come into her cave, her abode, her safe house, guard
house, cathedral, whatever it is, wherever women go to before
they let you into them. What a damned fool I am. I know
them, especially Lauren Bacall types who look tough on the
outside and exude softness, who say with what seems to be

their soul, I could love you, you special man, hold the potential to have your child, to do the simple things, to share, to return to the days before school and growing up and work, to feel real again.

A damned fool I am. I know they want you to be aloof; show them you want them, but not too much, don't expose your needs, your desire to love, it's not manly, doesn't fit into their fantasies. A good looking woman, though, perfect mate for a man ready to settle into a soft routine of adventure mixed with love, a touch of domestic bliss.

What a damned fool I am.

We ate, waited in a short line, she stayed, didn't go to some other guy; but one came around now and again, one of the local roommates, tall, kind of wimpy, they didn't seem too close, right before my eyes, a big brother type. She stayed and talked and that was what counted. The good looking, smart, sophisticated wordly woman, and me, damned fool, falling again against the odds on a Caribbean cruise ship tightly circling the bay bathed by the Bajun moon. She played it well, lay back away from me, made me come to her, drew me in, the eyes down, the hand thrust upward boldly through her hair, the smile, the glance from the crisp, lean eyes, the aloof roof of her mind laid out like a rope to tug, a thug's weakness, a gun mall's soft side glidingly by me after dinner to the boat's stern deck where the band played.

"What do you do?" she asked as we danced.

"I'm a writer."

"Really?"

"I am more than a writer."

"What are you?" she asked.

"Don't laugh."

"No, I don't will not, laugh."

"Then," I said, "first, I am a thinker. I think slowly, long and carefully, like on little cat's paws."

She was onto me now. She knew. She'd tripped me up, trapped my me; and my game was off. A sap. What a damned sap. But I held on, oh did I not hold on, for was she not, yes she was, beautiful! Those legs. Trim waist, smile, hair blondly cascading over her downcast eyes, and me wanting her, imagining a flight from my home in Monterey to Toronto, a weekend in Canada, enticing her to Monterey, a horse ride to the wilds of Big Sur, the natural beauty of the dashing mountains, lone, grazing stallions on the bald mountain peaks' lower plateau, over the Pacific at Nepenthe's. Explaining my thoughts to her. A good looking woman. A woman a man could love. If she would let him.

Close now. We were a point of fact. And so we danced, at first only I dancing, she gone off inside herself some where away from us, escaped, a wounded lady slighted by some previous damned fool who had hurt her like I too had hurt other women. Then soon her reentry, hand to my elbow. My bare skin. And gently on my arm, softly, on my skin, relaxing to me. And here I should have been strong and held back, become too elusive for her to grasp so she would have been openly required to get to me, but I failed. Damned fool. I drew her close and held her close to me, her swaying hips, her high, taut breasts against my upper stomach. So tall I was over her, this beautiful woman, and I, in the West Indies foolishly falling. On a cruise ship. Summer. In the Caribbean.

Dancing now before the boat docked, ten or twelve dances, no one else cutting in, we alone, we danced. Lauren Bacall could not have been so fine. I was so proud the fault again to be with her. Afterward on the dock I lost all my cards, became lost, lost the advantage.

"Come meet me later with my friends," she said. "Don't come with me now. I'll find my way with them. Find yours. And meet me later. We'll be at the Carlisle Club. "

And I, damned fool, pushed it and blew it. It seems I blew it, she was so beautiful, my perfect woman once again.

"Let's go together," I said. "Why part? Why should we part?"

"Do part. Let me go," she said. "Come separately. I will be there. Don't push. Please, you are too persistent."

I wanting her, her closeness, her maturity, her adult self, so bad that I did push, and she gave in and we rode on a small mini bus together to the port gates, where her cool Canadian friends, who did not seem to find her overly beautiful, picked us up to drive us grandly to the Carlisle Club where we danced some more. But I had disturbed, it seems, the spell. Mad about her. I was mad about her. Outwardly I remained so calm; I willed calmness to divert her attention from my anxiety. We were alone again, not that wimpy guy, only she and I. I thought we had kept something. What a damned fool. We sat down and drank and talked. I took her to the disco room where the records were played for the dance floor. She thanked me and seemed to warm to me again. We stepped down to the beach to watch the band play. Abruptly, the lights flickered, filtered, then died. We were buried in darkness.

"The electricity is out! The power plant has broken," someone exclaimed.

No more music. She, feet naked in the sand, waiting while I ventured into the new darkness looking for matches or candles, seeking a solution, and on my return, found her…gone. I searched. Restroom. Bar. Hallway. Bar. Beach. Sand. Water. Bar. Dance floor. And there she was, undulating with some new guy, his bulging belly hanging limply over his belly. She finished with him like a quick beer, a good looking woman, and went to the ladies' room, then came down to me below where I waited, she now ready to go home, ready to rest, to sleep, perchance to dream.

"May I see you again?"

"I think not."

"Why?"

"I don't want to."

"The whole night. "We've spent the whole night," I said. "I like you. I want to know you. I really want to know you badly."

A ragged conversation.

"Why?"

"Because."

"Because why?"

"Because."

But never the real reason, hidden behind her downcast eyes, under the cascading blonde hair, I still lost in my damned foolishness; and then, he came, the wimpy one, and took her off into the night. Some bookish clerk, a stockbroker, a concrete salesman, I don't know what, his arm around her, she with him, and I abandoned. After all those hopeful hours. My hopes lost in a cloud of smoke from the leftover hangers on at the bar, outside in the warm Bajun Summer night.

Lauren Bacall from Canada. So fine, a damned fine looking woman.

But I, no Bogart. Not yet, anyway.

Taking Care Of Business

He was a large, black man. About six feet two, big shoulders, handsome, with penetrating eyes, not aggressive, but perceptive. He seemed to be judging whether I held an attitude toward him. His white wife followed him through the door of the Big Sur Pub, where I tended bar, carrying their beautiful beige daughter in her arms. They took the table to the right of the doorway, the one nearest the fireplace, and he picked up menus and, seeing our board on the wall, asked me if we had any darts.

I showed him the magnificent ones with the English flag feathers.

"These belong to the manager," I said. "Our house darts are all broken. He gave me explicit instructions not to let anyone use these. Be careful, will you?" I asked as I handed them to him. He smiled.

"Sure."

He played darts alone while his wife tried to cheer up their little girl. She seemed out of sorts at first, but under her mothers' persistent touch, she opened up and soon was laughing. He said they would order in a few minutes.

The bikers in their black leather riding gear ambled in about two minutes later. They were white, beige, red, a real mixture. The black guy glanced over at them and they looked back without any overt mutual communication. The first biker was at least six feet four inches, and looked like he'd be a tough basketball player. The others were smaller, but in their black pants and jackets looked mean enough. The bar air didn't register any contentious vibrations, and the black guy went on with his darts. The bikers continued a conversation they had brought in with them after getting off their black Harleys out in the parking lot. Everybody settled in quietly among the vague background sounds of the TV playing in the corner.

The dappled, old, pink-skinned couple did not enter as much as they materialized. Nothing particularly distinguished them except the age marks on their faces and hands. He was in his eighties. She too. They did not look around but kept that self-centered control that comes so naturally to older people. They were at home inside their own skin. They picked up the menu and looked at it intensely together for a long time, literally at least five minutes. It was as if they had to study every single word, perhaps every letter of the alphabet, to decide if they wanted to stay and eat.

Something in the menu finally appealed to them. They discussed it in more detail. I couldn't hear their words, but they must have speculated on the nuances of the Taquitos, or the potential richness of the Enchiladas. They conferred upon the Cheeseburger, perhaps, whether to have Coke or diet Coke or lemonade or root beer, I suppose. They seemed to make up their minds and together raised their heads to identify seats.

Then they saw the black and his family and the bikers.

Fear oozed from them like water from a reservoir whose gates have been slightly opened. They whispered into the menu as if it were a hymnal. Their eyes darted. Their lips fluttered. They did not leave the bar so much as they dematerialized, quietly, softly, as if they had never been there. I looked over at the black and the bikers. They had not even noticed the old couple had been in the room with them.

Walking up to the black's table, I nodded over at the bikers to indicate I would be with them shortly. They smiled their acknowledgment and continued their talk. "What'll it be?" I asked.

"My wife would like a salad, and I think I'll take a hamburger," he said. "The little one will eat out of ours. And a couple of Cokes, please."

"That it?"

"That'll do it."

"How'd you like the burger? Raw, medium, or fried to a crisp?"

"Medium rare possible?"

"We'll give it a try."

I walked into the darts' physical pathway without any immediate danger, since the black guy had given up his game of solitaire, aware that someday when I least expected it I would receive a sharp tang in the back of my neck indicating I'd been penetrated by one of the little spears. Would it be enough to kill me, I speculated? What was inside the back of a neck that could cause death? A major artery? Some obscure gland connected to a basic life support mechanism? A nerve that could unbalance one's mind?

The cook studied the order as if it were a problem in nuclear physics.

"What's the trouble?" I asked.

"Ah, shit, my wife is causing me pains. I think I'm going to leave her."

"All right with me so long's the burgers get cooked."

"Damn women!"

"Indeed," I said.

I poured the two Cokes from the automated liquid dispenser and delivered them to the black guy's table. His daughter squealed in festive delight at the sight of the Coca Cola. His wife gently restrained her groping fingers.

"Hey, you guy's able to keep it quiet?" one of the bikers barked.

The Black turned his head toward the bikers and immediately stood up and walked over to them. He stood looking down at them with both his hands in his pockets. They all looked up at him and seemed surprised he had reacted so instantly to their outspoken one's comment.

"You gonna say something?" the talkative biker said.

"You going to apologize?" the black guy said.

"You got a screw loose?" the biker answered.

"I don't know. I'll look if you don't answer me."

"Well, I'd look if I was you," the biker said. "Cause I ain't planning on answering no black faggot with a half breed kid, you dig?"

"Gosh, sir," the black said. "I didn't mean to offend you. I'll do that. I'll look to see if I've got a loose screw."

The biker glanced at his buddies, not showing he was surprised at the sudden fear he figured the black guy was showing him, and then grinned so wide it bared his gums. The grin evaporated when the black guy pulled a small automatic pistol from his pocket and pointed it neatly into the biker's face.

"You see any loose screws in this?" the Black asked.

The biker was speechless. The black guy cocked the hammer with his thumb.

"I asked you if you see any loose screws."

The biker's eyes dilated. From my position behind the bar I could see the pupils getting bigger. The rims of his eyelids seemed to pull back from the whites to give enough room to accommodate the pupils. The eyes' owner's hands rose up before his face and fluttered like they were trying to talk for him.

"Put your hands on the table, flat!"

The biker did so with a slap.

"Now, what we have here is not a failure to communicate," the black guy said. "This ain't Paul Newman in *Cool Hand Luke*. What we got is a dumb ass biker who hasn't ever run into an educated black man who doesn't like to be fucked with. What's going to happen is this. You and your friends are going to get up, and I am going to escort you to your bikes, and you are riding into the setting sun. Do it! Now!"

The bikers rose in unison, like a choir singing. They quietly marched outside with the black closely following, and got on their bikes and started them. The roar of the machines filled the parking lot. After motioning them to hold still, the Black pulled a cell phone from his pocket and dialed three digits. It took about thirty seconds before he spoke again. I had walked up close beside him.

"Please connect me to an officer," he said. "I have an emergency to report."

The bikers didn't move a muscle.

"Lieutenant. I'm Jonathon Barker. I'm at the Big Sur Pub and some big mean looking bikers have been threatening me and my wife. They're riding North on Highway One, back toward Carmel. I'm a Captain of L. A. P. D. Could you try to intersect them and deliver a lecture about courtesy to other races? Three black Harley's They're all in black. One's got red hair, one's bald. The other just looks generally sleazy. Yeah. I appreciate it. My cell's 310-Bad-Buck. Thanks. We'll be here eating another thirty or forty-five minutes. No, I didn't check ID's. All right. I'll tell them."

He hung up.

"Lieutenant says if you guys will ride quietly through Carmel and Monterey on toward San Jose or San Francisco, he'll stay in his office and finish his coffee. What do you say?"

The three bikers nodded and waited for permission to leave. The black guy gave them the nod. As he came back in with me to join his wife and daughter, he pulled his badge out and showed it to me.

"Sorry," he said.

"No problem," I said.

The two old people walked in then from the side door, the one off the hallway to the two bathrooms in the back.

"Hungry?" I asked.

"They gone?"

"Yes."

"Yes, we are hungry."

"You could of have eaten next door, you know," I said.

"We know. But we kind of wanted to see what the little girl is like. She's so cute."

"Well, sit down," I said. "And we'll all see how it plays out."

She ordered a Chicken Taquito and he an Enchilada. They both got a Corona with lime.

"What's her name?" the old woman asked.

"Margarita," said the black guy's wife.

"What a pretty name."

The black guy and his white wife and the old couple had a nice time playing with the little girl and eating and with me refilling their glasses with Coke and beer. I'd never served a black guy with a white wife and their kid having fun with two old white people before. It was a unique experience, I guess you would call it. And the bikers didn't come back, although I hadn't expected them.

Everybody left nice tips too.

The Fog

When the fog wraps itself around you in Monterey there is no describing it. Words fail. What can you say? I'm not even going to attempt it. There's a feeling, however, of safety in the Monterey fog. It's a gentle hugging by the elements. Cars emerge through it on the highway, slowly, in miniature traffic jams, dropping down off the mountain into Carmel Valley on the way to Big Sur. Going to work isn't a big deal in Monterey County; it's like the peeling of old paint off the walls: it just happens. It's something you do and you're glad you have the right to do it, that you're allowed, that it's permitted. Dropping into Carmel Valley, the road narrows and, unlike in Los Angeles, drivers don't battle to be first in line, but compete to give way one to another, like human beings in a time capsule where courtesy has been preserved as possessing value.

Ginger Patousky, a six foot three, two hundred twenty-six pound, blond entrepreneuress of Monterey's 'Valiant Effort' bookstore, guided her 2003 VW bug down the hill. As she passed Carmel Valley Road and curved off to the right, her eyes dropped to her lap. Her one hand, the one not on the steering wheel, lay placidly, its long, crimson fingernails neatly manicured and painted. It was a dainty little mitt that used to crash into line-backers when she was quarterback for a Southwestern university college team twenty years ago. That was before she discerned she was not really quarterback material. Her high, taut breasts might be manufactured, and her meaty arms and muscular back and legs might, from at least a half block away, look tough for such a dainty lady. She was in truth, however, an immensely sensitive soul with a heart of, if not gold, at least bronze. It would probably have been of gold but for the pain of being what she was, a pain she carried with delicate aplomb when dealing with others whose well-concealed disapproval she clearly recognized, but graciously ignored.

Her lapped hand reached into her purse, lying on its side in the navigator seat, and she plucked out a stick of Dentyne. She popped it into her mouth and began to chew. She turned on the radio, switched channels through several variations of the American theme, and settled in on a classical piece; it happened this morning to be Beethoven's violin concerto. She was concerned. Barry Barrigan, her boy friend, had not called as he promised, and she wondered if he had been successful or had failed. The silence implied failure. If not failure, it implied an obstacle had arisen in their joint project to adopt a child.

She had met Barry on the gridiron when he was line backer for a neighboring state's college. Their relationship hadn't developed quickly, but after three seasons between their sophomore and senior years, they had both noticed something across the scrimmage line: a non-competitive twinkle of the eyes. One day Barry had called to ask if she'd like to have a cup of coffee at Starbucks. He was in town to see a musical. And that's how it started.

The army had rejected both of them, and the navy, and the air force, so they were both free to pair up, which they did. To avoid complications with old teammates they figured would never understand, they had agreed to hide away on California's central coast. This had been going on now for seven years and, rather than slacking, it had become serious in both their minds as they learned to appreciate one another's more intriguing qualities. Yes, of course, sex had been there in the beginning, and remained, but the relationship was not about sex; the relationship was about things they had discovered were hard to find. Old fashioned things like caring, empathy, appreciation for one another's differences, resiliency, and patience. It was a good relationship. It developed love, kindness, and integrity. Neither was on the forefront of the sexual revolution. It was irrelevant to them whether they were married or not. They understood the obstacles in the world, and felt no need to take a public stand. Theirs was a quiet stance, not a defiant one.

Barry was smaller than Ginger, although she was the more assertive, the more masculine, if a term is needed.

"Big Patousky," Barry said, "you're my rosebud, my delicate rosebud."

"Oh, Barry," Patousky always murmered when he said such things. "Let me feel your muscle."

"You little witch, you," Barry said, and gave her a hug.

This is not a real moment we're talking about, not a specific moment, rather. It's a prototype of many moments they shared; it's a reaching out for a description so you may get some idea of them. Physical descriptions don't mean much. Patousky, as I commented, was a blond or, if I didn't say it I'll say it now: she was a blond. But that was a wig. She was really a brunette, more an auburn maned thing. Although big, she was still lean and muscular, her waist cinched in by a little girdle that made her hips and shoulders look larger, that gave her breasts some sense of credibility. Her teeth were even, but not exactly white, more like golden rod. She had lean ankles, had had when playing football, and they had grown leaner as she aged.

Barry was shorter by a few inches, broader, thicker, stockier. Flaming red headed, he had big ears that stuck out on either side, but not distastefully. He had big feet too, and big legs. His hands were lean and delicate, however. Sensitive hands. While Patousky tended her antique books every day, Barry was a lineman for the phone company, drove his truck all over

Monterey County, preparing phones for people as far away as Big Sur and, sometimes, when a local was missing with a cold or some other illness, in Gilroy, where he always enjoyed the deep whiff of garlic in the air.

Patousky checked her cell phone to make sure she hadn't missed a call. Barry was in San Francisco, where the adoption agency kept its office, and where various governmental bureaus maintained a presence.

This instant the phone rang. She hesitated, but quickly pressed the talk button.

"Yes."

"It's me, Babe."

"Yes."

"Ah…"

"Yes…?"

"Oh…"

"Yes…"

"It's no."

"No."

"Yes."

"Oh, well, we suspected, right?"

"We did."

"Where are you?"

"I'm halfway back on Highway One. I thought I'd take the slow way home, to think about it."

"Don't think too hard, darling."

"I'll try not to."

"Are you OK with it?"

"Hey, guy, we know the rules. We break the rules, we have to live with the rules."

"We could fight."

"Maybe, but not yet. Let's think about it."

"All right."

"You want me to pick up something on the way home?"

"Sure. A bottle of cheap champagne and a filet mignon. I'll fix us a super supper. A fixer upper."

"Of course."

"Love you."

"Love you too."

"Bye."

"Goodbye."

Patousky continued the drive on Highway One toward Big Sur. She had with her a signed copy of John Steinbeck's 'To A God Unknown,' which she was delivering to Patty Kowalsky, the ancient, invalid grandmother of Tommy Kowalsky, the young man from Seaside, who periodically bought books from her. It was a gift Granny wanted to give to Tommy on her ninetieth birthday. As she drove along, she came to the point where, off to her right and forward, sitting lonely on the coast, the navy lighthouse splashed a beam over the ocean. The air was clearing here, the fog lightening.

Barry returned to her thoughts, and she equated some-how their relationship to the lighthouse, and briefly wondered whether that made any sense, but then noticed as she drew closer to it, that the coastal mountains obscured the island, which – slice by slice – began to recede. The thought of Barry faded too, and, as she cruised off markedly to the left down into the valley preceding the side road approach to the lighthouse on the island, all thought of Barry, and both the island and lighthouse, disappeared. It took a few seconds, as she dropped swiftly into the curve over the bridge, to realize she was simply here now, driving along the coast, observing the Cyprus trees, the sky, the ocean, and the speed sign, which at the curve to the left announced thirty miles per hour.

Sand dunes to the left, golden as the midday sun in the morning mist, vaulted to the sky. Deep, dark orange flames of coastal growth cascaded over both sides of the road, gargan-tuan balls of fire plummeting down the hill to the sea. When she came around the curve, Barry's image instantly reentered her mind, and the island reappeared, suddenly, ten times as big as it had been. Its mountain was so like a pregnant woman's belly, she wondered why it was so and why she had been burdened with this desire that she knew was biologically impossible and politically problematic. For the hundredth time she decided there was no answer to this.

The rider on the high bluff to the left lightly rode his trotting horse along the coast. She considered what he might be thinking, and she knew that whatever it was, it was a reflection of her thoughts and all the thoughts of anybody, anywhere. It was a fragment of existence. And both his and her unanswered questions still remained. They were as enduring as, now off to the right between her and the sea, the cattle: who, synchronously, accompanied her Dentyne habit, gently nipping the grass and chewing.

The Hand of God

The lemon lay on the side of the street. I picked it up and scratched its surface with my thumbnail and tasted it. Since it was still pungent, I carried it until I came to the ocean, thinking to take it to Judith so we could use it later in the day on something to eat or to make lemonade. From a seawall, it dropped into the water as I tossed it hand-to-hand. I watched the waves tug it in and out, looked away momentarily for a path down to retrieve it and, upon looking back, found it gone.

I jumped down to the water's edge and looked all around, but it had disappeared. What could have taken it? I wondered. A fish, an eel, an undertow, a crab, a quick small water rat? Just as I had picked it up a few minutes before, rearranged a piece of the universe, some other piece of that universe had abducted it during one of my brief, unguarded moments and altered my perception of my place in that universe.

Should I look more thoroughly? Does it matter? I thought not looking would be a sign of my own weakness, my inability aggressively to control my life. But there again: *Did it matter?* Was it not possibly wiser, more worldly, to just let it go? *Of course.* It was only a lemon. But it was too, my mind insisted, symbolic of larger struggles. Would I not let real tests of character and endurance find me wanting if I now let a lemon defeat me?

Of course not. How foolish, I decided. It was only a lemon or, if it was more, at least it was over and done as a piece of my reality and I would not make it come back. My camera bag, hanging heavy on my shoulder, drew my attention away from this citric intrigue, and the thought of taking a picture appropriated my attention. I pulled the camera out of the bag, deleted the lemonesque problem from its conundrum by ignoring it, and I photographed the beach and the rocks lying next to the beach before I packed the camera away and walked up the street toward Judith's.

As I walked, I remembered the U.S. Naval Cruiser which had lain at anchor in the harbor all week until Thursday. Its presence had been felt in Bridgetown the whole week like a visiting uncle. Intrusively big, it had periodically disgorged its sailors, who had entered the bars and bought rum and food and had wandered off later in the evenings to buy women. When Thursday dawned, the sun rose, looking all the world like an overgrown lemon, and – in another unguarded moment – the ship silently headed out to sea and disappeared. Gone were the lemon and the cruiser and the rocks and the beach I had photographed before I walked up the street to Judith's. Worldly things these, kidnapping my attention while my invisible serious thoughts groped for her.

She, a not unusual woman, rather ordinary in her thinking and her ways. She, wanting to be married, having twice married, twice lost, but having gained a daughter now eight, pretty, well spoken, haughty. She a little woman, less than one hundred pounds.

"Do you like me small?"

"Yes."

"Why?"

Why indeed? The tiny waist so inviting to encircling hands, the slender hips just a mite larger than the waist – a perfect figure, just small and manageable. I guess. I guess that was the answer. Feminine being fine and small in my mind. That must be why. Indeed.

A biting tongue when she felt like it, but almost always soft in tone and volume, not belligerent. Stark disagreement from her felt like mild reproach. A charming trait. A small, tight mouth when thinking and full soft lips when relaxed, pouty. She was moody. Her moods were like the tide ebbing and flowing; others might say like a word processing machine thinking with electronic, barely discernible clicks without clackingly printing out hard copy.

A smart woman, protecting herself and her daughter, defending herself from me, the serious one, which trait she said she liked, I treading the waters of introduction cautiously too, as cautious – every bit! – as her, moreso possibly, I not wanting to make a mistake. I too wanting . . .

After we met on Saturday night by chance, introduced by a friend of hers who owned the café we were in, I reentered her life on Sunday morning for breakfast, which I ate alone while she and her daughter built a doll house. We had been intimate the first night. Far too much intensity too soon. We gently argued an inconsequential point that Sunday morning, and agreed to part for the day. To let us think about us.

And I took up where I had left off, returning to the beach alone where the hot sun's cloud-filtered rays whipped by the wind catapulted the sand, each grain like a scathing sword point, against my sandy white arms. Sixteen year old bikini-clad girls in green and red and blue dashed into the surf.

Damn! I thought as the old world interrupted by producing another of its lessons in reality: choosing rain – thin, cool droplets threatening to soak my towel, which I gathered up for a dash to the ever-present beachside bar, God's earthly decompression chamber for earth-bound aspiring angels

I bettered the situation with a coffee and a cute, button-nosed, freckle-faced nurse from Ohio. *Ooh!* Lost her boyfriend last night – and more! – left him and moved out to another hotel, and I now the father confessor hearing the whole tale from beginning to end, her chunky little body next to mine, a bruised cheek bottom black as a crow's toe, asking for oil after we make it from the bar back to the beach, a paradoxical bag: forbidden fruit.

Advice? Sure. Why not? My strongest suit, the pinnacle of my proficiency, especially knowing no-one ever takes it anyhow, and a few minutes amusement from it, my cynical side showing today. A good respite from the serious dialogue with dear Judith, my potential wife.

This little one on the beach now needing a sounding board. Me as well as anyone else I guess, and listening with a kindly ear for near to an hour or more, and then a swim and a "maybe" dinner together.

"I'll call at six to see. OK?"

"OK."

Sprightly bounce to her step; she wants a little fatherly flirt, I think, an older man's controlled touch, that way we have of being very good in bed while not attaching sticky strings. It works so well – when our emotions are not involved.

I walk back to my cottage and eat a bread and butter and honey sandwich. Yum Yum. The perpetual clown I seem inside myself – and outside? What do *you* see, I wonder? How do I appear to you? The father figure? A deceitful uncle? She hugged me close, the freckle-faced nurse, when I said goodbye, needing closeness. That was more than Judith had offered. A good round house loving between cool sheets would help nurse and me both, perhaps.

But what of Judith? Why this infernal obsession with a mate? This was the question, wasn't it? Certainly not the existential condition of the world. Damn the Goddamned world! It is incorrigible, after all. And all that seems to make sense is getting on with someone else. No! Not with someone else. *Plainly said.* With a woman. With that opposite life, that possible other side of myself, that strangely indefinable creature of my yearning. I wonder, do other men feel the same way? Are ten million bachelor lives wasted because we are free agents rampaging about? How many nameless women have we known? Loved for a few minutes in the molten furnace of our simple groin's lust? God bless Lust, it perpetuates the race. But does this sound like a cheap paperback novel or a tormented monk's final Koan? I wonder how it would read as an after thought to a lengthy novel, or as a preface to a short poem; or the appendix to a cash-flow chart?

And that damned little lemon!

Where did it go? Will I see it again, squeeze its yellowy insides onto the freshly slaughtered body of a filleted fish? Or will it wash out to sea and be swept to Miami, ending up in a rum and coke of an escaped Cuban plotting to regain his country? Or get salty waterlogged and sink to the ocean bottom to be eaten by a shark intent on a little vitamin C before attacking an unsuspecting swimmer too far offshore of some other sandy beach?

This internally-debilitating quest for a simple, good-natured, steadfast, semi-consistent female member of the species. What contrived essence of our male selves do we weak livered men have to conjure to tickle their impalpable fancies? Are all marriageable women homely as sheep, as boring as bridge tournaments? Are we doomed to finding some flat-brained, heavy-chested Collie as a mate in our waning years? Or do we need again to grab them, blameless, helpless creatures, by the hair, dragging their delectable, bumping asses bruisedly down the street, one good solid club to the cranium, and – once home – a long-term hump to the crotch to show them who's boss, then off into the night to find a dark cave where the boys are playing a set of toss the rock against the wall and drink fermented coconut juice and fresh squeezed oranges? Do they understand our own illusory needs? It appears to be an endless lineup of totally unacceptable alternatives. To be true to one of the creatures with her mascara and sweet perfumes is to sound your own death knell. To play freely around is to turn her onto you like a *non compos mentis* German Shephard. Bless us! We men *are* trying!

But there is no middle ground attainable from them. They demand time be infinite. Infinity be finite. If we try to determine what they really want, we are setting ourselves up for a long-term ride on the trail of futility. If we let that happen, we are forced to permit our world to turn at their closely-guarded clandestine pace until our own sense of male self worth is broken in two, split fairly amidships, floundered on a sea of insecurities because we even dared think of starting to be the one good man the sweet, gentle, desirable, intelligent, sensitive Contessas say they want. Excuse me! I apologize for violating good taste, for disturbing the peace. You may ask rightly now am I angry at women? No. I am not. *I am hurt. Goddamn, it hurts!*

But, having said it, I know, at least I suspect, our internal pain is only seen by them as immaturity, and I am ludicrous again. It's God's little twist, that sneaky rite imposed upon the process of life.

Then again, I suppose it remains a fun game after all, about as serious as a found lemon, they fall away so easily. Pungently they depart like the lemon, like passing yellow buses in traffic. To love one well and deeply would be sweet. To let one inside you, inside your man, and to have her realize she was inside you, and inside another world. And then to have her cherish it and give you strength and make you feel good when you lose the big sale to the snot-nosed competition across town you know is bribing the purchasing agents big time, but you can't prove it. And to listen to you when you give up your childlike ways and don't need her strength? And to nod when you make a parental pronouncement, then tell you you're too serious.

"Go drink a beer with the boys, because I don't want to hear your guff anymore. I'll be here when you get back. Maybe."

To trip you up with her embarrassingly adult reaction when you, on rare occasion, say or do something entirely mature. Or better yet, to have her actually meditate beside you silently without embarrassment, sit wordless and listen to her thoughts as you listen to yours, then get up and – while cooking breakfast with you – compare notes on what you meditated about; and after washing dishes make love with you on the couch before you go to work; and even be home at six when you return, a rum punch on a tray with hors d'oeuvres; or send you a telegram at work telling you to have a rum punch ready for her when she gets home, and be hot, or she's going to spend the night out with the girls.

Most likely the bleeding lemon was right there in the water, caught invisibly under a passing wave, some freak optical trick of light concealing it while the hand of God covered up the page of the book of life which states: "You are now to leap into the ocean and grapple blindly among the waves and rocks until you find the lemon, no matter what other thoughts you have, no matter what alternatives present themselves, no matter anything else, and you will finally be rewarded a honey-sweet glass of natural lemonade."

I wanting to be with older mother Judith. Knowing to call her again so soon to be the beginning of the end, and needing a woman, wanting a woman, not wanting once again to be alone, and calling the little freckle-faced nurse who lay patiently waiting for a short joust in the sheets before returning to Ohio to marry her boyfriend in a Presbyterian ceremony on the lawn of the town park – a daring departure from the tradition, my late semen stealthily lurking in her nether regions as her beau plunges home his ceremonial shaft to consecrate their sacred vows.

And afterward the juice of one lemon she found on the beach in Barbados, and sneaked home past all the fruit and customs inspectors, is squeezed into water and used to douche her tender little love lips and leave her fresh as an unpicked rose, and God reaches into his book of life again and tears out the page of instructions I was required to follow, crunches it into a ball, and drops it down the mail chute to hell, where old Lucifer adds it to the flames and sends his Swat team out to find me for violating the pretty nurse's warm thighs that Sunday night in the cool evening's wallowing hours, her last night before leaving me, sand between my toes, the faint scent of her cologne on my cheek, right between the sad twinkle of my eye and the thinly veiled grin above my stubble-bearded chin.

After all is contemplated, would it have been so rare a life to have taken the lemon to Judith and made a lemonade and drunk it with her and shared it with her and her dear daughter and eventually to have said our own vows on some lawn somewhere, another's semen lurking in her, the leftover love of some other yesterday's bright promise? It might have been very good lemonade. However, that is for God to say. And God plays his cards close to his vest.

Very close.

The Great White Shark

C al bends to his knees and loosens the bow line from its cleat. Tandy Clannighan, features editor of the *San Francisco Monitor,* who's tasked him to photograph the annual Fall feeding frenzy of the great white sharks on wayward seals in the North Pacific, balances himself with two malleable legs on the swaying dock and yells:

"You two rickety septuagenarians stay out of trouble, you hear?"

The tide immediately pulls the sailboat from the dock, slipping the line from Cal's hand, and he is compelled to jump aboard to go along. He is prepared for this. He has ridden the tide for many years. He knows of its many tricks. It is ebbing now, flowing west toward and under the bridge, where it is beginning to become briefly the largest river of the country and join again the capacious North Pacific.

Capacious is well chosen from the Latin meaning capable, for this ocean possesses indeed the capacity to achieve efficiently whatever it chooses to accomplish. It has long earned his fearful respect. He pulls the bow line on board, moves forward, and secures it to the stanchion near the red port running light. He needs the ebb to clear the bridge and join with the sea. His friend, the good Doctor, at the wheel, guides the stern earnestly back toward the wharf, checks its movement, reverses gently the gears, and urges back the wheel to guide the bow straight down the way to the concrete barrier that protects the harbor. One smart turn right and to the end of the concrete, a one hundred eighty degree reversal, and they are set directly to enter the bay.

Their goal is Los Farallones, the jagged island jaws that jut upward twenty seven miles out at sea beyond the Golden Gate: that inexorable western edge of the country where the continental shelf abruptly plunges into mile deep green depths, where the border line of man's knowledge murkily fades and – if he has the aptitude for it – his sense of security trembles fragilely in his breast. It is, they both know, this humility before the ocean that has always prolonged man's life when he goes down to the sea in ships. Sailors, they both know, are not made; they are born. They may be trained, but no amount of training can produce the innate instinct certain men and women have for the sea that others never learn.

While the Doctor mans the wheel, Cal whips the halyard around the winch and raises the main sail. It is heavy and this takes some time as the boat circles still within the protection of the inner harbor. When the main is set, Cal joins his mate in the cockpit and, taking the sheet well in hand, furls out a meter of the jib, and cleats it down. As they clear the protective end of the concrete, a twenty knot wind fills the jib and main, and beckons them to port. Cal takes the wheel, allows the boat to veer left, halting it with a soft touch to define a course toward the north end of the bridge. The boat heels over moderately to starboard and quickly gains speed to near five knots. The bow prances shyly through the waves blowing into the bay. He cuts the engine and the wind begins to ply its magic trade.

"With wind and ebb battling one another, it'll take us about an hour to clear the bridge, I estimate," the Doctor says.

"Yes," Cal says. "But we'll have no fight. We'll get out easy."

"Probably. But *how* will depend on where the true ocean breeze is coming from as we clear land's end: whether from due west or northwest, as is usual. Swooping in over the mountains as it now is, it confuses the insides here."

"And I doubt we'll find it's from the southwest this time of year," Cal adds.

"Unlikely. So, wanting to head due west as we do, we may have a time of it gaining the islands."

"No matter. We've lots of food and water and drink and time and a sturdy engine. Speed is not the issue."

"Indeed, Captain," the Doctor intones in his most possibly pronounced professorial voice. "And I suggest we open the first bottles of that virgin Czech Pilsner I got us to initiate our formal withdrawal from the strain of civilization. Have I the Captain's permission?"

"As you will, First Mate. I defer to your superior education."

"You sot. You're too easy."

"So've the ladies always said."

"And in such matters," the Doctor insists, "*I defer* to the superior intuition of women."

"Mutinous talk!"

"Hah!" the Doctor exclaims as he goes below to fetch the beer.

"We'll have this out, I warn you!" Cal yells down.

"And I'll bury you in supporting scientific evidence!"

Doctor Konrad Koch is neither physician nor chef, but a retired physics professor and all around bon vivant. He habitually observes Cal with the singular attention he affords every one he talks to, a technique he has over long years nurtured, which serves two purposes. If his present companion of any time holds toward him any disguised evil intent – however unknowingly or innocently – he sees it coming a mile away and prepares some obscure scientific fact with which rhetorically to parry or, if necessary, retaliate. Or, if his luck holds and the person is truly guileless, as he judges Cal to be, his technique permits him at least to impart a new fact into his friend's life. This enriches him as a person and makes the Doctor feel that he too is a more valuable human being. Born a Russian, raised a German, Konrad learned his craft over many years at the University of Munich, taught more years at the University of California, but more pertinently, has a steady helmsman's hand. His value to Cal, the responsible Captain of his own ocean sloop, is not his scientific knowledge but his practical experience as an ocean sailor, the certainty he brings that he too knows many of the ways of the prodigiously salty master of the earth. He is a singular character, who when sailing draws on a Bedouin like Kaffiyeh to defend his thinning gray hair and naked neck against the rigors of the brine.

Cal is a simpler example of the sailor's art. Six months younger than his seventy-two year old colleague, he is a free-lance photographer and stringer reporter to various publications on matters of the sea. In keeping with the meager pay of such a job, he lives economically on his sailboat. When talking to others, Konrad included, he is unaware that guile is one of the tools of conversation. It puts him, unknowingly, in a defensive position, but fits well within his personal philosophy of life, for although he is generally an inoffensive fellow, he is not an unassertive one. He wears a tough, wool, Greek sailor's cap, smokes Partagas cigars, and is a self taught ocean sailor with two decades of salt in his silver beard and hair.

It is October, the season of the whales' migration to the south, the weaning of young seals on the islands, and Cal's objective: the great white sharks, the lethal consequence of millions of years of evolution in the sea, long before life's subsequent migration to land, where eventually the delusions of man relegated his real history to the evasive profundity of the deep. The tide has been virile of late, gripping Cal's sloop, scourging it, straining its dock lines, exacting upon its cleats the utmost test of their strength. So far, all has held. The boat has maintained her structural integrity and withstood all trials the sea has advanced upon her.

Wild Goose is her name. She is an indomitable long distance flier, soul mate to the albatross, ready at a moment's whim to engage any course and all its weather elements in the quest of adventure and, hopefully, wisdom. Breaking beyond land's end, she directly confronts the North Pacific Ocean where the wind blows sharply from the northwest against her prow. The Pilsner is forgotten, sweaters are drawn on, and the men grapple with the ocean's potential. Here beyond the safety of the bay is where sailing begins. Within a mile of their present position lie the ruins of hundreds of ships. Whether driven by sail or machine, they have all succumbed to the indisputable jurisdiction of the sea. The law giver here is clear. As Joseph Conrad said, this is the sailor's shadow line.

They have now been for several hours laboriously heading north under sail and engine. The wind's unfavorable direction permits them only to beat back east toward the nearby shore or southwest out to sea. Neither direction moves them directly toward The Farallones. The western sky darkens. Day falters. The sun provocatively falls steadily into a rising horizon. The sky transforms from blue to blue-red, to blue-wine, to brilliant red, to abruptly deepening wine-red, to wine-blue, wine-black, then magically spreads out like cake icing of molten red-gold over the entire horizon, becoming as burnt orange before evaporating into a moonless dome of tenuous black. The stars have not yet broken through the reflected white light of departing day. Neptune calls. Then, they do. Dark returns. A trillion diamonds beckon.

"We can't get to the islands easy now. Let's head southwest under sail the whole night," Cal says.

"That'll take us completely off the chart," Konrad remarks.

"Great! We'll backtrack to the Farralones tomorrow morning. Maybe we'll get there in time for the sharks' breakfast."

"OK by me."

"It'll give the engine a rest. No point burning diesel to get north when north doesn't want us."

"Aye, mein Herr."

"Helm's alee," Cal says.

He swings the wheel left and the main sail centers and flaps and coughs and wheezes and the wind grabs the jib and various cantankerous lines possessing minds of their own whip briefly against one another. Eventually, the two men find themselves headed west-south-west. Cal hanks down the jib sheet, secures the main, leans back, and looks up at the stars.

"Goddamned, that's the prettiest thing in the world."

"Do you want to take the wheel first, or shall I?" Konrad asks.

"Neither. I'll turn on the automatic pilot."

"Splendid concept."

"Take the wheel. I'll go below to the control panel. Yell me our magnetic course, and I'll set the pilot. Then, let's eat. I'm starving. How about you"

"Yawohl, Herr Kapitan."

Cal goes below, and benevolent Neptune permits them to engage the auto pilot. Cal creates sandwiches, frees beer, and returns. Now come the good times; uninhibited by the seductive grace of women, alone on the ocean, able freely to talk and speculate on every prohibited thought of life on earth, they sit wordlessly for half an hour.

"What's going on here?" Cal asks, finally.

"Now? Here on the water? Or is yours a more metaphysically empowered question?"

"The latter."

"You mean the ultimate question of existing? Being here?"

"You got it."

"Hah! It's an inscrutable phenomenon."

"Konrad, you're a Ph.D Physics professor. Your job is speculating on philosophically untenable theories to explain in experimentally practical terms what's going on. Well, I'm asking you. What do you think is going on? Practically?"

"I am paralyzed by your wish for an honest answer."

"Cold blooded! Cut to the quick! I won't judge you. I'm just curious."

"Well, like all scientists, I can only say, who knows?"

"Why are you paid a huge pension?"

"I possess a marketable share of continental savoir faire."

"Well, I wish we had some women on board."

"It *would* add life to the party."

They consider the liberating power of the stars.

"What I really think is going on?" Konrad asks, after awhile.

"That is the question."

"This is only an informal guess you understand; however, it appears that this physical presence we experience is all we can count on. The restless imaginings we create bring us only intermittent triumphs destabilized by disasters."

"Don't we make progress?"

"Possibly. Painfully, however."

"I like that part…so long as it's balanced with pleasure."

"It appears to arrive in a million to one ration."

"The pain dominating?"

"Unquestionably."

"Didn't some old wise man come up with a concrete solution?"

"Pascal said if you believe in a god, and you win, you gain all."

"And if you lose?"

"You lose nothing."

"Except."

"Except?"

"The integrity of your mind."

"True believers discount the validity of the mind."

"And minds discount the validity of belief."

"Just living is the winning."

"Precisely what the world needs, a philosophical physicist."

"Do I disappoint you?"

"On the contrary. It's a good answer."

"Please don't tell me you're going to force me to like your company because you're smart. I was hoping you'd remain just a simple sailor."

"I'll see if I can dumb me down. Shall we change the subject?"

"The point of sailing *is* to empty the mind, not aggravate it."

"I do it better by talking sometimes."

"And I can banter with the best, if required"

"No moon tonight"

". . . Not visible, but there all the same..."

". . . Can't destroy matter, eh...?"

". . . Allegedly, out of sight is not really out of mind."

"I think we've beat the subject into submission. Want another beer?"

"I'd rather have coffee."

Konrad scans the horizon as Wild Goose strives steadily on, her bow dipping and rising back to dip again and again in hypnotic rhythm. Cal brings up coffee *and* cigars, and they smoke awhile. The night is cool, but not yet cold, and there is no hint of rain. The yet unforgotten vexations of life do not force themselves upon the men and, other than the occasional comment on the sky, the waves, the elusive message of the ocean, they resist idle talk for a couple of hours.

"I'm tired," Cal finally says. "You feel like taking first watch?"

"Fine."

Cal goes below, crawls into the bow berth, and quickly falls into a dreamless sleep. When he later awakes, the boat still beats rhythmically against the wind and sea. He uses the head, brushes his hair, pulls on a jacket, and clambers back into the cockpit. The black sky remains, pierced only by the countless stars.

"Any problems?"

"Smooth as silk."

"Want to rest?"

"Yes. I was about to wake you up. I'm getting fuzzy."

Konrad goes below. Cal glances about. The horizon seamlessly joins the sky, defining their course as a continuous path into an indefinable black void, whose saving grace is the reprisal of the stars in elusively wavering sparkles on the surface of the water. It grows colder and dampness worms its way into his body. He jumps below, determines that Konrad has successfully tied himself into a side bunk and sleeps, finds a scarf, and returns to the cockpit. Turning around toward land, he views the faint San Francisco skylight, glowing warmly and vaulting into a restricted dome over the city. About four, Konrad relieves him again, and he accepts once more the night's offer of sleep. When he next awakes, it is light outside. It seems to be about six O'Clock. He climbs back into the cockpit and looks around. Sometime in the early morning as he slept they have crossed over the curve of the earth, and now for the full three hundred sixty degrees exists only water. They have become an integral part of the three quarters of the watery earth aloof from land, and they sail now over the submerged mountains and valleys of marine societies still largely an enigma to man.

"Let's take a GPS fix on our position," Cal says.

Konrad takes the fix and plots it on the chart.

"We're sixty-five miles out," he yells from below. "West south west of the Farallones...and our depth is over a mile and deepening."

"We should have packed parachutes."

"If we come about now, we'll gain the Farallones by one this afternoon – by sail, if the wind holds steady."

"Let's do it."

They reverse direction and head back toward the islands. Cal fixes bacon, eggs, crepes, and coffee. When they've finished eating, Konrad washes up. In a couple of hours with binoculars Cal sights the tops of the islands' miniscule hills. The northwest wind pushes Wild Goose deliberately at five knots, so that the hilltops methodically develop triangular bases. The Farallones' raggedness confirms their fearsome nature, and as they approach, the islands grip Cal's emotions. As morning fog nears the small, foreboding archipelago, a surrounding circle of open water holds it at bay, as if large unseen hands encircle the land, protecting it from the weather. The men absorb the islands' unique power.

"No seals," Cal says. "No fins."

"It's early. The young seals are still safe by their mothers ashore. They'll start their own sea explorations soon, but it may stay quiet for awhile."

"Let's get in the dinghy and tow some bait. Maybe we'll stir up some action.'"

"Why not?"

The men anchor Wild Goose off the islands and lower the dinghy. Konrad gets in first, then helps Cal, loaded with his camera. Settled in, Cal drops a large gunny sack of bleeding fish scrap and entrails over board, lets out a twenty foot rope, and they paddle the dinghy slowly through the off shore hunting grounds, trailing their bait behind. It leaves a slick of oil and blood on the water. Half an hour nothing breaks the smooth swells rolling in from the west. Then a single fin cuts the water's surface and circles the bait bag.

"We got a visitor," Cal says.

"More," Konrad says. "Look!"

The single fin has been joined by two others. The trio are inspecting the gunny sack with serious consideration. Methodically, they cross back and forth as if uncertain of their strategy, then one alters his course and glides directly under the eight foot dinghy, jostling it with more than casual interest. The dinghy lifts a few inches off the water and slaps down with a jerk.

"Sheisse!" Konrad says.

"Shit is right," Cal answers.

The other two fins join the lone hunter and all three inspect the tiny rubber dinghy, roughly bumping it as they pass around, repeatedly upsetting its stability and the men's equilibrium. Finally, one dives to abruptly explode the gunny sack, tearing it to pieces. Bits of fish scatter on the surface and the oil and blood spread. The brother sharks react in a frenzy, splitting their renewed attention between the remaining dregs of the gunny sack and the dinghy. One giant head swims directly to the dinghy, crashing against it, lifting an edge half a foot before retreating.

"Goddamn!" Cal says.

"I'm for getting back to the boat," Konrad says.

"You got that right," Cal responds.

They drop the line to the gunny sack and paddle swiftly to Wild Goose, The shark fins circle them continuously, backing away only when the pair have clambered aboard the sloop and drawn up the dinghy to the deck.

"Did you get a photo?" Konrad asks.

"You've got to be kidding," Cal says.

"Those sons of bitches are serious."

"We'd better be too."

"How'd you get this job at your age?"

"Our age, you mean?"

'Whatever."

"Clannighan owes me. I bailed him out of a story or two when I'd got my hands on the facts his reporters had missed."

"I hope he's paying big time for the risk."

"He didn't ask me to take a risk, just a photo."

"The risk was your idea?"

"I should have brought a hard dinghy, I guess."

"I guess too."

"The water's calm again. Looks like they're gone."

"Want to hang out awhile?"

"If they don't come back, let's head up to Tomales Bay."

"We'll have to kick the engine in again."

"I'll leave the sails up; that'll help."

An hour later, Cal starts the diesel and points up nearly direct into the wind, steering a course to Point Reyes through scoops of whitecaps that introduce the peninsula lying out into the Pacific some fifteen miles north.

"Those guys were onto us, big time," Konrad says.

"Had me thinking we might take a deep swim, I'll tell you."

"I was scared."

"Scared? I'm afraid to check my drawers."

"I don't think we should try that again."

"No. We'll use the telescope on the camera next time and do it from the fantail."

"Safe and dry."

With that, Konrad again defines the heading, Cal sets the automatic pilot, and they relax. After a few minutes, Cal asks:

"How are you and Raia getting on?"

"Now you've opened a can of worms."

"You filled it."

"Hah! How can I explain? She is afraid of her own breath."

"You've been with her a long time, no?"

"Ten years or more."

"Was she always so fearful?"

"Her timidity matures with age. She's presently praying for us today, so we won't sink."

"She's really afraid for us?"

"Certain we're doomed."

"I don't understand how a diehard Catholic can be afraid. Doesn't she feel any security from her belief?"

"She does not connect the two."

"Has she ever sailed with you?"

"In Florida, where the water's about ten feet deep and flat as a pancake."

"Perhaps we should take her out and teach her."

"You know not what you propose. Besides, we now have another issue. She was alone the other day when my other lady friend called from Florida, the one you talked to by phone when I was last there. It infuriated her."

"Does that surprise you, Lothario?"

"Why should she suspect any indiscretion on my part?"

"Konrad . . ."

"It *could* be Platonic."

"You are delusional. Even if it were, no woman would ever believe that of a man, especially one who likes to gamble with life, as Raia knows you do. She can only suspect you of the worst. And, accurately so, as it is."

"I am trapped by my own appetites."

"Aren't we all?"

"If only she would engage in life. Risk something. I feel alone when I'm with her."

"She feels she's risking enough just being with you."

"She's driving me to distraction."

"My friend, you're too old to permit that. You have a decision to make. Preserve your decade old relationship with her or bail out for the rich Florida lady."

"The temptations of affluent flesh *are* hard to resist."

"Your lack of character appalls me. If *I* had more, I'd toss you overboard."

"You need me to navigate. And if a blow comes up."

"Saved by a hair. You are a lucky man."

About four O'Clock they reach Point Reyes.

"If we go north around her, we'll have another fifteen miles to Tomales Bay," Cal says.

"That will put us in at about seven."

"To get over the bar into Tomales, we've got to enter on a flood. Check the tide times for me. I called the Coast Guard. They said we can use San Francisco times for Tomales."

Cal scans the horizon again. The weather is holding clear. Konrad checks the GPS and sees the electronically unwavering track of the tiny V confirms their path toward Reyes. If only, he thinks, the simple affairs of man were so reliable. It is a fleeting thought. The great void-producing effect of the open ocean is starting to work. Pursuing the thought looms as too strenuous even to consider. He forgets it in an instant.

"We should enter Tomales about eleven tomorrow morning," he reports.

"Let's anchor at Pt. Reyes tonight and cook a hot meal."

"I admire the discipline you bring to your appetites."

"At least I don't get dangerous phone calls."

"I bet you have tales to tell."

"Over a sincere drunk, sometime, perhaps."

"Have you ever anchored at Reyes?"

"Yes. It's got a good bottom. And it's shallow near shore. The cliffs create a great barrier to the sea. We could safely sit out a mean storm there. . . hey, it's called Drake's Bay. The old English admiral actually parked his ship there. And he had no engine to pull him out."

By five, late afternoon headwinds increase. Before they are ready to drop anchor it is almost eight. Just after the inner buoy's whistle, they skirt Point Reyes' bayside shore, discover two other sailboats at anchor, and, after inspecting a few hundred yards of coastline, draw to within fifty yards of the second one, deeply in the curve of the cliffs, where docile cattle graze oblivious to the approaching dark.

"Picture perfect," Cal says. "Hold the wheel and I'll do the honors."

Konrad holds them steady as Cal goes forward, frees the Scottish cast iron anchor, and lets it slide into the bay. They've nine feet to bottom and another thirty-five feet of chain to secure them. Konrad edges the boat backward as the chain plays out. Cal shouts.

"Push her hard now and hook her in!"

Konrad prompts the engine to two thousand rpm's and Wild Goose sinks the anchor into a firm bottom; she stops dead in the water. He shuts the diesel down. As the sun slides behind the cliff, its plunge into the ocean is less pronounced than last night. Quickly, however, it is again dark as they settle in below. It's getting colder and the cabin lights are low, so Cal fires the oil lamp and the propane heater amidship near the mainmast, where it plunges below the deck to the keel below.

"Want wine now, or when the chicken's done?" Cal queries.

"Let's do first prime our pumps with wine. It does the heart good and sensitizes the cook. We'll get a better meal that way."

"And you call me a sot?"

"It takes a genius to recognize another."

The raw bay headlands circle about them like huge, protective arms, and over the water spreads a no nonsense blanket of silence. Sipping wine on deck, while dissected chicken and two dozen white pearl onions simmer in cocoanut milk in the galley, the men – far beyond any futile need of introspection – regard the bay with that quiet thoughtlessness the sea brings to fatigued souls.

"I'm tired," Konrad says.

"Beating against the damn wind for a day'll do it to you."

"Does it ever come from the southwest when you need it?"

"Only to the sober and pure of heart."

"That's a discouraging observation."

They eat. They sleep. Next morning, the sun rises from the east, suggesting the universe proceeds confidently on its way. They sleep in late. Once awake, they note one of the other boats is gone. The second has swung about in the shifting tide. Looking closely, Cal sees its hatch is locked.

"No one on board."

"Must be a good bottom for them to leave it alone like that."

"It is. Except sometimes there's a lot of seaweed. Last time I anchored here I had to cut it off with a knife."

On shore a party of several cars drives down off the road and parks near the water. Its members are dressed in hiking gear and gather soon into a circle, where a man in a red stocking cap speaks to them. They listen, then immediately spread out to explore the waterline. They look like a long thread of working ants intent on something serious to their preservation. Cal raises the anchor, which pulls clean without seaweed this time, but coming around the inner point of the bay and circling the outer prominence of Point Reyes takes much longer than he has figured. Upon clearing the westernmost spit of land to clearly sight in on Tomales Bluff, he's used up most of their morning. Konrad checks the tide book as Cal studies the bluff through his binoculars.

"We'll miss our mid day entrance into Tomales. Want to try to go in at sunset?" Konrad asks.

"No. I've never been in there before. They tell me the bar's tricky. Let's just anchor again in Bodega Bay across the way, and go in tomorrow at eleven."

"Sounds like a plan."

"If you would demonstrate your navigational skills and give me a magnetic heading to the inner shore of Bodega, please! We'll not go inside the fishing boat harbor. It's a thin channel. We won't anchor inside without paying for it. Besides, the beachfront is as nice as Drake's, if not nicer. Let's just hang out and kill time eating and drinking some more. I'll tell you what. If your course proves accurate, I'll cook again.

"If?"

"Just keeping you on your toes."

"Impugning my competency, sir."

Konrad produces a high-powered, battery-operated spotlight from his duffel bag. He clicks it on and a sharply-focused beam pierces the impending darkness, bringing into relief the shore's water line. Firefly-like pinpoints of light bob from the beach, and a dozen voices laugh out at them.

"Sailors, ahoy! Take us aboard!"

"We're pirates. We take no prisoners," Cal shouts.

More laughter. The faint smell of marijuana reaches the boat.

"Civilization," he says.

"I smell it," Konrad replies.

They anchor. They eat and drink. It is late when they have cleaned the galley gear, and they quickly fall asleep. Inside the bay, the tide disperses evenly over the broad expanse of water and, each man communing with his solitary dream, the night passes undisturbed. With scarcely noticeable effort, the sea leaves them be and focuses its energy on the fate of others, who – for whatever reasons – have been unable to find safe harbor for the night.

Circling seagulls bark over the sleeping sailors.

Fall has begun.

———

A prehistoric convulsion of the earth created Tomales Bay, an inner lagoon fifteen miles long, half a mile wide at its fattest, splattered with a half dozen little islands here and there, home to wayward birds and independent ground creatures, and a few hardy human souls who prize their solitude. Conformity here is not to the corporate world. Locals do not wonder if

Nietzsche is a brand of soap. Our sailors nearly miss it next morning when, instead of assigning the exacting navigation task to Konrad, Cal himself plots the short course from Bodega Bay. When land to port too long persists, Konrad speaks up.

"We've missed the entrance."

"Can't be."

"I'll put money on it."

"All right. Do a GPS check."

Konrad reports.

"We've passed it."

Cal reverses course and a half hour later finds the entrance. He studies the chart closer.

"I see what happens. It's a mile inside the peninsula before the entrance. I'll bet we're not the first to miss it."

"You didn't adjust for magnetic correction. It put you off a hundred yards."

"One of my several inadequacies."

"Your contrition is admirable."

"How about more coffee?"

"I'll get it."

Wild Goose threads through the proscenium of this marine sanctuary between Sandy Point off her port side, and Avalis Beach off to starboard; her sounder determines the depth varies from three to thirty-seven feet. Inches left or right determine whether she will pass on or ground. Cal idles the engine and Wild Goose glides stealthily forward as if infiltrating a hunter's blind. Temporarily the water deepens. At the second mile, shoals again appear irregularly to as low as three and four feet. Wild Goose drafts six. It is like threading a needle. They hold their breath and listen. It is not a matter of hope or will. It is a matter of patience and luck. Once, the keel scrapes bottom as faintly as fingers scratching a sailor's beard.

"Starboard!" Konrad whispers hoarsely.

Cal strokes the wheel gently right. They advance and glide

clear again. The sounder indicates increasing depths…then it is done. Safely through, they are into depths of fifteen to fifty-five feet for the next ten miles. Beneath the benign surface, nature's underwater plan, like a country quilt, is bewilderingly unpredictable. The lagoon is superb, every sailor's ideal: placid, elegant, exclusive. Before night, they find a quiet inlet, and well before dark drop anchor. Off the land comes a light breeze. The little valley cups the early evening sun like a ball and tosses its heat back and forth, warming the air and water above the temperatures of the outside ocean. Cal stares up to the Moon for a long time. Konrad watches him without speaking. Finally, Cal says:

"What's the German word for translucent?"

"Describe its meaning."

"It's when you can see through something, like those Moonrays, for instance. Like when you can look through cellophane. You know, when you can see the Moonrays or the cellophane but you can still look right through them and see the world?"

"It's called *Lichtdurchlaessigkeit* in German."

"Light – through – let . . . *the ability to allow light through.*"

"Exactly."

"Can it also mean to seek the truth?"

"That cantankerous old contender is always on the scene."

"Is that a scholarly consideration, or are you speaking as a humble peasant member of the human race?"

"*Darwin knows.*"

"*Darwin knows*? What's that mean?"

"People say '*God knows*' when they don't know. I say '*Darwin knows.*'

"I appreciate your courage. It is not an easy life to buck the ever invisible Gods."

"And their braying promoters and financiers."

"The smart money has always invested in the promotion of God."

"Do you know the history of the corporatization of Christianity?"

"I know the Knight Templars and Crusaders and Inquisitioners killed people by uncountable numbers who refused to believe their dogma."

"Supported by a lot of Kings, Popes, and bank presidents."

"Caution, Herr Doctor lest you upset the politicians of the world."

"Hah! Not I. I'm no longer a physicist working for my government. I have arrived at that ripely rare phase of life when I am mandated by my own earned self authority to use my mind for myself."

"You're assuming a heavy responsibility."

"Figuring out how to get by is man's most sacred obligation."

The *translucent Lichtdurchlaessigkeit* of the Moon's Rays shine down on them and wordlessly they view the heaven in perpetual awe. Eventually Konrad transports the spell to a new level.

"May I drastically change the subject and ask why you took on this job photographing and writing about the great white shark?"

"I am intrigued by the process of living and dieing."

"It is your soul you're concerned with?"

"No."

"It's not about a possible afterlife?"

"Not at all."

"You've got that figured out?"

"I believe so."

"And…"

"…I suspect both the body and mind give it up when we die."

"Doesn't leave a lot of room for a God."

"Not a lot."

"You're not doubtful?"

"Several tons of archeological evidence tend to support my theory."

"So…?"

"So…the real issue is how do we persuade humans to conduct ourselves sensibly while here."

"In relation to…"

"… not butchering ourselves in the name of the Lord."

'That's a pretty broad field of research."

"Yes."

"Simple acceptance of the most obvious reality."

"That this here life on earth is it."

"A one time pass-through."

"Yes."

"Without benefit of a tangible God?"

"I borrowed the idea from others, of course."

"You plan to try to sell it to people?"

"I have no desire to start another church. The market's already flooded."

"And you call me cynical?"

"Besides, *The Monitor* won't pay me for metaphysical speculation."

"You have to have a journalistic angle for them, don't you?"

"It's called a strong lead."

"And yours is?"

"I don't know yet. That's why I want to see the great white shark doing his thing. I want to experience his expertise up close, and form an opinion from it."

"Conduct a little personal empirical research."

"I like to think of it as a close up watery look at the ultimate metaphor for the ultimate metaphysical experience we all eventually share."

"If that rhymed you'd make dieing sound almost like poetry."

"Which deep thought, I hope, leads us to another beer."

"Now, that's a really good idea. I'll get us a couple."

The next morning, Konrad announces:

'I'm going swimming."

He is climbing up into the cockpit devoid of clothing other than an old pair of khaki shorts; an olive green towel on his shoulder quickly transfers to the wheel as, rubbing his hand through his hair, he eyes the drowsy water.

"It is rumored, you know, this is breeding ground for the great white shark," Cal says.

"Since they and their offspring are now at the Farallones, the breeding is long over. The females are with them on the islands."

"And the males?"

"I missed that part of the lesson."

"Some might be here."

"I accept the odds," Konrad concludes.

He plunges into the light green water, disappears below the surface, and for a long time the water sends circles out to near and far banks. Finally, his head pops up nearby the undergrowth of the neighboring shore, and he grins back at Cal. Several minutes more he braves the water, while Cal soaks up the rising sun; then, with a bluster of energy, he scrambles up the side ladder back aboard.

"Shit, it's cold!"

"Are there really supposed to be sharks here?"

"That's what they say."

"It was worth the chance."

"As Raia says, you like to gamble."

"Let's avoid that subject."

"You also avoid answering my request for the ultimate meaning of life."

"I stated clearly it is inscrutably unknowable."

"Why do I feel unsatisfied."

"It's the bed you've made."

"Is that what Nietzsche meant by *overcoming* oneself?"

"He meant simply that self pity is not acceptable behavior."

"Have some coffee."

"Thanks."

They sip the hot brew noisily to cool it as the morning warms. Konrad dries and dresses; they eat and assess the day.

"You know there's absolutely nothing to do here but do nothing," Konrad says.

"We've ten miles of lagoon to explore."

They slowly skirt the lagoon's lucid inner shore. Little man-made beaches periodically appear, already filled with mothers and children in canoes and paddle boats. Small sailboats come out and lollygaggle, and along the far shore of Highway One a few cars on all fours crawl along. At the end of the lagoon, various paraphernalia signal the presence of the local oyster farm.

"We've got to eat some of these," Cal says.

"No argument from me."

Late afternoon, they return to within a mile of the entrance, and anchor directly off the far shore by the lone reputable restaurant of the bay. A trawler lies at anchor.

"Looks legitimate," Konrad says.

"Let's dinghy in and find out."

Cal paddles. By the boat dock on the end of the pier to the restaurant, a tiny shingled shack – well weathered with gray wooden planks, awash in rusted old fishing gear, anchors, oil lamps, chain, and a fairly new cast iron wood stove, ablaze – charms them into more serious hunger. A well worn menu, clinging desperately to life, rests on an old rusted tub bottom that lies on pine two by fours.

"This is clever marketing. I could eat a raw frog," Konrad admits.

"I doubt that's necessary."

Walking up the long pier, they view the row of rental cabins on the waterfront: yellow, blue, gold, white. Scaling the coastal highway's edge, Eucalyptus trees rise tall behind them.

The restaurant is too well designed to be a mistake. The outside is rough and plain. Inside, also from rough planked walls, hang wild stuffed animals: deer, foxes, coyotes, a bear head, wild fowl, their glass eyes studying the handful of early evening guests as they sip wine and skim the menu. Very old oil paintings depict dark sea scenes of spectacularly serene secularity. The floor too, unsacredly, is of rough, wide, wooden planking. The high-vaulted ceiling is braced by comparable planking in thicker dimensions. Expensive crystal chandeliers give the game away. The prices substantiate it.

"I think we'd best tread lightly here," Cal says.

"Either that or charm the waitress into fiscal irresponsibility."

"That works for me."

"What'll it be, gents," the well-bosomed, raven-maned waitress asks, bumping her amply sculptured hip against their table.

"Such beauty have I rarely seen on this earth," Konrad offers in his lowest Russian/German accent.

"It's nice here, isn't it?" she replies, innocently, looking out the window with them.

Gazing intently into her eyes, he proceeds with the con.

"I meant you, my dear."

"Thank you; but no discounts," she responds, smiling him into quivering submission.

"Gad, you've found me out."

"We're isolated here, but not entirely unaware of the devious world."

"What about me?" Cal says. I'm on Social Security. Can't you make me a special deal?'"

"Sure. Can you wash dishes?"

"You drive a hard bargain."

"I'm on Social Security too."

"We want oysters," Konrad says, "and are but poor, wayfaring sailors just in from the sea."

"I thought I'd heard it all. Wait'll I tell my husband. How's about two dozen raw ones for twenty-five percent off so long you do a couple of expensive wines each. No free side orders."

"Done!" Cal says.

"I knew you had soul the minute I saw you," adds Konrad.

"No smoked ones either! Just raw. I'll throw in the lemons and horse radish for free. But I expect a hell of a tip."

"You got it, Dulcinea," Cal says.

Wild Goose bobs obediently at the end of the pier. Near her, a big man with a big belly, and a beaming big blonde woman, climb down from their trawler into a skiff, motor by outboard to shore, and walk up the pier to the restaurant. The man goes immediately inside, but the blonde spontaneously stops at their table and touches them both on the arm with well manicured hands. She has that telling gleam in her eye that speaks of drink, but she is sparklingly charming.

"You two beautiful men. We live in Napa and are holding a party in a month. There are more mature, earnestly languishing, lonely women who'll attend than fish in the sea. Would you care to join us?"

Lustily, Konrad smiles his most seditious smile.

"Madam, you misconstrue our characters."

"Really? Then I retract the offer."

"Let's not be hasty," he says.

While they flirt with the lady, the man regales the waiters and waitresses inside, who gather about him like seagulls to discarded cake crumbs. He gesticulates like a Shakespearean actor. His entourage is hypnotized.

"My boyfriend owns the place," the blond explains. Come have a drink when you're through eating," she bubbles before joining her equally ebullient benefactor.

They do that half an hour later. He's of the consistently exuberant, congenial chef genus, and it soon comes out he owns six such places, most in San Francisco, each an icon of the city's restaurant scene. Visiting the head later, Cal discovers several carefully framed articles from well known gourmet magazines proclaiming their host's talent for designing unique places to please your tummy. He refrains from revealing his occupation, but exchanges phone numbers with the lady, who swears she'll have them fixed up with warm blooded women shortly after they arrive at her party. Multiple visits by other guests to the chef's private table augment the evening. Ever so briefly they all become part of the owner's inner circle. Near ten, Cal and Konrad pack it in and row back to Wild Goose to sleep.

Next morning the trawler has moved on.

"What's say, Kapitan?" Konrad says.

"I guess we head back."

'We could wait a day."

"I want to visit the Farallones again. I've an appointment in the city day after tomorrow. If we wait 'till tomorrow, and weather comes up, I might miss it."

Konrad consults the tide chart. Two hours from now will be slack after flood, allowing them back out into the Pacific.

"Do we need to refuel?" he asks.

"We ought to have enough."

Cal gets his measuring stick and checks the tank.

"It's half full. That'll do us."

They snug lines up, stuff loose kit away, tie down rebellious objects, the enemies of order on the waves, make their head trips, and – finally – the time is right, and they creep back out the channel the way they came, feeling their way over the secret bottom. When they depart the proscenium and leave the bay behind, they turn left around Tomales Bluff and motor west to clear the point.

"Do you feel the wind?" Cal asks.

"Not yet."

"It's not coming from northwest anymore."

"We'll be heading south. What did you expect?"

Two miles out, the land no longer blocks the wind, which announces its direction.

"Southwest! Can you believe it?" Cal exclaims.

"It's a law of physics. Invisible phenomena are cantankerous."

"Son of a bitch. We motor all the way up, and now we've got to motor back."

"I am not personally a proponent of Bhuddist philosophy," Konrad says, "however, I believe this is where we are supposed to relax and go with the flow."

"Shit!" Cal says.

"I'm going to drink a beer," Konrad declares.

"Get me one too."

They motor until Point Reyes, and off that venerable landmark, the wind conducts some clandestine incantation and dance that shifts it more westerly so Cal is able to define a tacking strategy that, theoretically, will take them to the Farallones. He raises sail and cuts the engine. It is slow but steady. They drink beer and smoke cigars again. Cal is looking out to sea when Konrad shouts.

"Look! A whale. He's spouting!"

Cal turns back toward land, where Konrad is pointing. For a brief second he imagines a vague plume of falling water that becomes a vapor and then a faded memory.

"Are you sure?" he asks.

"Yes! It was a whale. I saw it spouting. There!"

Nothing interrupts the calm of the coastal water.

"It was there! I'm serious."

"I believe you. It's the season. I just missed it," Cal says.

Despite their abstract attention, the solid whale does not reappear. Sometime between four and five they near the Farallones again. Western swells scallop the waters about the islands this clear, crisp, sunny day. Cal sails past the north and middle islands, and circles close up, just outside Mirounga Bay of the Southeast Farallon.

"They call this the hunting grounds," Cal says. "They hunt together here."

Konrad gets his camera and with a short telephoto lens begins to capture the canvass before them. Cal views the scene through his binoculars.

"There's a seal," Cal says.

"Where?"

"There."

Konrad focuses his lens on Cal's discovery.

"It's an adult," he says.

The seal is alone in the sea, not far offshore, heading toward Jordan Channel, the thin waterway dividing two lips of land.

"There's a fin," Konrad says.

The black triangle cuts the water neatly without a trace of wake, coming at the seal from the left rear quarter of his vision – if he were looking. But the seal is swimming in an alternate dimension. In a moment of exaltation, he has dispelled all fear of the ocean's dangers, intent on some other goal concealed in his private heart. Now, it is a matter of trigonometry, the short distance of the seal from the land, the angle from which the fin approaches, its distance and speed, and the speed of the seal. Konrad resolutely aims his camera at the apex of the converging vectors. Paralyzed by the drama, Cal's mouth gapes. The fin speeds up and narrows the distance. The seal has almost made land; a few more supple moves of his powerful fins and . . .

"He's going to make it," Konrad says.

"Maybe," Cal responds.

Below, from the opposite direction of the closing fin, behind and under the seal, the ocean abruptly explodes in a rushing cylinder of rising water, as if an undersea volcanic eruption is occurring. The water lifts the seal, raises it as onto an alter, and offers it to the misty air. The seal rests unmindfully in its embrace, unaware anything has changed. The cylinder of ocean as it rises breaks water off; and as it cascades it reveals the triangular, pointed teeth of the mouth encircling the seal. The sea column vaults six feet into the air, the white belly of the shark standing upright as the giant tail forces gravity to its limit, to a point where the mouth simply hangs, arrested by time; and, for this split second before clamping its teeth together, the ancient killing machine appears to contemplate itself. The click of Konrad's camera returns Cal to his senses.

The great fish and the seal's body disappear. The water boils. Two other sharks, the original fin, and another, circle. The water calms. Floating on the surface are the seal's head and tail flipper; instantly, the fins converge and their spasm removes them. But the crimson blood remains, spreading like petroleum over the water, calming it, as if to document the event, as if to declare itself the sole, lingering evidence, the only witness, except for the two stunned men. Cal swallows. Konrad lowers the camera and stares at the bloody water as if viewing the final curtain of the final act of the final play.

Neptune has been placated. Fresh winds arise from the northwest, Wild Goose flies swiftly home, downwind. Astern, Cal spies in the distance an approaching sailboat, a swarthy, red-hulled sloop, speeding to them. It takes only a half hour before it catches up and passes to their left. Four women in colorful foul weather gear crowd the boat's cockpit. They are young and vibrant and look as strong as Amazons. They are running downwind under full sails and screaming engine, but they slow long enough to parallel Cal's course a moment, and smile.

"Where you from?" Cal yells.

"Just crossed from Hawaii."

"Damn!" Cal blurts.

"Piece of cake."

"Where're you going?"

"Pier 39, San Francisco."

"That's where we park."

"See you there," the helmslady cries.

She advances the throttle, and rapidly becomes a disappearing dot on the water.

"So much for man's supremacy of the sea," Konrad observes.

"They're shooting for the midnight tide."

"We'll not make that under sail."

"No."

———

About three AM, offshore yet a good two miles, they near the outer bay of the Golden Gate. Konrad is below listening to *The Pilgrim's Chorus* on the CD player. Wagner has jogged his childhood memories and he is singing along with vivid gusto.

"We're nearly home," Cal yells down.

"Except for the tide. The ebb's beginning."

"I'll continue south. When can we enter on the flood?"

"It turns back full about nine."

"That means we can motor in about seven."

"Hah! I'm going to sleep. Call if you need me."

It has clouded over and the moon has disappeared. Crossing the southern outbound traffic lane, Cal senses more than hears the deep throb of giant diesels. Faint running lights of a massive black freighter's hull emerge, just clear of the outer harbor before the bridge. The behemoth passes before him, unaware he even exists. At five, he turns back, starts his engine, and retraces his steps. The eastern sun begins to lighten the sky. Konrad wakes and joins him. He's made coffee and brings up a cup.

"Time yet?" he asks.

"Almost. We've got to give the ebb another hour, then I can get us in against it with the engine."

At seven, Cal enters the bay just to right of the southern inbound lane. The sun is up off the horizon now, backlighting the San Francisco skyline. It gleams through some of the windows of the tall shorefront highrises. The mild ebb bucks them as they motor in, but Wild Goose's diesel stems the tide and they pass under the Golden Gate as early workers cross the bridge from Marin into the city.

After bending into Pier 39's outer bay and reversing around the concrete barrier of the inner bay, they spot the ladies' sailboat snugged into the outer slip of "A" dock. By this time, the ebb has decreased, and docking presents no problem. When finally the lines are tied and the engine stilled, they sit below a few moments mulling things over. Konrad picks up his camera and reviews his shots.

"Take a look," he says.

Cal takes the camera in hand and inspects the viewfinder. The outer frame of the picture contains the shark's teeth. It is though they grow out of the frame rather than from the mouth of the animal. The shot is remarkably sharp, clear, and well lighted. The seal at center stage still swims, very much alive, oblivious of his fate. *Or unconcerned?*

Konrad has captured – no, the camera has captured, the moment the eye could never see: that luminous split second when the instinctive agendas of two distinct, living creatures, totally dependent upon one another for the completion of their inevitable destinies, meet to enact that finite instant of time.

"See how the teeth completely surround the seal?" Konrad asks. "They're like a fine Swiss watch, so precise they are. There is no margin for error. None can possibly exist. No alternative to the conclusion is feasible. It is perfect physics. The seal cannot escape."

"He has nothing to escape," Cal says. "Look closely. He's so engrossed in living, he's smiling. It makes no difference that he doesn't know what's happening. He's intently at the peak of his life, of his living. He is totally absorbed with being."

"So is the shark," Konrad insists.

"That's the point."

Konrad considers this before speaking again.

"It's very much like when you jump on board as the tide tears the boat from the slip...when you kick one leg forward, and push with the other, and the dock's left behind, momentarily, and suddenly there you are, hanging in space directly over the gap between the boat and dock. You've made a decision, and if you're off by a fraction of a second it will crush you. But you're not. You look down, and you know that you've calculated everything just right. The seal miscalculated."

"It's something else."

"What?"

"It's his knowing smile of life. It's the keen insight that does not allow for the existence of the shark."

"That doesn't make any sense."

"It's the only thing that makes sense in the world."

"Your point eludes me."

"It is simple. Life is all that exists. Nothing else does, before or after. Life fully lived precludes its own loss. Life is eternal.

"I need to conduct an experiment to test your theory."

"You're conducting it right now. Each of us is."

"That is a vague concept."

"You weary my brain. Check if we have any beer left."

"Aye aye, Captain."

Hunky and Cappy

Christmas Eve of a recent year Hunky Badeker and Cappy Cornelius were stretched diagonally across the grassy creek bank below the Big Sur Village Pub, which establishment Hunky happens to own, on the central coast of California, preparing to speculate on metaphysical questions and such to a depth normally unexplored by philosophers, publishers, or media pundits.

Hunky started the conversation with this annihilating gambit:

"Those sure appear to be serious boots you're wearing, Cappy. Are they Wolverines?"

Cappy paused in the tasting of the grass stem he was chewing, and considered this pithy question. His classically trained literary mind churned.

"Well, no, Hunky, actually they are not. They are called Big Macs."

"Huh!"

"Yep."

"I thought that was a type of hamburger."

"It's that too, but it's also a brand of climbing boot. And that's what mine are."

All six foot three of the moderately domesticated, former biker, Hunky, rolled from his left to his right elbow in the grass and pondered this fact. The mole under his left eye, hidden by his large sunglasses, darkened a shade, the irises of both eyeballs dilated a fraction, the bristles of his bushlike black eyebrows fluttered ever so slightly, a passing breeze whisked the foretop from his forehead to the side of his brow near the ear, which hank of hair he then brushed back in place with one hand, and an ensuing intensity of concentration materialized from the totality of his being not entirely unlike a Stephan Hawkin's galaxy emerging in the starry night of the universal void.

"What," he finally asked with incisive precision, "is the key trait of a Big Mac boot?"

"It's a thinker," Cappy replied.

Hunky could not instantaneously conceive of anything germane to respond, and convinced that the intellectually appropriate attitude would be restraint, remained silent.

"Yep," Cappy said when it was apparent Hunky did not intend to comment further at the moment, "I been living with these boots several years now, and I'm certain they're first class thinkers."

"What do they think about?" asked Hunky, warming to the notion.

"'Bout near everything, I believe."

"Do they talk about what they're thinking?"

"No; they aren't talking boots. Just thinkers."

"Then, how do you know what they're thinking?"

"Dreams."

"Would it unduly strain you to elucidate on this matter?"

"Hunky, as an old friend, it would please me no end to help satisfy your insatiable curiosity for the deeper meanings of life. As a matter of fact, how it happens is I hear their unspoken thoughts in my dreams. Just the other night, for instance, I dreamt I heard them thinking about politics."

"What kinda politics?"

"Oh, just the ordinary backyard garden variety kind, you know, about people figuring out how to get control of things so they can be the ones calling all the shots instead of somebody else who might do it all different from what they would like."

Hunky scratched the outer edge of skin near his left eye, and then that of his right eye, dropped his hand down to his chin, stroked it contemplatively, and cogitated a few moments.

"I would not want to endanger our deep seated and long established friendship," he said, "but I have got to tell you that what you just told me has raised a potentially controversial subject in my mind."

"Shoot, Hunky. What are friends for if not to test one another's deepest sentiments?".

"I appreciate that. What it is, this thought that's come to me, is – let me say it this way: don't it strike you as slightly odd you'd hear your boots conveying to you in dreams ideas about things like politics?"

"Naw. It strikes me rather that your questioning the fact before even listening to what they convey to me is a close-minded attitude typical of the rightist times we live in, leading eventually to the exposure of ignorance on your part if you don't learn how to open up your intellectual apparatus wider to new ideas. I mean, Goddammit, Hunky, who are you to question me on such an issue you don't yet know anything about?"

"Don't get all het up now, Cappy. It's just a question."

"Well, it's a damned uppity one, I think."

"You just said a minute ago what are friends for if not to test one another's deepest thoughts."

"But I didn't know you were going to attack me."

"Attack you? Who in the hell attacked anybody? I just asked a question."

"You sure could have phrased it more diplomatically."

"And you sure could of took it more graciously."

Cappy sat up at this point, and then stood up, walked down to the creek edge, looked at the water flowing for a bit, turned back, returned, sat back down beside Hunky, and seemed to battle with his insides a time. Finally, he spoke again.

"I reckon you have a point. I'm not saying you're right.

But you do have a point. Expecting it to sound sensible for my boots to communicate to me in dreams without my having explained at least part of what they communicate is somewhat of a stretch of credibility on my part, I imagine."

"Thanks for the consideration," Hunky said.

"Not at all."

"So, all that behind us," Hunky ventured, "what do they convey about politics to you in your dreams?"

"Let me think on it…the other night, for instance, the left boot – in one of my dreams – woke me up mumbling about some dude named O'Reilly he'd seen on TV recently when I'd set him down beside his brother near the edge of the couch I was sitting on."

"O'Reilly's brother? You mean the brother of that diarrhea mouthed Irish-American pundit who snaps at everybody invited to his show like he has divine knowledge of everything in the known universe?"

"Wait, Hunky! You're getting mixed up. I meant I'd set down the left boot beside its brother, the right boot, after taking them off to watch O'Reilly."

"Oh. I was close then to your meaning, anyhow. I assumed from your last comment you'd seen the feller yourself pontificating on various and sundry matters."

"I have done that too."

"But in your dream your boot talked about him."

'That is correct."

And how does O'Reilly strike you?"

"That isn't the issue, Hunky. Remember, we're discussing the opinion of my left thinking boot and its observations about Mr. O'Reilly, not mine."

"Must have misspoke myself."

"Happens in the heat of conversation. Well, to get on with it: the boot was cussing, and it wasn't until I woke up that I understood that the cuss words it was saying were words this

O'Reilly fellow had designated on some recent show as having been said by a current Democratic presidential candidate, and his – O'Reilly's, that is – opinion, which he articulated quite forcefully, was that no man running for the presidency who cussed should be seriously considered for that august position. When I was clearly awake and revisiting the dream, I remembered that the boot said some other fellow on the TV show, a professor of some kind, had sat back and listened to O'Reilly spouting off so piously, and when O'Reilly had finally shut up, which takes him sometime quite a while, had pointed out to him a fact of history relevant to O'Reilly's point."

When Cappy did not immediately explain the point in question, Hunky, yearning to obtain adequate facts to enable him to judge the validity of the concept of thinking boots, urged him on.

"Well?"

"Well what?"

"What was the cuss words?"

'What the cuss words were isn't the point. The point is what the professor said."

"Then what did the damned professor say?"

"The professor pointed out to O'Reilly that a substantial number of famous American patriots have been either avid or occasional cussers, including Benjamin Franklin, George Washington, Franklin Delano Roosevelt, Teddy Roosevelt; and that his personal secretary had even reported that now and again Abraham Lincoln had been known to toss out a loose word or two, had actually used the word 'damn' in a public debate to make a point about slavery to Mr. Douglas – all of which proved to the professor's satisfaction that summarily chastising and discarding Democratic presidential candidates for using cuss words was a weak means of discrediting them in favor of allegedly more clean mouthed Republicans, and – furthermore – that Mr. O'Reilly would do well to study American history before mouthing off his singularly biased opinions."

"Good for him!" Hunky declared.

This conjuncture of agreed-upon viewpoints established, and Cappy's wife, Bernadette, having arrived on the scene, the two wisely interrupted their discussion to see what effect the presence of a female would have on the peace of the day, both experienced with the opposite sex enough to know that such an appearance in their immediate personal environs by a woman having temporarily abandoned the security of her home could take the fine edge off the comfort of their talk.

Bernie's defining trait was immense physical cuteness, augmented by dimples the size of small lemons on her cheeks. Her eyes twinkled like Fourth of July sparklers and nestled under a bush of raggedy curly hair the shade of white corn, before boiling. Her lips were full and pouty without benefit of injections, and when standing arms akimbo, stretched tall to her full five foot three stature, as she now was, presented a formidably intimidating adversary.

"Cappy, are you coming home for dinner tonight, or are you and Hunky thinking of hanging out at his bar again like you did last night until two this morning while I was home sniffling with the cold, and my rheumatism acting up again, as if you'd really care what happened to me or not in this world?"

Hunky and Cappy exchanged glances. Hunky demurred to Cappy, since it was his issue, and wife, to be dealt with.

"Bernie, darling," Cappy responded in his deepest *I-still-love-you* voice, how are you? It's so good to see you again."

"Don't you try to divert me from my question, Dr. Cornelius. After twenty three years sharing your often empty bed, I am wise to your ways. Now you answer up. Are you planning on coming home tonight or not?"

Cappy caught on this was a serious moment for his spouse, and rose to the occasion.

"Darling, it being Christmas Eve, could I ever leave you alone as the annually recurring miracle is celebrated among our midst? As a matter of fact, I was just telling Hunky, right Hunky? that since I need to hurry into Pacific Grove to pick up your presents at Holman's Department Store, I'd better get on with it."

Cappy rose to his feet, and made as if to find his car.

"You just hold on there a minute, Cappy Cornelius. If you're going to drive to Pacific Grove, I am going along with you, or my name is not Bernadette Peguine Padua Cornelius."

Whenever Bernie used full names, Cappy knew she was serious. He turned to her and, drawing on his deepest reserves of empathetic understanding, appealed to the love he suspected still lurked in her heart for him.

"You got it, Babe. Come along. We'll go together."

"You sure?" she asked, incredulously.

"Bernie, would I spoof you? Let's have one eggnog at Hunky's though, before we hit the road, to fortify our stomachs. It's about sixty miles round trip, and we can't make it if we're short on energy."

It being Christmas Eve, and eggnog being a fairly mild drink, even with a dollop of sour mash injected, Bernie acquiesced, and she, Cappy, and Hunky walked up the bank to Hunky's establishment and entered into the ambience starting to develop among the dozen or so locals who were tipping a few from the back pool room to the fireplace in the corner.

It was warm inside, smelled of pine cones and mud, it having rained the night before and everybody's boots having acquired the results from the forest floor. Two women lounged at the corner of the bar, energetically discussing the rights of females, and how to further secure them in a world still dominated by evil men. These were Belle Thomas and Alice Constance. Belle was about fifty-five, bleached [actually streaked], slightly chunky, but still attractive in her way; Alice, not what you'd call a beauty, but at thirty-five with a fine figure, long brown hair, and a gentle demeanor, supported by full, soft, moist lips, was an enticing package to any man.

Bernadette watched her man as he greeted the pair, then busied himself ordering their eggnog. Cappy was a lean sixty-five year old transplanted New England scholar whose short silver and black hair reminded her of salt and pepper scattered on hamburger meat. Not that she thought of Cappy's head like hamburger, but the texture of his cropped mane was almost as rough as fresh ground beef, and so – for her, a butcher's daughter with a fine arts degree from Monterey College – the comparison seemed sufficiently apt. His lips were lean, but soft, pliant, and imaginative, she knew, when he felt so inclined to pleasure her. His eyes were brushed aluminum grey, his nose as aristocratic as a Poodle's snout. He maneuvered through life with the humbly self assured air of a cynically enlightened Zen monk who, when bolstered by booze, was known occasionally to philander with the ladies.

"Here's to you, kid," he said, and Bernie and he toasted Christmas.

They didn't linger long. Cappy sensed that any hesitation on his part would meet with fervent negative reaction from his spouse, so – after a single eggnog – he suggested they get on their way. Cappy led Bernie outside, opened the door for her, closed it slowly so not to entrap the hem of her coat, and clambered into the driver's seat of his 1951 Ford. This model Ford had always fascinated Cappy, first when he was completing his Ph.D. at Harvard, and later when he'd picked up his postgraduate auto mechanics degree at a Dodge dealership in Bakersfield. He liked its simplicity. The flathead V-8, the three-speed gearbox, the straight clean boxlike lines.

They drove all the way to Pacific Grove silently listening to Christmas carols because the eggnog had set a mood upon them and neither wished to disrupt it by chancing a difference of opinion about some unimportant topic or the other. Bernie even slipped her hand onto Cappy's leg and left it there while he maneuvered the Ford through Monterey and Pacific Grove traffic. When they got to Holman's, the manager, Sally Crandle, personally retrieved Cappy's layaway boxes of wrapped presents and wished them both a Merry Christmas. Bernie, disoriented by Cappy's generosity, nodded a meek thank you, and kept her tongue. It all implied a pleasant holiday. Cappy decided to take the hilltop road past the hospital to bypass the highway between Monterey and Carmel, and connect directly to Highway One back to Big Sur.

Near the hospital, Highway Patrolman Danny Terwilliger was hiding behind a clump of bushes. Although Cappy was not speeding, Danny recognized his car and, knowing Cappy's fondness for spirits and creative driving, figured that if he'd follow him, he'd likely catch him in a transgression of one driving law or another. Danny was bucking for Lieutenant and needed a few more ticket quota points to look good on next year's promotion list. He slipped his cruiser into low, and gently crept up onto the road. A couple of cars separated him from Cappy, and he was sure he'd arrived on the scene unnoticed by his prey.

"There's that damned Terwilliger again," Cappy said to Bernie, who turned in her seat and spied the patrol car a hundred yards back.

"He sure is a cantankerous soul," Bernie said.

"Son of a bitch is mean spirited."

"Drive carefully now, dear," Bernie said, squeezing Cappy's free hand.

"It won't make make any difference. He's determined."

"Why don't you stop in Carmel, and let's drink a cup of coffee, just in case he's got an alcohol measurer with him?"

"Damn him! I'm not gonna give him the consideration. It's Christmas. Let fate take care of it."

Cappy crossed the river just south of Carmel and pushed the Ford up into the hills overlooking the Pacific Ocean. Behind him, Danny's predatory instincts told him he was onto a winning strategy. But Cappy drove very carefully, and as he reached the flats heading South to home, the mighty Pacific basking in the unlikely winter sun to his right, he thought maybe Danny would give up and he and Bernie could get back among their friends at Hunky's for another eggnog without provocation.

He didn't count on Danny's mood, though. Christmas did not weigh heavy on the patrolman's mind. It irritated him Cappy was driving so sanely. It festered in his gut that maybe he'd been spotted in his dedication to duty and was being outsmarted. No, by God, he figured, he was not going to be cheated out of his kill. He lay back and persistently followed Cappy, who righteously continued to observe all local, state, and national laws to the best of his ability as he trekked homeward, Bernadette glowing warmly beside him and anticipating the awaiting presents concealed within the packages on the back seat.

After he'd passed under the arching trees that magically signaled he'd made it home unscathed by Danny's power lust, Cappy turned briskly off to the right and parked the Ford in front of Hunky's bar. He sat quietly a moment, then turned to Bernie, who was gently stroking his hand.

"Bernie, I know I'm not the best man in the world, but you're still a good woman and as bad as I know you figure I am, I am still massively fond of you. It's Christmas, darling. Forgive me my weaknesses. I do the best I can, I promise. And I never want to hurt you, really, I just slip sometime and that's the way I am and I'm sorry. But I'll keep trying if you will."

"Cappy," she murmured, and leaned over and kissed him on the chin.

All of a sudden the red and blue lights of Danny's cruiser engulfed them and his voice pierced the crisp air and the pristine silence of the woods as he projected it with the amplified speaker of his vehicle.

"Stay where you are!" his voice thundered.

"I'll be Goddamned, that cracker's still here," Cappy said, ignoring Danny's order and climbing out his car. Bernie followed.

Danny marched over to Cappy and Bernie, and stood before them like all tyrants: emotionally insecure, but bullying, nonetheless.

"What the hell you think you're going?" Danny barked.

"I'm looking at a fool, I think," Cappy said.

"You calling me a fool?"

"I am considering it."

"Look how you got that damned car of yours parked. Looks out a line to me."

"Out a line? There aren't any lines in Big Sur. Anyhow, this isn't your jurisdiction. What do you want?"

"I want to know what you're up to?"

"I'm up to getting an eggnog."

The ruckus had made its way into the bar and, while Cappy and Danny had been verbally sparring, the inhabitants of Hunky's popular pub had emptied themselves into the parking lot. The crowd of twenty happy folks silently surrounded the battlefield, waiting to see what happened. The sun had dropped below the waters of the Pacific, and the crackle of the creek where Hunky and Cappy had lain not more than three hours before filtered up to the gathering. Gradually Danny became aware he and Cappy were not alone. He turned back to his car when its flashing lights went black, and saw Hunky climbing out of it. Klay Dornweiler standing by the front of Danny's cruiser, had lifted the hood, and was fiddling around inside with the motor.

"What the hell you doing there?" Danny cried, and reached impulsively for the nine millimeter automatic on his hip.

Klay turned to him, walked calmly up to his face, and grinned. He raised his hand, and showed Danny a hunk of electrical apparatus that looked like it might be a vital part of his car's engine.

"What's that?" Danny asked.

"A twist of fate if you don't lighten up," Klay said, and he flung the tangled wire thirty feet down the bank into the creek's coldly flowing waters.

Danny pulled his gun.

"Don't do that!" Hunky's voice carried to Danny's ears.

Danny turned to the sound, and looked into the business end of Hunky's eyes.

"Now these folks here are having a Christmas celebration in my place, Officer Terwilliger," Hunky said, "and you're welcome inside, if you'd care to join us. They're real peaceable people, but you know as well as I do I used to be a biker. I'm not so given to just standing by when someone pushes on me. I'd suggest you put your nine millimeter in its holster and we all go inside and celebrate the death and rebirth of Christ for awhile, just to carry on the traditions of our country, if nothing else."

"By God, I'll call for backup, you ignorant booze seller."

"I don't think so. That wire tangle Klay hitched into the creek turned your radio off too."

Danny looked down at the creek, and the truth of Hunky's explanation struck home. He was thirty miles from the nearest town, and Big Sur hadn't a resident policemen or sheriff. It was dark, he was the stranger, and the nine-millimeter only held a few rounds. Besides, he knew there was no justifying bloodshed in the situation. He'd simply overplayed his cards. He looked around him. Twenty men and women, give or take a few one way or another, surrounded him. Hunky kept his eyes on him and his hands in his pockets. The ten remaining men appeared calm, but didn't look like they'd take kindly to any further demonstrations of authoritarian rule.

"Danny Terwilliger," Hunky said, "I ain't sure what you think you stand for here with that pistol of yours in your hand. I don't know who you think you're protecting back there in Monterey where they pay your salary to you. I don't have the foggiest idea what you believe in. To be honest, I don't even pretend anymore to know what's going on in this county, let alone the whole misguided country."

Everyone stood listening with an earnest curiosity to Hunky's words. They'd never heard him say anything much but 'want another drink,' or 'what channel you want to watch?' before, but he sure seemed for the moment to have something on his mind.

"What are you saying to me?" Danny said.

"I'm saying you're out of place here, and it strikes me some honest talk is due to occur between us. You just followed Cappy thirty miles as an officer of the law to rag his ass. And now, to put it bluntly, you got your tit in a bit of a wringer."

Danny swallowed uneasily. Hunky continued.

"This ain't Monterey or San Francisco, or New York. It sure as hell ain't Washington, D.C. Up here, we're tired of what's going on nowadays in America. We don't particularly like you Danny. We don't like your attitude. We don't like how you think you got the right to tell us whether we're living right or not. We were all once taught that this country belonged to us. We think we're a group of people bound one to the other by constitutionally legal contract to hold us all together. We don't figure we're some kind of semi work slaves required to kowtow to and kiss the ass of every millionaire corporate trollop who ambles down the pike. And for damned sure not the ass of his paid flunky."

Danny tensely considered the people calmly surrounding him, sipping their drinks. Then he turned back to Hunky's never wavering eyes. He reviewed the condition of his cruiser, disabled by Klay's handiwork, and, although he didn't completely understand, he understood one thing: his nine-millimeter wasn't much of a solution to the situation. He thought a minute, and then he put the pistol back in its holster. Something sunk in. Some fraction of the scene clicked in place within his brain. And he took the buckle of this belt holding the holster, and he undid it, and took off his belt and gun, and he walked behind his cruiser and opened the trunk, and tossed the gun in, and closed the trunk hatch. Then he walked back to the group, unarmed.

"Maybe I ought to have a drink with you?" he asked, uncertainly.

Hunky smiled.

"Sure," he said, and led Danny into the bar. The others followed, an inaudible sigh accompanying them. Alice Constance, the aforementioned not really pretty woman, but still the most desirable unattached lady in attendance, stepped out of the group and approached Danny. She took his hand and guided him to a seat at the counter. After close consultation with her, Danny ordered two steam beers and a plate of nachos. Bernie and Cappy got a couple of hamburgers and two pale ales. Everyone else ordered whatever it was they wanted: chili, onion rings, French fries, peanuts, and a wide variety of liquid refreshments.

Hunky turned the TV on. As everyone started to relax, Fox news erupted.

First O'Reilly, then Greta Van Susteren, interviewing a sleek blue pen-striped two star army general who obviously didn't buy his suits at the post PX.

Klay, a dedicated bachelor, turned to Cappy and said: "You know, she's not a bad looking woman. I like her lean cheeks and the crooked turn of her mouth when she talks, and I always figured she'd have small, perky breasts. There's something sexy about her, but she's hard. She's like Danny. She seems to have misplaced her sensitivity somewhere, seems she's lost any understanding about ordinary people, those who do all the grunt work, the guys who empty her trash and wash her onions for her before she buys them so clean at the supermarket. I'd like to sleep with her, though, if she picked up some gentleness. Do you know what I mean?"

"Yeah, I know what you mean," Cappy agreed.

Bernie, who'd overheard this exchange, reached over and patted Klay's cheek.

"She's not got the right balance between bawdiness and braininess for you Klay. Hell, she's got more testosterone than Governor Arnold."

"Damn, Bernie," Cappy said. "I wouldn't have put her down that flat myself."

"Must be the ale," Bernie said. "But, I like my women as emotionally well balanced as my men. I mean, *soft-smart* is better than *hard-smart* for any woman wanting to plumb the heart of a good man."

Cappy slapped her on the butt, and said, "Honey draws better than vinegar, eh?"

Bernie slapped his butt right back, then she put her face up close to his and blew lightly into his mouth.

"Poooooooof!"

Cappy rolled back on his heels and laughed.

Meanwhile, Alice had slipped her hand into Danny Terwilliger's pants pocket.

"Bernie, my faithful lady," Cappy said. " How'd you like to open your presents right now?"

"Oh!" Bernie exploded, ejecting Cappy into the parking lot to retrieve her gifts from the Ford. He returned, sheepishly handed them to her, and retired to the back pool room with Klay.

Belle Thomas escorted Bernie to the corner fireplace and watched as she unwrapped each present. When Bernie had finished, she was bawling her eyes out, and Belle was hugging her in support. Before her lay the complete works of Emily Dickinson, bound in wine red leather, a single hand painted ceramic rose book mark, and a pair of one eighth carrot diamond earrings perched each on the end of a platinum pendant. Belle spoke.

"You two must love each other a lot."

"Yeah, I guess so, sometimes," Bernie said.

"You mean you guess sometimes you love each other, or sometimes you love each other, you guess?"

"Christ, Belle, how do I know?"

Bernie marched into the poolroom, flung her arms around Cappy's neck and kissed him. Then she stepped back, and gave him a full knuckled roundhouse slug on the chin that rocked him back on his heels again.

"Green peas, Bernie. Why'd you do that?"

"For being so Goddamned inconsistent."

Bernie turned on her heel and abandoned Cappy to feebly reconsidering exactly how the female mind operates. When by the end of the next pool game, he'd figured part of it out, he returned to her in the main room, and it seemed, for the time being at least, familial peace had been restored.

Belle and Klay, being the only two local singles, started mixing it up, and Hunky's broad-hipped, broad-shouldered woman, Flora, who worked the kitchen, came out and had a drink with her man. Danny, warmed up by Alice Constance's constancy, slid over to Hunky finally and said he was having a good time.

"Yep?" Hunky asked.

"Yes. Really. Except…one thing. What is it all of you want? Everybody living here alone, in the woods? In this lonely place?"

"That's simple," Hunky said.

"Well?"

"I ain't sure you'r ready for it, Danny."

"Try me."

"First, Big Sur ain't lonely. And second…"

Alice squeezed Danny's privates at this point, and he turned to her and grinned, silly, like a monkey on a string held by an accordion player.

Hunky noted this aside, and waited.

After a few seconds, Danny remembered he and Hunky were talking and he turned back to him.

"What were you saying?"

"You asked what we want."

"Yeah."

"I said it's simple."

"I'm listening."

"We'd kinda like our country back again."

Danny looked down into his glass and watched the foam dissolve gradually like soap bubbles do in a wash basin after they've lifted off all the dirty scum.

O'Reilly's voice from the television, sounding like jack boots marching on dry gravel, snapped a rebuke to his visiting guest as his hand clicked off the man's microphone in mid speech.

"We don't allow any loose talk here, you understand?" he barked.

The man got up and walked off the TV set, leaving O'Reilly alone.

"Some people just can't stand the heat," O'Reilly blustered.

The TV snapped to a commercial for imported breakfast sausages.

"I think I'm beginning to see what you mean," Danny said to Hunky.

"You think?"

"Some, anyhow. You know what's needed?" Danny said.

"A plan."

"Well, that would certainly be a start," Hunky conceded.

"Have another beer?"

"Believe I will."

Cappy and Bernie walked up behind Danny and Hunky.

"How are things going now?" Cappy asked.

"Getting there," Hunky said. "Danny," he continued, "Cappy here's got a pair of pretty smart boots that might help you with your plan idea."

"Boots? How's that?"

"Ask Cappy. It's his boots."

Danny hung his arm around Cappy's shoulder, and they started discussing the phenomenon of thinking boots. Bernie and Belle repaired to the fireplace, where they read Emily Dickinson's poems to one another and wept a lot. Everybody, continuing to explore – with all its failings, with all its pain and disappointments, with all its reluctant but obstinate beauty – the infinite mystery of human brother and sister hood, talked and drank together until three-thirty. Then, they all hugged one another and departed for home to exchange gifts with those they lusted after, loved, and, more often than not, worried about.

Sammy's Epiphany

Sammy Samoschevitz, previously of Flatbush, Brooklyn, was distraught. His brother-in-law-to-have-been, Curly O'Toole, of Boston's County Cork clan, had broken his word. It's like this: although Curly was vaguely aware the Internet existed, and the host of other modern twists of life the rest of us have adjusted to, he was fundamentally detached from the chaotic mayhem of the digital world.

Curly, who still wore corduroy knickers and plaid knee-length wool stockings mailed to him annually by his Uncle O'Faolain from Dublin, also still clung, albeit it tenuously, to Rome's Holy Grail, while Sammy had finally tossed his Star of David and no longer clung to anything any more other than his own devices. His loss of faith had coincided with the death of Curly's beloved: Sammy's younger sister, Ida, who had perished of pneumonia a year hence, this occurring while she was becalmed dead center of the Indian Ocean in her thirty-three foot sailboat, "Out Here," during a 'round-the-world navigation sponsored by San Francisco's Seven Seas Software Society.

Sammy hadn't minded Ida's involvement with a son of the old sod, but he had been concerned because Curly was an unemployed poet, wordsmiths not being major drawing cards in the high tech job market, security being a prime requisite of ladies in uncertain times like these, and him knowing it would reflect upon his personal character if he permitted a sister of his to end up in this kind of romantic liaison in a world already fraught with peril. Curly had at least tried. Once he spent his last quarters to buy a lingering copy of the dematerializing *San Francisco Chronicle* only to find that the employment section, which he called Section "E," was not present in his copy of the paper. Whether it lay on the floor of the *Chronicle's* pressroom, had dropped in the corner of the delivery truck, or had inevitably moved on to its Internet incarnation was irrelevant to Curly. What was relevant to his mind was – according to Sammy's mind – that he, Curly, was looking for "a way out" and had divined this missing section "E" to affirm that mankind's sense of a universal presence was informing him simple work was not his purpose in life, a leaning Curly had long held as gospel anyhow. So, missing section "E," Curly, over his morning Starbucks, penned a fresh piece of doggerel to add to his compendium of growing works of art.

> *Life 'tis very rough*
> *When "E" ain't there;*
> *If thinks you it is fair,*
> *You ain't astute enough.*

Dante's Inferno it was not. But, it delivered a certain down-to earth mysteriousness replete with psychological undertones, so Curly filed it away, perhaps to embellish, and even publish, the theme at some point in the undefined future.

What word to Sammy might Curly have broken? a tenacious and curious mind could inquire. It was simply that he *would* find a job during the week to earn money, and would start writing poetry only on weekends. Ida, however, eventually decided that rather than Curly being her ideal man, he was a bum, and consequently had opted to sail around the world. Sammy, possessing unique cognitive powers, therefore blamed Curly for Ida's demise on the cold and lonely sea.

Distraught was not precisely speaking what Sammy felt. He felt more, like, well – to maintain accuracy, we'd have to call it "anxiety ridden." The source of his discontent was that in addition to Curly's unsatisfactory relationship with the former Ida, he also owed Sammy some money from an ancient loan, which he could not repay due to his chronic impoverishment. Sammy, not being a major labor aficionado himself, could not get together the twenty-five dollar bet he wanted to place on the filly, *America's Soul*, running at five to one odds Saturday at Pimlico. Sammy wanted to place the bet because if his horse won, at five-to-one odds the twenty-five dollars would magically multiply into one hundred twenty-five dollars, this being precisely how much he owed on a parking ticket he had incurred on Broadway one night a year before when he had temporarily possessed a 1965 Plymouth convertible, won in a China Town poker game off Fung Wow Ding.

Fung Wow – ah, but that's another story for another day. Pertinent to the moment is that Santio de Chile, the upwardly mobile North Beach cop, had recently reminded Sammy of the ticket, specifying if the fine was not paid in full by a deadline soon upcoming, he, Santio, would be obliged to slap him, Sammy, in the city lockup for a month as just retribution for his heinous crime.

Sammy was not enamored of the concept of sleeping thirty nights on a hard slab in San Francisco's finest municipal accommodations. He had only recently conquered a lifelong bout with alcoholism, aided by the help of the local substance abuse program, and wanted to get on with his life. One twelfth of a year's incarceration did not fit into his career gameplan.

So, in its elusively charming manner, infinity had impelled into Sammy's evolving consciousness the notion that if he could find Curly a job, then Curly would be obliged to pay him back the borrowed twenty-five dollars, hopefully saving him the embarrassment and discomfiture of jail. To this end, Sammy had convinced Arnie, the owner of *Arnie's Burger Shop & Lottery Emporium* in North Beach, to offer Curly the four-day-a-week job minding his place on the days Arnie liked

to take off and play Bocce Ball with the local retired Mafiosi
– mostly just former low level bag guys for the family, who'd
never hurt a flea, and too were seeking peace of mind in their
old age.

Arnie, a fifty-four year old cook who had emigrated from
Gaza thirty-five years ago, needed a new helper because Tootsies, his former second-in-command, had abruptly abandoned
the job following three year's faithful servitude to move to New
York City, "needing," he proclaimed, "a change of scene," and
because, "it is time I started taking my ballet career seriously."

Tootsies, being an 'artiste,' and having set a high standard,
not only of cookery, but attention to the needs of customers,
had invested in the job a certain level of challenge and com-
pensation to any would-be applicant. The point here, lest it
may have eluded you in the mounting passion of the narrative,
is that the convergence of Arnie's need for a helper with Sammy's need for twenty-five dollars, and Curly's availability to
potentially satisfy both their needs, was – in Sammy's view – a
veritable gift from the all mighty, the being he was no longer
sure existed, but who in times like this was of value to Sammy
as a last ditch refuge. If this sounds like Sammy was at a spiritual crossroads in life, you have intuitively grasped the essence
of events to this point in time.

It was outside the toilet at the Trieste Café in Sausalito,
on the other end of the Golden Gate Bridge from North Beach,
Sammy eventually confronted the conclusion that he was ulti-
mately destined for sobriety. This past occurrence is not an idle
aside. Rather, it constitutes the germ of the eventual redemp-
tive transformation to take place in Sammy's character, the arc
of his mid-life crisis one might propose, saving and confirming
his continued companionship with Curly.

It happened in this manner. He had tried the toilet door
and, finding it locked, had stood outside five minutes patiently
waiting for the present occupant to finish his business and

emerge. When, after the allotted five minutes, no one had exited the John, he had tried the door again – again to no avail. His bladder was nearing the failsafe point. Abruptly then, but gently, the bathroom door had fluffed open, and then fluffed closed. Fluffed was the only word that came to Sammy's mind to describe how the door had wafted out and back shut, as a ghost might have sallied forth.

Sammy had waited a minute after this phenomenon, assuming the former inhabitant might have changed his mind, and was still inside the toilet. He considered, perhaps the occupant had returned to some last minute forgotten ritual, like zipping his fly or adjusting the hair of his temples to fall over a bald spot. After the minute, he had tried the door handle again, and found it was unlocked. He had entered. The toilet was empty!

While ministering to his needs, he concluded that under the influence of fermented sour mash he had just become too mentally confused to master the intricacies of the doorknob, and in a trice he discerned it was time to investigate the possibilities of life without inebriates. This might seem to the sober soul a far-fetched idea, but not from Sammy's perspective. This simple event was like a Zen Buddhist Koan: it was the key to his enlightenment. However, as Sammy had been socking down a fifth of Jim Beam a day for one-half his life, instantaneously coping ethically with the solution to his potential jail term was not entirely a slam-dunk.

It's a task I tell you," Sammy explained to police sergeant de Chile as the officer ticketed a Kansas-plated Toyota on a side street next day.

Really? " answered Santio, who had never allowed spirits of the bottle either to cross his pallet or open a toilet door for him in his twenty-seven years of devotion to defending mankind against traffic criminals while studying at night school to become a full detective.

"Give me some time while I work on Curly's new job," Sammy pleaded to de Chile.

"No," answered Santio.

"The reason I took to drink," Sammy blundered on, "was my father."

Santio stepped to the next car, a Honda Accord, and prepared another ticket.

"Dad was a devout Rabbi," Sammy persisted, "the full-bearded, ear-ringleted, fervently persuaded, orthodox variety who immigrated to America from Armenia in order to return the keys of the faith to the Jews of the New World. He figured if he could cleanse the upstart bastions of Capitalism of their moneyed taint, he would someday sit on the right hand of God and bask eternally blissful."

"You going somewhere with this, Sammy? Why don't you can it?"

Santio moved on to a green Mustang convertible.

"Come on, Santio. Have some compassion. I need your help."

"I think maybe you need cooling out in the freezer."

"Mother of Moses. You got dried ice for a heart. From the time I was three years old, my old man hounded me that steadfast adherence to temperance was the salvation of a young man's future."

"Sounds right to me," Santio said, emphatically.

"But the moral pressure was too much for me. In high school I fell one Saturday night outside in the parking lot after a basketball game to the lurking genie in the bottle. A buddy gave me a beer, actually in a can, and bet me a dollar I couldn't down it in one swig."

"You won the buck?" Santio asked.

"Yeah."

"Well, you're gonna win thirty days if you don't find the twenty-five bucks, pal," Santio said, and started stalking off.

"You ain't gonna help me?"

"Why don't you get a job, Sammy, and just pay the damned ticket?"

"You wanna know why? I'll tell you why. It's cause I got the original $25 fine for being two minutes late pluggin' the meter with a quarter. And when I couldn't pay it right off, the late fees ran it to the $125 mark, which is a 500% return on the original quarter if you do the math, all of which we know goes to a bunch of rich guys who run the city, right?"

'Maybe," de Chile admitted.

"Maybe, my ass. So, I don't get off grindin' my butt into mincemeat to make some rich guys richer off my hard labor. You know what I'm sayin' to you?"

"Whatever," de Chile said.

And this time, he did stalk off. Unable to divert de Chile from his duty, Sammy's salvation now depended on immediately maneuvering Curly into accepting Arnie's hash slinging job. He knew the four hundred dollars a week Curly would earn, a substantial portion of which Sammy would surely acquire with some regularity if he played his cards right, would introduce to both a new lease on life.

Instinctively certain, however, that filthy lucre alone would not spark Curly's interest, he endeavored to delve into the revelations of poetry composition as an insight of how to motivate him. For the first thirty minutes he drew a blank. Eventually, however, progress emerged. There was obviously the element of rhyming and the joys to be gotten from the successful pairing of words. Sammy had never himself tried to put his internal experiences into words, let alone rhyme them. Where in all of life's trials truth resided had never before been an issue of serious concern to him. But now, meditation on what might motivate an Irish poet for the first time brought to the forefront of his brain the wonder of metaphysics: the relationship of the human state of being to the universe – in other

words, where we come from, why we are here, and where we
are headed.

He got *inside* poetry. It was…what was it? It was, he
groaned, in his newly discovered process of thinking: holes. It
was the spaces in between normal words and sentences, what
was left out more than what was put in, the *in-between* of
communication, the not-quite-articulated, or even consciously
thought of, that which was…what word could describe it?
Undescribable." That was it.

Probing further he considered *emotions* might in some
peculiar fashion play a part, exactly how he wasn't sure, but at
this stage of his intellectual development precise applicability
was not the object, it being first more important to identify the
living thoughts he was dealing with in order to make real progress. This realization alone to his mind constituted progress.
He warmed to the subject.

Curly, he considered, might be seeking personal substantiation. Perhaps, poetry gave him a foundation for being. If so,
what did this mean to him? What precisely did he feel needed
substantiating? What was it inside himself that demanded
this? For that matter, what was substantiation? For a moment
Sammy thought he was going crazy circling about these ideas.
Then he took a deep breath and felt he might have gotten it.
Was what Curly needed possibly exactly the same as what he
had needed and found in alcohol? Might not it be some kind of
universal something people need to make them feel right about
themselves, that which some find in God, others in service to
fellow beings, yet others in self-denial, and some not so rare
creatures in blatant acts of evil?

If he could identify in himself what that need had been,
he reasoned, might not he understand Curly's motivation
as a poet? Flatbush practicality merged with North Beach
intuition. New York and California cultures experienced a
momentary merging within his cells, between the nerve

synapses, among the enigmas of his brain. Now that he was on the leading edge of a roll, as they say in California, he decided to go for it.

Santio, having now finished his punitive rounds, returned to the scene at this point and brusquely insinuated himself into Sammy's meditations.

"You haven't got a lot more time, you know, until I'm obliged to take you in."

"I'm working on it!" Sammy exclaimed.

Sammy headed over to Curly's, a room behind and above Ching Loo's duck and goose butcher shop on Little Puddle Lane, where China Town merged with the backside of North Beach. The neighborhood is called Patusan for some unknown reason by the local residents, and is infamous for harboring leaders of a handful of competing Asian gangs, which methodically run rampant vying for criminal control of the area.

Arriving unannounced at Curly's abode, Sammy sensed something was amiss.

Ching Loo was not in attendance as usual, having left two pimpled youth whacking away with machetes at the fresh ducks and geese lying limply on the cutting tables. The air was filled with the scent of blood and an aura of foreboding. Nevertheless, ever courageous in his task, Sammy slipped around the back of the place, and climbed up the stairs to Curly's. He squeaked open the screen and tapped on the door.

Nothing.

He tapped again.

A muffled shuffle arrived, and the door opened. Two beady little eyes, glistening with moisture, peered out at him. Curly didn't look very good at all.

"Are you all right?" Sammy inquired.

"What do you want?" Curly said.

"To introduce your muse," Sammy answered.

"Introduce…"

"Let me in," Sammy said, grabbing the edge of the door with curved fingers and thumb, nudging Curly gently aside as he invaded his privacy.

"I'm not well..." Curly attempted.

"I can see that. What is wrong with your self? Are you ill?"

"My soul, it's my everlasting..."

"That's what I've come about, actually," Sammy said, placing a kettle on Curly's one hot plate to boil tea water. "Sit down, I'll take care of you."

Curly seemed stunned by the intrusion and sat down at the kitchen table. After Sammy had got the water boiling, dipped the teabags, and spooned the sugar, Curly found his voice again.

"It wasn't my fault. I've been thinking...she had something to do with it..."

"What are you talking about?" Sammy asked.

"Ida..."

"Now, that's OK. I didn't come here to rag you anymore about Ida."

"But that's what I've been thinking about...thinking...no, dreaming...or something. She had an idea...I didn't listen... or she didn't..."

Sammy gathered Curly was truly not content at the moment. If he was to persuade Curly to his plan, he must first deal with this surprise issue and help Curly work his way through his present state of mind.

"You're concerned with something about Ida?"

"I can't talk here. Let's go outside."

"What about the tea?"

"Let's get out of here," Curly blurted, and he bolted out the door and down the stairs, knocking his teacup off the table and onto the floor where the tea mingled with the yellowing pile of classified Chronicle ads in the corner, causing them ever so slightly to rearrange themselves, as though they were living things.

Sammy followed Curly as he crunched himself through the milling throngs of China Town, down Grant Street past the many open-faced shops, among the gaping tourists, the bearded old Chinese gentlemen guarding their front doors and enticing wanderers in to their wares, their women, arms laden with fresh veggies and fruit, patrolling their swarming children toward home. Eventually, they reached California Street, a long, jagged walk taken in silence by Sammy as he obediently followed the irrational Curly.

A cable car arrived and Curly jumped on. Sammy clambered after him. They found seats inside. This was good, because a light mist was falling and a chill was on the bay breeze skirting the buildings.

They rode in silence a block.

"There was more to it…" Curly attempted, then shut up, clamping his lips together as though he had committed a blasphemy.

"It's all right. I'm listening" Sammy urged.

Curly looked up close right into Sammy's eyes, attempting – it seemed – to determine if he were safe saying what he wanted to release from his fevered mind.

"She…"

"Ida…"

"Yes…"

"Go on…"

"She…I…we…"

"Out with it…"

"You must understand…I tried…I really did try."

The conductor clanged the bell loudly as the car crossed an intersection.

"I wanta go back again," Curly said.

"Back where?" Sammy asked.

"Back to where Ida and I…"

Again, Curly became mute, staring into nothingness. Sammy looked hard at him, then slapped his face. The conductor and other passengers glanced out of the edges of their eyes, and Sammy put up both his hands, palms outward to all of them.

"Shuuhh," he whispered. "It's all right, I'm his friend. He's had a hard time, needs a jolt to come out of it. I didn't hurt him none."

The passengers seemed to understand, and slunk back behind their newspapers, engrossed in the more fascinating misfortunes of the world. Discretely, and without taking Sammy's and Curly's fares, the conductor stepped outside. He seemed to understand that the crisis needed spiritual space to alleviate itself.

"Let's get out here," Sammy insisted and, taking Curly by the arm, he guided him safely onto the street. They were at the peak of Nob Hill on the corner where the Mark Hopkins sits, austerely independent, enshrouded now in the afternoon summer fog. The sun shone meekly through the mist like a failed benediction.

He walked Curly past the ruddy red millionaires' mansion, and directed him into the park where they carefully inspected for several minutes the delicate flow of the fountain, and then sat down on one of the benches.

Curly seemed to come to his senses.

"I've got to tell you something."

"Anything," Sammy said.

"You blame me for…"

"No more…"

"You *blamed* me then, for…don't stop me…for her death."

"I did," Sammy said, finally.

"Well, it was this way, maybe I was partially to blame, but I loved her, and I wanted her, and I tried, but it was hard…and

I had problems…but, see now, she did too…it was about us being afraid to be…to enter into one another's being, to be… close, I guess must be the word, I can't think of any other…of her wanting to be…and I when I tried…finding that my trying caused…something to happen to her…that I could not measure, something unfathomable…"

He looked up from his hands to a little boy who had made his way out of the sand pile to come stand before them and stare, his toy steam shovel hanging from his grimy little hands.

"Go away, kid," Curly said.

The little boy continued to stare.

"I mean it, scram!"

The kid flipped sand on Curly's lap.

"Bugger off, you little creep!"

The child's mother approached, a sweet understanding smile on her face.

"I hope little Johnny's not bothering you gentlemen," she said.

"He's driving me nuts, lady," Curly said. "Take him away. Now! Fast!"

"Well I never!" she exclaimed, escorting her son to safety.

"Well now you have, dammit!"

Sammy waited while Curly regained his composure.

"Before she left," Curly continued, "…three months before…we were home one night. We'd been…" he looked at Sammy as he revealed this information "…lovers for awhile. We'd made love, that is, several times, and it had been good. Everything seemed fine. We were happy, we were lost in one another."

"I understand," Sammy encouraged him.

"But, this night, she was suddenly distant. She sat reading a…some kind of Philosophy book, and she ignored me. I walked over and…lightly…touched her shoulder, but she ignored me, as if I were not there…touching her. 'Is something wrong?' I asked."

She looked up at me.

"'I don't think you understand me,' she said.

"What don't I understand?

"'See! You have to be so specific. I mean, down inside me.'

"I dropped to my knee to be close to her. I never done anything like that before, you know what I mean?"

"'Don't condescend to me,' she said, and got up.

"What's the matter?" I asked.

"'Goddammit, you men are all alike. About as sensitive as tire tools.'

"Honey," I said, "I don't understand."

"'I know,' she said.

"I didn't know what to do or say. Nothing was making any sense to me. I was lost for words. It was more like inside my head was a filling up with pressure that pushed out all thought. She looked at me a long time, and then picked up her coat and walked out the door. Things were never the same after that. We just sort of fell apart. She grew more and more distant, then she started planning the sailing trip. She wouldn't talk to me. I didn't know what to do."

"Why didn't you tell me?"

"I thought she'd come around. ...I don't know... I thought...maybe...she would just change back to the way she was. But, she didn't. She left."

"Gee, I'm sorry, Curly."

"You know what you wanted? I did it."

"What?"

"I'd found a job."

"No!"

"Yeah. Macy's said I could sell socks."

"You'd signed up at Macy's?"

"Full-time."

"She knew?"

"Yes."

"Did you tell anyone else?"

"Father O'Leary. He said, give her time. I gave her time. I kept quiet, waiting for her to change back the way she was. But the day came, and she got in the boat and sailed away."

"I never knew about the job," Sammy said.

They kept quiet a long time.

"What did you want to see me about?" Curly finally asked.

"I...I've..."

"It's your turn."

"I was wondering...if you could help Arnie out."

"What's Arnie need?"

"Tootsie's left town."

"So?"

"Arnie needs a replacement."

"I think I could have helped her...if I'd been quicker. She needed me to understand."

"You did the best you could."

"I didn't know how to do better."

It's all right."

"Yeah. I guess. . . Arnie needs someone?"

"To run the place...when he's gone, playing Bocce, four days a week. Pays really good, hundred a day, that's sixteen hundred a month."

"What would I do?"

"You know. Cook."

"I don't know how to cook."

"It's easy. He'll learn you. Go see him."

"When?"

"Now. I told him about you. He's waiting."

"Sammy..."

"...Yeah?..."

"...I met a new lady..."

"It's alright. I understand."

Curly mulled this over a minute, jumped up, and said: "I'll do it. I'll go now. I'll make a new way for myself. I will. It'll work. I'll make it work."

And he left, immediately, just like that. Like fate turning on a dime. Sammy watched him walk down the street, wondering at how easy it had all been. He didn't see Curly for a week; then, he dropped by Arnie's one day, and there he was, flipping burgers. Sammy ordered a beer and a hotdog.

"How's it going?" he asked.

"Fine," Curly said with enthusiasm.

"You got the hang of it, real good."

"Piece of cake."

Curly had a way of tossing a bun over his shoulder, and it landing open side down on the grill beside the wiener, that was absolutely amazing. Then, he'd swirl both around with the spatula like a Benihana cook does shrimp, and twirl the spatula in the air and catch it – God's truth! – in his teeth by the handle, after which he'd jump in the air and click his heels together. Damnedest thing you ever saw.

"I'll tell you, man," Sammy said.

"Don't bother…I know…it's good…but, when you get a chance, things like this can happen, you know?"

"Guess so," Sammy said, looking around the café.

The other customers were a mixed bag: an old Chinese guy with one of those long, straggly white goatees, a sloe-eyed Italian laborer type, a thin, wan lady of indiscriminate background wearing an equally thin cotton dress with holes in it and a yellow bow in her hair, a couple of fat teenage boys with skateboards at their feet, and one really rough looking oriental guy in a T-shirt bulging with biceps, a mean ass look on his face, scars, that kind of thing. When Curly set the hotdog before him, Sammy whispered:

"Who's the scuzz down at the end?"

Shit, man, keep it down. That's Shar Pei, head of a local Gang. He's one mean mother, you know what I mean? I mean, he's a bad dude, been putting the protection make on Arnie. I'm trying to chill him out."

Sammy kept his mouth shut, except to chew the dog, didn't talk anymore, just let Curly do his thing. When he had finished, he got up and fumbled in his jeans for some money.

On me," Curly said.

"Thanks, say…could I...?"

"What?"

"I..."

"You need some money?" Curly said.

He fished in his pants and pushed a small wad of cash at Sammy.

How much you need?"

"Would..."

"Whatever..."

"Twenty-five dollars?"

Curly shoved three tens into into Sammy's hands and turned back to the grill to roll a wiener over and flip its bun on the side.

"Thanks." said Sammy.

Get outa here," Curly said, and Sammy left.

Sammy put twenty-five on the five-to-one longshot at Pimlico, but the little scamp ran last, and the remaining five wasn't enough to prevent Santio from doing his job. So, Sammy spent thirty days on ice. It wasn't so bad. The mattress was razor thin and the food wasn't even up to McDonald's, but at least he had a toilet in the room and a sink and hot water.

While inside, Tony Tabasa told him Curly had come head on with this Shar Pei guy and, bully for him, had gotten some other guys together to help, and they had knocked some sense into the Chink one night. Shar Pei had left town after his beating, moved to Chicago where the scene was cooler. Curly overnight had become the hero of Patusan, its savior, a mythical modern day protector of the local downtrodden.

"Hey," Sammy intoned sometime later, sitting down on one of the stools Friday night after all the hookers and the strippers had finished their midnight chili fix to fire 'em up for the early Saturday morning bumps and grinds.

"Sammy, baby," Curly said

Hear you're a big dude hereabouts these days."

"Got a little status."

"Why you still flippin' burgers?

"World needs more humble leaders."

"Well said."

"You all right? Heard you…was… 'in' for awhile."

"For a month. Yeah. I was in. It's OK. I'm…I'm OK."

"Good…bitch of a world, huh"

"Has its moments."

"I'll say…you want?"

"Chili."

"Good choice. Just killed the cow yesterday. Cooked it all night. It's the best."

While Curly prepared his cuisine, Sammy noticed Arnie's place looked like it had enjoyed a face lift. New paint, new green stool covers, floor was clean, menu no longer chalked on a blackboard, but printed off a computer, windows washed, grease wiped off the ceilings, the grill neat and tidy, icebox door hinges repaired, paper napkins – green, not white, to match the stools.

"You been interior decorating?" Sammy asked.

"Yeah, now the gang war's under control."

"Good job."

Curly set the chili on the counter and doused it with cheese and raw onions, just the way Sammy liked it, gave him a bottle of Tabasco and a cup of coffee, and watched Sammy dive in.

"You know, Sammy…"

" …Good chili, man!"

"…Thanks. You know, Sammy, you gave me a new lease on life. I'm somebody, nobody big, but …I'm…somebody, anyhow, now…somebody."

"I'm glad for you," Sammy said.

"You're a real Bro."

"Man's gotta believe in something. I believe in you, Curly."

"You oughta believe in something bigger than me, Sammy."

"You keep fingering the beads, buddy. I'll take strength from you. Believe me, Curly, in this world, you're not a bad guy to bank on."

"Gee, thanks, Sammy."

"Don't mention it."

"Say, Curly ventured. "I don't wanta impose on you, but the Chinaman's had a change of heart. Says he's gonna paint my place. Can I, maybe sack with you tomorrow night while the paint dries?"

"Need you ask?"

Next day, Curly moved in for the evening. It was his day off, and he settled in on the couch with the latest sports mags. Sammy gave him a set of sheets and a pillow, and repaired to the bedroom. He thought how lucky he was to have found such a friend as Curly and sleep wrapped around him. When finally he dreamed, his dream was more real than real.

He didn't hear from Curly for awhile. He had to find some steady money himself, somewhere, and taking a clue from Curly, applied for a sales job at The Fisherman Wharf boat shop, and started hawking bottom paint and chains and floats, that kind of stuff, to the sailors and the fishing guys down on the docks. Now and then he got word of how well Curly was doing at the job. Arnie'd let him buy in half of the place, and they were investing part of the profits together in computer stocks, and now and then taking a fling with currencies and commodity futures. He heard Curly was getting along well with his new lady. He was happy for him.

It was Santio who told Sammy. He came by one day on his day off, wearing his chinos and deck shoes, and his blue sailing cap, to buy some varnish.

Sammy."

Sergeant de Chile."

I need to talk to you."

They went next door to the fish and chips place and had a beer.

I got something to show you," Santio said. "Curly got a letter the other day... from some far away place. Ida left it in the boat, it seems. After they found her, later some time, somebody put a stamp on it, and mailed it to Curly. Here, look at it."

"What…"

"You need to read it."

"What are you doing reading Curly's mail?"

"I'm gonna tell you. But you gotta read it first. This is important. I'll explain. Trust me on this."

He handed the letter to Sammy and watched him while he read it.

"Dear Curly," it said. "You couldn't help it…I couldn't try…because of my…that which I still can't talk about…the something inside that wouldn't figure out…I wanted to be near you, Curly, but the fear…it was, the fear…and I remember the smothering of it all…you were dear, but understand…do, do try…I'll come back. Someday …maybe, but the wind is up now and the sail needs trimming…I'll write more…later…I want you to have this now, though…perhaps it will make up… in some part for what I …"

And there as abruptly as it started, it stopped.

It don't make no sense," Sammy said.

Something was wrong with her, that's all," Santio said. He pointed at his head. Up here. You know? Something just went wrong. It happens sometimes."

"I guess so, Sammy said. But that don't explain how you got the letter."

Shar Pei, he came back in town. This morning about one, while Curly was wiping down the grill, Shar Pei drilled him in the back with a '45…"

"Ahhhhhhrrrrhhhh . . ."

" I finally got upped to detective, you know. . .they sent me to Arnie's ... to investigate the scene. The letter was in Curly's pocket. I figured you need to see it.
You understand?"

"Yeah, I understand...Thanks Santio. That's nice of you to do."

"There's something else," Santio said, and handed Sammy an envelope. "Curly left something for you."

Inside the envelope was Curly's handwritten will leaving Sammy $3,000 worth of IBM.

"Jesus!" Sammy exclaimed.

"You need anything, you call on me...hear?" Santio said.

He got up and left Sammy alone with his beer. As he walked down the docks, Sammy called after him.

"You be a good cop!"

Santio nodded and gave him a thumbs up.

The gave Curly a real nice funeral, cremated him. That really flustered Father O'Leary when he heard, he likes real burials with caskets and pomp, but they put Curly's ashes in a silver urn, and everybody got to toss some over the bay from one of the ferry boats, about a hundred neighbors, while Father said a nice prayer about them being thankful, Curly had tried, anyhow...to help them with the gangs.

"And he was still trying," Santio said. He was seeking purity. I know he was. I know the type."

"Amen," said Father O'Leary.

"We're gonna work it out," Arnie said. "Tony Tabasa and my 'Bocco buddies are tracking down Shar Pei. Justice will be done."

Curly's ashes lay on the waters of the bay a whole day, held in by the flood and slack, before the ebb sucked them under and carried them out to sea late in the afternoon. As they disappeared, Sammy broke down and started crying. He sat on a deck chair and bawled like a baby. Santio took charge and, grabbing him by the arms, pulled him up to his feet.

"Cut it out, Sammy," he said. "Get yourself together."

Sammy just went crazy, crying harder and harder. Santio started shaking him harder and harder. Sammy finally looked up at Santio and screamed.

"Leave me alone, Santio!"

He looked up at Santio, and...it wasn't Santio. It was Curly.

"Sammy, you're dreaming. You're having a nightmare. Wake up!"

Sammy sat upright in his bed to face Curly head on.

"What are you doing here?" Sammy said. "You're dead!"

"I ain't dead. What are you talking about?" Curly said.

Sammy looked around. He was in his own bed, and it was Curly shaking him awake out of the dream. He couldn't believe it. It had all been so real. After Curly went back to the couch, Sammy lay awake thinking it was really time he got his act together. Next day on a whim he went to the Fisherman Wharf boat shop, and there in the window was a sign: "Help Wanted." In an hour, he was employed. A week later work still felt good to him. Finally, he was on his way.

The gangs are still in Patusan. The local pols still rail against them every election or so. Hasn't much changed. Ida and Sammy's Rabbi dad was both kinda nuts if you want to know the truth. After all, who can handle orthodoxy and real love in this day and age? Even Sammy's mom, hey, she thought her Rabbi husband was a throwback too, and had left Ida and Sammy when they were only eleven and thirteen to honey up to a jazz sax guy in New Orleans.

Curly just hadn't been able to make out what Ida needed, no more than anybody can make out anybody who has faced the inner fears of love and found them insurmountable. But there in Arnie's, he had found himself, and taking on Shar Pei in the alley where the fancy politicians don't go, he tried, that's what counts. On all counts, he had tried.

The neighborhood was even thinking of running him for city council in the next election.

Sammy?

He hasn't quite figured it all out yet.

He does his job, the fisherman fish, the sailors sail. Things go on pretty much like they been for ages. His Flatbush relatives send him post cards and he sends them postcards back. Just the other day, Curly gave him an autographed copy of all thirty seven poems he'd got printed up for him. He'd entitled it: *" 'E,' The Collected Works of Curly O'Toole."* Sammy's favorite is the introductory poem:

> *Life, 'tis very rough*
> *When "E" ain't there;*
> *If thinks you it is fair*
> *You ain't astute enough.*

Sometimes Sammy still looks in the *Chronicle* for a better job. But, most of the time it seems better just to stay in place… on the waterfront, selling boat stuff. Now and then, he gives in, takes a shower, combs his hair, dons his Yarmulke, and on a crisp, foggy Saturday goes to Synagogue to be with his people. Still doesn't believe, of course. But nowadays, he likes to keep his options open.

The Pinky Caper

He was a swarthy eighteen or so, with greasy black hair and a flame in his eye like he was losing the battle with his inner demons. I had just inched over the Golden Gate Bridge in the Friday night traffic, late for my meeting with Testy O'Donnell in Chinatown, and figured I'd take the shortcut between Fu Lane and Soy Long Street. This appeared to have been a mistake. Shaking in his hand, the gun appeared close up to my nose. It was a small automatic. Not as hefty as a .38, I guessed it was a .380, maybe a Bernadelli. He had it so near, my eyes couldn't focus on the small print etched into the barrel. It was a neat little gun. Nice choice for an intimate alley robbery. He grinned, baring yellow teeth with a half inch gap in front. His breath smelled like marine diesel exhaust. His movements weren't really controlled like a professional thief. Rather, he twitched a lot and it seemed he would explode and do something crazy any moment. Although wearing a light blue Dior tie with his denim shirt, he'd obviously never made it to the Wilkes Bashford gentlemen's store off Union Square. He struck me as what a displaced Somalian pirate might look like if he'd been smuggled into civilization and taken a quick mail order course on Western male fashion trends.

"My wallet's inside my right coat pocket," I offered, reading his mind.

"Lift it out, slowly," he said.

He had a strange accent I couldn't place. It took me awhile to raise my hand to my chest. I didn't want to help him pull his trigger. His crazed gaze also said he might have a vague idea how to use the little cannon. When I could see he figured our eyes were looking directly into each other's souls, I slowly moved my left hand to the right and slipped it under my jacket. His Adam's apple bobbed once before I willed my arm to catapult from the elbow, arcing the back of my hand into his throat. Something collapsed under my hand that felt like mildly tough Chicken Tempura. He dropped his gun, and both hands went to his throat, which was gurgling like a clogged scupper. So much for his ability to read my soul.

Over his head a water pipe ran across the top of the door frame. I pulled both ends of his Dior over the pipe and tied them together. I bent over, picked up his gun (it *was* a .380 Bernadelli) and smacked his head good with it. He let go of his throat and hung, his knees bent, feet dragging the pavement, arms limp at his sides. I pushed his gun under my belt in the back, shook my coat free from its grip, and walked on down the alley. After ten steps, I reconsidered, returned, and cut his Dior with my Swiss Army knife. He dropped into a grateful heap and started breathing again. I like to do my little bit to encourage continued U.S. immigration.

When I got to Wing Chow's restaurant, Testy accepted my apology for being late and ordered a pot of Oolong tea for us.

"Have any trouble gettin' here?" he asked.

"Lots of cars coming in from Marin," I replied. "Otherwise, no problem."

"Good. How about Won Ton soup?" he said, nodding at Wing Chow who was peeking out the serving window of his kitchen.

We sipped our tea and waited for our Won Ton.

"Happy birthday," Testy said.

Testy is a San Francisco narcotics cop. We go back a long ways. We were in Army Intelligence in Paris together before and after Vietnam. I guess that makes us battle weary old farts. Whatever. We trust one another. And, to an extent, America's philosophically sound democracy, as decapitated from Thomas Jefferson's original concept as it is. That gives us an edge over the duds we have to deal with. After Intelligence, he decided on the police because his dad was a cop. I decided to run a boat brokerage because my dad was a Navy guy and I like to sail. Testy graduated to plain clothes awhile back. We share the same mother, which makes us half brothers, I guess. He feels like a whole brother to me.

"Here," he said, pushing a brown paper bag across the table to me.

"What's this?" I asked, pulling out a paperback book with dog-eared corners.

"It's your present. Le Carre's latest spy novel. I read it. It's good."

"Thanks. Can I expense it off my tax return as a professional publication?"

"Fuck the IRS. Do what feels good."

"Eat your Won Ton."

We eat in China Town because the food's good and cheap. Testy and I share a common failing: we tend to be honest and, consequently, poor. Frugality is important to us. After Won Ton, we shared a couple of other dishes together: sweet and sour pork and almond chicken. Testy's fortune cookie said he was going to be a ladies' man. Mine said I would take a long journey. Testy's been faithfully married to Myrtle twenty-five years. I resist traveling outside the Bay area anymore. What's the point? It's all right here.

After cookies we talked.

"Evelyn Glennie is in town," Testy said.

"Who's she?" I asked.

"She's a deaf percussionist."

"A what?"

"She plays the drums, barefoot. With the symphony. She'll be at Davies Hall tonight at eight. I've got cheap onstage tickets for Myrtle and me. We gotta talk fast or I'm gonna be late.

"That's OK," I said. "I'm gonna eat popcorn and watch Fox and MSNBC duke it out on my I-Phone.

I daubed a cookie crumb off my lip with my napkin as Testy wiped his mouth with his shirt sleeve.

"Pansy," Testy said.

"Slob," I answered.

We grinned together, then Testy stopped. I kept grinning and chewed a hangnail while watching him think about what he wanted to say. When he thinks too hard, Testy exudes an aura that makes him look like he's dumb. He's not, and a couple of dozen drug dealers rotting in prison know it for fact.

"I wanna discuss something."

"We going to have a meaningful conversation, for a change?"

"'Something like that."

Why not?"

"I'm pissed off how the economy's still pumping up the financial guys, but so many others are homeless. And since I'm obliquely a part of the system that makes it that way. It's bothering me."

Testy's been taking night sociology college courses.

"I mean, at my age, do you think I could still change my profession?"

"You need a vacation."

"Yeah, maybe that's it."

I waited.

"You can't watch Countdown and Rachel Maddow tonight," Testy said.

"Why not?"

"Because I've got something for you to do."

Sometimes I do things for Testy that I learned in the Army, which help him out. It brings in a little extra money and keeps life interesting. Sailboat selling can be a pretty slow business. Again, I waited. Testy likes to take his time. He thought some more, as if he wasn't sure I would like what he was going to say.

"There's a dope deal going down tonight. Smugglers. We're buying from them with marked money and I need someone to deliver it and pick up the stuff for us."

"Why me?"

"I need someone who can't be traced to the department. I'll pay you $100 and give you a quarter of the reward out on the guy we're fingering – if we catch him. The reward's $25,000.

I figured silently for a minute. Math's not my strong suit.

"That's $6,250."

Thoroughness is.

"Who gets the rest?" I asked.

"None of your business."

He slid a cheap imitation leather briefcase out from under the table to my side.

"Don't open this now. It's got a hundred thousand cash in it. Deliver it to the Alistair Cook Suite, 1204, at the Huntington Hotel tonight, and pick up the stuff and a signed receipt from a Madame Françoise Caron.

"Anything else?"

"Stay with her awhile, probe for information. See if you can find out if Abdullah means anything to her."

"Abdullah?"

"It's a name keeps popping up."

"Whose?"

"Don't know."

"The boss?"

"Maybe."

"What's his game?"

"Something else's happening with the drug profits."

"Like?"

"Politics, maybe."

"What kind?"

"You know, Mideastern shit."

"What's the lady look like?" I asked, changing the subject.

"She's a looker."

"My turn in the barrel, huh?"

"Yeah."

"Why don't you do the job yourself?"

"It'd blow my cover. She thinks I'm something else."

"What?"

"You don't need to know."

"What if she falls for me?"

"Marry her and have kids."

As I chugged up steep California street later from China Town to Nob Hill, and passed my car off to the Huntington's doorman, even as I entered the sedate foyer of the Hotel and took in the elevator's tastefully designed interior while rising to Caron's top floor suite, I was not emotionally prepared for the real woman. She was tall. Her hair was buff brown, long, thick, and straight. She was Eurasian, and her skin was the color of mature Cognac. She was clearly an experienced weight lifter. One who had not pushed it too far. Her arms were bare, resonant, highly toned, rippling with gaunt muscle, but smooth, not knotty. She was wearing a thin, white, silk dress. She was barefoot.

Her perfume was Joy. Her legs were architecturally significant. The thighs were the kind, which kiss one another when she stood erect. Which she was doing. They were strong and teeming. Their muscles spoke paragraphs. Her knees were glib, and flowed into her calves, which traced the most impossibly graceful arcs down to her ankles, connecting to modestly sized feet: aquiline, tensile, desirable. Her bare toes were sensuous. Her hips were like sculpted Michelangelo marble. Her mouth was open, the lips were moist, beige, her tongue resting slightly behind them, vaguely quivering in her gently nervous smile. Her eyes resembled nothing so much as the deep green side eddies of a sparkling mountain brook. She looked out through them into the innermost, deeply-hidden part of my being.

I am a grown man, reasonably intelligent, six foot even, one hundred ninety pounds, have lifted a few weights also, am mildly cynical, and too experienced to expect anything out of life but the daily grind. So she nudged me off balance. I tried not to let her notice. I suspect I failed. It didn't make any difference. She was the kind of woman any man worth his Jung, or his Freud, would want to tip him over. I hate to admit it, but my good sense was overcome by my baser instincts. She stood in the doorway of the suite and eyed me briefly before asking if I would like to come in.

Would I? Indeed.

"Yes," I said, and stepped through the doorway.

"You're with the hotel?" she asked.

"No," I answered. "I'm not."

She looked at me and contemplated.

"Then," she replied, "may I make you a drink?"

She opened the bar, revealing scotch, bourbon, gin, vodka, rum, and Pernod. A bucket of ice and a bowl of oranges and lemons sat next to a silver thing filled with olives, cherries, and small, pearl onions. A jar of bitters existed quietly beside it all, as unassuming and discrete as carefully guarded incest. Pachelbel's Canon was playing on a CD. Dark red roses filled eight or ten vases positioned throughout the room. I sniffed. They really smelled good.

She mixed the Pernod and water I requested, poured herself an icy vodka with a Maraschino cherry in it, guided me to the couch, and sat down beside me with her beautiful bare feet tucked under her lovely buttocks. She rested her left hand upon my right shoulder and drank her vodka and continued to unnerve me. I continued to endeavor not to let it show.

"Do you like this music?" she asked me.

"Pachelbel? I like Pachelbel."

"You know this music."

It was a statement, not a question.

"Yes."

"And?"

It was a question, not a statement. I hesitated before revealing an intimate piece of myself.

"I am quite fond of classical music. It helps ground me..."

She smiled, quizzically.

"...it provides me a base of operations, so to speak, in what I perceive to be a chaotic world."

"It is a chaotic world," she answered.

Pachelbel concluded, and we sat in silence for a couple of heartbeats.

"I suppose I should ask who you are, " she said.

"You know who I am."

"You think me impetuous?"

"Just confident."

"I believe I'm foolhardy," she admitted. "I've always liked to take chances. I think it may get me in trouble some day."

She paused. I waited. It is a technique I learned in Intelligence. Others often say things to see how you react. f you don't react, they continue their thought in other or additional words, and you have gained the edge. They are revealing themselves; you are not. She did not take the bait. Instead, she probed, delicately.

"Do you agree?"

Her eyes were actually hazel, flecked with green.

"I imagine you would like it to," I replied, sipping my drink.

"My name is Françoise."

She was clever. She would not push the issue and ask me my name point blank. Her eyes showed no fear. She revealed no anger. Her presence was unintimidating, unaggressive. She did not use masculine tricks against men. She was a real woman. A rarity of her sex. I thought about what I could say to prove I was a rarity of mine.

"You don't have to tell me your name," she said, finally.

"I know why you're here, of course. I've been expecting you. You're supposed to deliver something to me, aren't you?"

"What if I'm not?"

"Then we have a far more interesting situation on our hands than I thought." Without waiting for a reaction, she got up and made me a second drink. She made a second for herself too, and sat down again. The air crackled with anticipation. Outside, a streetcar bell clanged. I stood and walked over to the window. Below, on the left, stood Grace Cathedral, before me the lovely park fronting the hotel, to the right the so-called Millionaire's Club, its smudgy red stone smudgy as ever, farther to the right, the Fairmont Hotel, flags a flying, limousines a flitting, tourists a gaping. The scent of her Joy ambushed me. I turned around.

"I like you," she said.

I knew we had business to attend to, but what was there really to do? She knew she was to receive the money. I knew I was to give it to her and take the drugs. The receipt. Of course, I was to obtain a receipt.

"Do you want a receipt?" she asked.

"Please."

She penned one on the Huntington note pad and put it in my hand. I pulled out my billfold and slipped it inside. She took my hand and guided me back to the couch.

"It's all under the bed. You can have it when we're finished."

I tried to think of something to say. It wouldn't come out, so I smiled and sipped my drink. Still holding my hand, she leaned over and kissed its palm. Then she guided it toward the top of her dress, which was a V-neck, slit not too low, but open, nonetheless. She guided my fingers up onto her throat until they were firmly in place, then removed her hand and placed it on my thigh. I paused, briefly, cupped my hand over her throat, let it slide down onto her breastbone, then halted. Her breasts were as perfect and soft as a comma. She sighed a luxurious, deep-throated sigh and smiled at me.

"Do you like me too?" she asked.

I didn't feel a lot like talking now, so I leaned over and kissed her on the mouth. Her lips were baking. She placed a hand behind my neck and drew me toward her. The insides of her mouth came into my mouth. Her hand skimmed up my thigh several inches, then stroked back down to my knee. This lady understood nuance. I breathed deeply – an involuntary reflex. I sat up, leaned back, picked up my drink, and took another sip. She put a finger to my lips with one hand, took my drink from me with the other. She set it on the coffee table and got up to do something with CD player.

Madonna started singing. Caron returned. I leaned my head back on the couch and looked up at the ceiling. She dropped her head on my neck and slipped her hand under my shirt and stroked my chest.

"Do you still want to know who I am?" I asked.

"I know who you are," she said. "You're the man who's supposed to be here now."

What could I say? Nothing intelligent came to mind. I said nothing. Now and then I make a smart move. If ever, I thought, this is the time for one. The smart move I made was to make no move. I left my head on the couch and listened to Madonna and smelled the roses and her Joy. After a bit, she stood, kneeled before the couch, squished herself up between my legs, put her arms around my hips, scrunched up, and looked into my eyes.

I forced my brain back into gear.

"I'd like to meet your boss," I said.

"Not now, my sweet."

"Later then."

She curved her lips into a faint smile. Sweet turned into knowledgeable.

"Later is good. Life is short. I hope you don't feel like I'm trying to use you."

"You've got to be kidding."

She sat down again, leaned against me, and rested her head on my shoulder. I put my arm around her. We sat that way for several minutes. She looked up and kissed me again softly on the lips. There was no sex in this kiss. She was just saying hello.

"We've not *completely* finished our business," she said.

"No?"

"The money in the briefcase."

"What?"

She retrieved the case, locked it in the closet, and then sat back down beside me.

"When are you supposed to pass it along?" I asked

"Not now. Now business *is* over."

She turned my torso from her, and placed her hands onto the small of my back. Then, deep into the muscles, she slowly worked her fingers up to my neck.

"That feels good," I admitted.

"I want you to like me."

She had a way with words.

"When are you due to pass the money along?" I repeated.

"Would you like to take a walk, get some fresh air?" she parried.

"Sure," I said.

We went out. Bob, the doorman, showed us his white teeth. His uniform gleamed in freshly pressed splendor. We jaywalked over California Street and climbed the stairs to the park. Having just been massaged by a beautiful woman, standing on top of Nob Hill in the most beautiful city in the world, not employed as a computer geek, and being reasonably healthy, I looked around me and took stock of the evening. The sky was clear, cloudless, star-packed. It was about sixty-five degrees

Fahrenheit, the scent of the salt-laden bay invaded my nostrils, the clean air excited my lungs. I felt vital and immensely lucky. Pride, I would have remembered from my boyhood Sunday School Bible classes, goeth before a great fall.

"Are you as hungry as I am?" she asked, squeezing my hand.

"Hungrier."

"Let's go."

"There's a delightful little cafe in this block."

"Marvelous! We won't have to drive."

Her laughter was as infectious as influenza.

I nodded, and we walked hand-in-hand to the little Italian café on Taylor a couple of blocks down from Grace Cathedral. She ordered spaghetti with a cube of unsalted butter, a dish of diced garlic on the side, a large Caeser Salad, bread, and olive oil. We agreed on a bottle of good French Champagne. I forget its name. One of those with the cool silver aluminum neck piece up over the cork. They had real imported Russian caviar, so we got some of that too. I marveled at her composure. She sat totally silent for what seemed a month, waiting for me to speak. The air in the café lay heavy with implication. Where would this beginning lead? My imagination loped. Was this the woman I had sought all my life? Was I the man she had sought? The waiter broke into my thoughts.

What?" I said.

"Would you care for a cocktail before your wine?" he repeated.

"Scotch," she answered, "Single malt, a good one, you choose."

Him too, a young man with sordid eyes, she held in the palm of her hand. He scurried away without asking me what I wanted to drink. I contemplated exactly how I might go about insulting him as I returned my eyes to hers. Hers were not sordid. They were mercurial. She scudded her hand across the table and I took it in mine. Through the café window we watched a cable car careen down the hill, its passengers screaming and acting ridiculously silly. A stray dog jumped out of the way. Two longhaired Latinos shuffled down the street, out of place in this Asian-flecked, but mainly white enclave of privilege, huddled at the top of the hills.

"You don't talk a lot," she said.

"Sometimes I'm quiet. Sometimes not."

"When are you quiet?"

"When talking might compromise me."

"We are cautious."

"Isn't cautious wise?"

"Perhaps. Not necessarily alluring."

"I though alluring was the woman's role."

"Times have changed."

The waiter reappeared with her scotch, setting it obsequiously before her.

"You forgot to ask my friend about his drink," she said.

He dissolved under her reprimand.

"I beg your pardon."

"It's alright," I said. "I understand."

You would like, sir?"

"Bourbon, over ice."

"Any special brand?"

"They all work for me."

"Surely you have a preference."

"I prefer you choose. Quickly," I said, a slight edge creeping into my voice.

He caught on and left. Quickly.

"Do you believe in the concept of an enlightened people?" she asked.

I had never been asked this question before, and I had to think for a moment before answering. She was clearly not a woman to whom one gave a shallow answer.

"Would I be equivocating to ask you to define your terms?" I answered.

"No," she responded. "I mean people worldwide joined by a common philosophy closely aligned with verifiable truth."

Beating her at conversation was not going to be easy.

"People," she continued, "who have discarded the varied beliefs they have been taught and have replaced them with their own."

"Sophisticated people," I ventured.

"Sort of."

The waiter returned with my drink and asked if we needed anything else.

"No," she said.

"Thank you, Madame."

He left us alone again.

"I believe," I said, "that a good many people who have seen much of life have reached a similar conclusion."

"Which is?"

"That there are as many conclusions to reach as there are people."

One of her eyebrows lifted, apparently without her guidance, for she smiled.

"When will your friend want to get the money?" I asked.

"When I'm ready to deliver it."

I sipped my bourbon and swallowed.

"He is busy elsewhere," she continued. "I am supposed to bring the money to him. Is it important you meet him?"

"It might enhance profits…His, mine, yours."

"Perhaps it can be arranged."

The waiter delivered our food and wine with proper deference and disappeared, this time, I hoped, for good. I ate in silence. I did not know what she knew and I did not know how to proceed. She did not speak. I thought about what I should say. She watched me think. I watched her watch me think. It became less important to know how to proceed, for she had removed a shoe and was caressing my ankle with her stocking foot.

"Arrange it for me," I suggested.

"For you, I will arrange it."

"Do you happen to know an Abdullah?

"No," she said, matter of factly. "I just know a Jacques. I am supposed to deliver the money to him day after tomorrow in Paris. You could come with me, if you'd like. Have you ever been there?"

"Paris?"

"Yes. He is at a DNA conference at the Sorbonne. DNA is one of his interests. He's conducting some experiments there."

"What kind of experiments?"

"He is identifying people from microscopic particles of their bodies."

"Why?"

"It's a complex subject. He'll explain."

I walked her back to the Huntington.

"I need to pick up some clothes," I said.

"Come back tonight?"

"Count on it."

Testy OK'd me going to Paris, advanced me fifteen hundred bucks, and one of his men drove me back to the Huntington about two in the morning. The night deskman, whom I have known for several years, showed me the record of Françoise's calls. She had called Paris just after I left. I wrote down the number and stuck it in my pocket.

"Darling?," she queried from behind the closed door when I knocked.

Not many women say darling these days.

"Yes," I answered.

She opened the door and I took her in my arms and drank in her lips. Then I picked her up and carried her to the bed. She had been sleeping in it and it was very warm. Next morning we took an Air France flight, arriving at Orly later than scheduled. The captain explained that he had had to contend with unusual headwinds in addition to the dateline change. Time and space always confuse me, so I took his word for it. Françoise's idea was to rent a limousine and a driver. I wanted more control over our transportation, so I told her how much I liked to drive. We compromised. She rented a Rolls Royce and I drove. I had never driven a Rolls before. It drove nice. We checked into a small three star hotel in St. Germain called the Odeon. Early spring flowers were budding in the window boxes, and ivy crawled down the building's walls.

She had wanted the Georges V, but I insisted on the left bank for its quaintness. She accepted my choice and gave in without struggling. She knew when and how to humor me. She had me beyond the putty stage. I was becoming gooey. Paris was exquisite: the air, the sky, the sun, the French ambiance. St. Germain smelled like wine and cheese. Pigeons scoured for crumbs, tourists scoured for excitement, Parisians accepted life and thrived. We showered and rested a day before getting down to affairs. In the evening we ate in a small restaurant across from the hotel.

After dinner, we walked down some decrepit steps to an underground jazz club where I was informed that a drink, any drink, would cost the equivalent of fifty American dollars. Françoise read the look in my eyes and suggested we leave. I agreed. As we ambled through the tiny streets, we did not discuss the barbarity of the price or the absurd attitude of the barman who had observed me as if I were a plumber. I could have cared no less about his opinion of me had he been a goat herder. Being taken financially in any language is a sign of stupidity. I may not be the swiftest guy in the world, but I work hard for my money, and in my books throwing it away promiscuously for pretension's sake indicates immaturity, plain and simple. It's an outmoded concept, but it's mine. I stick by it. In a nearby restaurant I bought us a bottle of Dom Perignon for just over $90. Real value is worth the price.

"What did you have in mind?" I asked. "How am I to meet Jacques?"

"He's at the Sorbonne, building a data base of DNA samples from conference participants. He will be working all day. We are to see him tomorrow afternoon or early evening. If you wish, we can visit the conference and become part of the data base.

"Which entails?"

"Giving a sample of our bodies, maybe a skin scraping. Then its DNA code will be stored on the Internet. If you ever need to identify yourself without a passport or other ID, you can refer to the data bank. A doctor can resample you for your DNA code and verify who you are in minutes. C'est ca."

"Why not?" I replied.

When we finished our champagne we walked back to the hotel and watched TV for awhile. Later on, after discussing the state of the world, the origin of the universe, and sharing our opinions of most governments [totally inept and insensitive was our summation] we identified one another's bodies without benefit of DNA. She was still definitely herself. She seemed satisfied I was still me.

"Shall we take breakfast near the university?" she asked next morning.

"Sure."

We drove to the Place de la Sorbonne, put the Rolls in a garage, and ordered petit dejeuner in a small café called L'Ecritoire. It was one of the tiny glassed-in cafes of which hundreds, maybe thousands, exist in Paris. It faced the Place, or plaza, although that seems a grandiose title for the unassuming square before us.

"Cafe au lait et croissants?" she beamed.

"Oui," I beamed back.

The waiter did not beam. He was one of those tiny, wiry, professional French café waiters who in America would probably have been a bookkeeper's assistant. He mumbled and shuffled off for our breakfast.

"Charming, no?" she laughed.

Later, the café au lait warming my insides, bringing life to my body, I absorbed the scene before me. Place de la Sorbonne is roughly one-third to one-half a city block long and 50 to 200 feet wide. It runs perpendicularly off the Boulevard St. Michel. On the far end opposite the Boulevard is the University of Paris, the Sorbonne. A tall statue of August Comte stands near the Boulevard. Actually, his is only a bust over two other full figures. I do not know who August was, but under him the two other figures are a woman with a child and a young man seated, thinking. I assume Monsieur Comte accomplished something singularly important in his life. I assume my not knowing what marks me as ignorant. I have my weak points. French philosophy is one of them. I make up for limited world knowledge with what I consider a relatively keen ability to intuit when something's missing.

"Why's your friend so interested in DNA? I asked.

"It's a way to identify people without exposing their origins or names."

"Why does he want to do that?"

"I prefer that he explain."

"But you know something…"

"Ready to go to school?" Françoise interrupted.

I nodded.

"Then follow that man."

She pointed to a professorially tweedy type energetically traversing the plaza.

"That is Jacques Carvalle."

He was my age. There the similarity ended. His hair was long, well trimmed, flowing back over his ears in the smooth manner of the European sophisticate. I'm sure he was one of her enlightened ones. His suit was gray, French, tailored, expensive. He was masculine, in a feminine sort of way, and exuded a cautious self confidence. Discretely, we followed him into the Sorbonne. Our footsteps blended in the corridors with those of many vibrant students variegated by every possible human color and accent.

Immediately upon Carvalle's entering a lecture hall, the gathered students, and some nurses in crisp white uniforms, organized themselves and sat down, the students on the bleachers, the nurses at a long table before the lecturer's platform. Carvalle began his lecture. He was well spoken, his voice tempered and even. He smiled easily and gestured freely with Gallic élan. He was the kind of man most women dream of. Françoise paid him little attention. She watched him talk, but put her hand in my pants pocket, to keep it warm I guess. It certainly kept me warm.

Later, one of the nurses, a plain woman in a white jacket, took a sample of skin from inside my mouth and gave me a card with a bar code on it, an address, a fax and phone number, and my name under a color Polaroid she personally took of me. I was eternally identified. It was easier than having my tonsils removed and made me hungry. Carvalle, surrounded by admiring students, fielded their questions, Françoise said we'd meet him later, and we returned to the Café L'Ecritoire for lunch.

She ordered Pave au Poivres, I got Cote d'Agneau. We shared a bottle of Moulin de Belot. She ate a Tarte Alsacienne and I a Gateau au Chocolat American. We had an espresso each. I felt full and sleepy. We walked down St. Michel to the Seine and spent the rest of the afternoon outside waking me up with fresh air and her fresh conversation.

At Shakespeare & Company, the English language bookstore, we browsed through a broad array of ancient and modern writers. Books, we reminded one another, were how we used to learn before TV and the Internet emerged. Obviously, we were not up to date. Several other couples in the store appeared obsolete, too. If not technically hip, we were happy. Today was our *temps perdues,* our lost times, our good old days, and we consumed them to the limit. Her perfume filled my nostrils with pleasure. So did her touch, her smile, her trembling ideas of life. My jaded self allowed something approximating contentment to take over.

"I believe the moment brings us our destinies," she explained. "The secret of life is to accept the direction it brings us, to follow it to its eventual conclusion. It will lead you if you will follow."

I followed her into the Luxumbourg Garden.

"When is our destiny going to lead us back to Carvalle?" I asked.

"It is arriving, " she said. "Be patient."

"Whenever."

"See, you're becoming an existentialist."

"Whatever."

"You're practically enlightened," she laughed.

We walked past the sailboat pond where a little girl sailed her boat with her father. A strong young Frenchwoman in running shorts jogged past us, cutting through the warming Spring air as if she were in the tropics. She was tough looking in the sense of possessing endurance, but her lean, taut face stretched over keen, sharply-defined features and her brilliant teeth flashed in the sun. As she passed us, she shot a quick glance into my eyes and my heart faltered. Françoise noticed her glance and – the only time I ever saw it – gently bristled with what I took for mild jealousy. Not a word passed her lips, but generations of breeding could not hide her concern. In an instant it disappeared.

"Wait here, or in the café," she said, consulting her watch. "I will find Andre and bring him to you."

She dropped me off at L'Ecritoire and walked toward the Sorbonne. I ordered a cognac and espresso. An hour later, Françoise had not returned, so I walked the thirty feet to the Sorbonne entrance and, inside, inquired of a guard about Monsieur Carvalle. He asked me to wait a moment, and stepped away. I leaned on the guardrail of his mobile office, scouring the wall for amusement. Someone tapped me on the shoulder.

"Monsieur?"

I turned to discover a broad-shouldered, slightly pudgy man with steely eyes, which were boring into mine.

"Please, to come with me," he said, rather than asked, taking my arm.

I did not argue, but followed him willingly. It seemed he was trying to guide me, not harm me. I trusted him even as he led me into the dark stairway leading to the basement. Under this famous institution of learning I now learned something new, something I would have preferred not to have learned. I learned the immediacy and accuracy of Carvalle's DNA identification technique. In the dark of the university's basement lay stretched out on the floor two dark green canvas tarpaulins.

"Monsieur Carvalle," my host said, lifting one of the tarps, under which, upon another tarp lying on the floor, spread out like a high school science exhibit, were the blackened, charred remains of what had been human bones. A skull as dead as the one in Hamlet, yet deader, since it was also charred as black as the cinders of Hell itself, confronted me. Its skeleton eyes inspected mine.

"It is Monsieur Carvalle," he assured me.

"Who is under the other tarp," I asked.

He lifted the second tarp. It too revealed charred bones and a skull burnt black as night.

"His accomplice, a certain Madame Caron."

My eyes blurred. Pain bolted through my head. I tried to stop my legs from crumbling, but failed. Our first night in the Huntington flashed before my eyes. When I came to, police Captain Pierre Broullard finally introduced himself.

"Monsieur is very sensitive," he said, "for an experienced man."

"I knew the lady," I stuttered.

"Oui, monsieur. I know."

"Let's talk," I said, starting to sit up.

A nurse pushed me back on the floor. She was big and strong. She did not smile at me. I did not protest, but gave in. Then she smiled and patted my shoulder. Broullard explained that he was Testy's French counterpart. He had been watching Carvalle from Paris while Testy fingered him from San Francisco. Together, they had planned this affair. But they had expected me to help them get Carvalle and Caron alive.

"Complicated drug scheme, huh?" I said.

"Partially," he answered.

"Partially?"

"Yes, the real commodity is not drugs. It is human beings."

"Human beings?"

"Indeed, monsieur. Jacques Carvalle and Françoise Caron were not primarily drug smugglers. That was only a sideline. Their real business is – was – smuggling people."

"People."

"Jacques and Françoise provided people to someone. They smuggled refugees out of various despoiled nations into new jobs.

"What for?"

"Money, monsieur."

"Of course. But why were they smuggled?"

"The people smuggled had work to do."

"Work?"

"It is big business today to smuggle poor people from politically explosive nations into, shall we say, opportunistic professions. Much money is involved. Millions of dollars. The people are economically motivated to agree to all kinds of work in the hope of eventual freedom."

"Doing what?"

"Piracy, terrorist support, prostitution, pimping, drug running, political agitation."

"What happened to Carvalle and Caron?"

"They were cheating their clients," Broullard explained. "They cheated your friend, O'Donnell too. He will find the drugs exchanged for the money in San Francisco were bogus. They are relatively benign chemicals which look and taste like heroin."

What could I say? I'd been taken. And so had Testy. They say a salesman is the easiest person to sell something to. I guess con men, cops, and spies are the easiest conned and deceived too. You never figure someone else is as well versed in deception as yourself. Not simple criminals, at least. Well, now I knew. A new generation had ascended the thug hierarchy and I was going to have to refresh my act. More than that. Since I'd been a long time without a woman, I had let my guard down. I'd let myself become involved with a lady I had no business messing around with. I'd let my professional life become personal. What a dope.

"Here in Europe," Broullard droned on, "your friend, Caron, and her colleague, Carvalle, recruited and organized members to help them smuggle people whom they delivered to their clients. Of course, they took a commission for the transfer. But, they got greedy and tried to take all the funds. Over $3 million."

"So, their clients killed them."

"Someone did."

"How are you certain it is them?"

"DNA."

"DNA?"

"Precisely."

Broullard produced a small box from his pocket and slid back the lid. Inside were two entire little fingers, the end of each blackened with congealed blood where it had been severed from the hand. One was a man's. The other a woman's. One could have been Françoise's: the polish was right, and the discolored shape seemed almost familiar.

"Whoever exterminated them left us these fingers when they put the bodies in the furnace."

He pointed to the oven in the far end of the basement. I hadn't even noticed it until now.

"And a note. We checked the DNA of the fingers with the data base at the conference; it seemed an obvious thing to do. There is no doubt. It is they."

I wished Broullard's English were less academic. I'd rather have heard that it was "them" than "they." Just the academically invalid "them" replacing the technically correct "they" would have made it all more human and acceptable. But his accuracy that it was, indeed, "they," one of them the lady I had most recently slept with, upset my guts.

"What did the note say?" I asked.

"Read it yourself," he said, and handed me a piece of wrinkled paper.

"Recycling by Abdullah."

"What is that about?"

"I don't know," Broullard said.

He took me to his office and we spent half a day trying to see if there was anything else we could find out about the deaths. There wasn't. In the end, he told me to go home and he'd call if anything new came up. I agreed that's all we could do. He pinned down a flight to San Francisco for me, and I drove the Rolls back to Orly. Caron had secured the car with a 5,000 Euro deposit. The bill was for 3,770. I pocketed the 1,230 Euro refund, not bothering to exchange it for dollars. A perk of my trade. I figured I might return to Europe again, sometime.

Next morning I was back home with Testy in his office on Bryant Street. It was misting and the bay's foghorns were braying.

"You knocked that out fast," Testy said.

"It knocked me out."

He gave me a check for my services. The reward was, he told me, for dead or alive. This was not very gratifying, but I needed the money, so – despite my personal discomfort – I pocketed it. I guess we all have to sell out to one degree or another. This was my degree. The mortgage had to be paid, even if over Françoise's barbecued body. I envisioned how her skin had looked. It had not been motley textured like burnt charcoal. It had been smooth and olive-colored, alive to the touch, truly sweet to the taste. *So long,* I thought.

"See you," Testy said.

On the way out, I saw the swarthy rat I had dealt with in Wang Chu Alley a few days before. He was being booked at the front desk.. I turned to Testy, who was accompanying me to the door.

"Ask why he's being booked."

Testy spent a moment with the booking sergeant, then returned.

"Found some explosives in his apartment. Plus drugs," he said.

"I should have left the bastard hanging by the pipe," I mumbled.

"What?"

"Nothing."

At the door we spent one of those brief moments wordlessly assessing our lives in general and our relationship to one another in particular. Testy looked at me, and I thought he was going to say he was sorry again about Françoise getting killed, so I started to interrupt but something in his eye was different so I kept still.

"Myrtle's filing for a divorce," he said. "Says she needs her space. Can you believe that shit? A quarter century we been together, and now she needs space."

I didn't know what to say. I mulled it over. Why would Myrtle…? When Testy could see I was almost about to say something, he stopped me.

"Don't say a fuckin' thing. Ain't nothing needs being said."

I nodded, turned away, and walked down Powell Street to the garage where my car sat with a $350 accumulated ticket. After I paid it off, and with my Rolls refund, I was left with a fairly healthy net from my work. Crossing the Golden Gate Bridge, I thought again of Françoise. Her Joy still clung to my clothes. Her taste still inhabited my mouth. I remembered the touch of her hand, the pliancy of her tongue, the scent of her hair. I looked out over the Bay and the glistening lights of San Francisco blurred through the fog and the thin film of tears upon my eyes. What a damned fool I was having started to fall for this dame. Same old story of my life. Fairly competent when it comes to my work, a sap when it comes to women.

She cared for me, I thought. *I think she really cared for me.*"

What I did not think, as the Pacific Ocean flowed into the Bay under me and the vision of her burnt bones seared the insides of my eyes, was that in a café on the West Indies island of Martinique, a couple sat drinking Champagne, their hands entwined.

"We've done well," the man said.

"The $100,000 I got in San Francisco."

"The $3 million we picked up in France."

"Yes, and the expense was not really *too* high," she said.

"Considering the net, no, not *too* high."

"Too bad we have to share."

"Abdullah made it possible."

"Nevertheless."

"Don't be greedy, Cheri."

She leaned over and cupped her hand around his neck. He leaned into her and they kissed, not even noticing the waiter as he refilled their glasses.

"An attractive couple," the busboy remarked to the waiter after he had returned to the kitchen and they were drinking espresso together.

"But," the waiter answered, "did you not notice they each have bandages on one hand over what appear to be missing little fingers?"

"Really?"

"Love can overcome all obstacles, eh?"

"Perhaps"

Spies and Lies

A Memoir

Half a century later, I still can't forget Tomaso Alfredo DiMarisi, III ("Il tertzo," he pronounced it) from Philadelphia, that gentle, Catholic, Italo-American student of comparative literature, who worked as an undercover Intelligence agent with me during the Cold War. We met in an old three story upper middle class house on a tree lined suburban street in Wiesbaden, Germany at the onset of a dark tense Kennedy winter preceding America's escalation of Vietnam.

Full lipped and fulsome, round faced and raven haired, short and stocky, Tomaso was a sensitive graduate of the University of Pennsylvania, a U. S. Army buck sergeant when we met, and I a discordant University of Oklahoma ROTC-manufactured lieutenant. The ranks were unimportant to us, but since we were civilian-attired agents they were probably of interest to Herr Brandt, our German language teacher, the big bellied, balding World War II Wehrmacht veteran who I suspect had been a Nazi and was, at the time, a Soviet agent. I have no evidence for this judgment other than instinct, which I'm inclined to trust in such matters. It's a gut thing I developed in the service that as often as not proved to be accurate. When Brandt introduced us, Tomaso responded before him with appropriate caution by respectfully honoring the implied chasm between enlisted man and officer.

"Have you been in Germany long, sir?"

"Just got here," I said.

"Me too."

"I guess this is where we start."

"Apparently."

The Army had acquired the house as an advanced German school for active field operatives, to whose ranks Tomaso and I hesitantly aspired. From the outside, it was commonplace, featuring steep gables and roof and winter winds which coursed through tree limbs that brusquely brushed overhanging eves. Nights they would whisk us to sleep. Truthfully, I can't remember any great detail. I recollect, however, that dark back stairways led us from floor to floor; a pristine, all white kitchen allowed us to prepare solid meals of meat and potatoes; and a once well-stocked wine cellar suggested the status of previous residents, possibly a former banker, or attorney perhaps, and family. The front ground floor door opened into a parlor, which abutted a good sized living room. The second floor in its entirety was a massive office and library where we took classes. It was filled with old, overstuffed, tapestry-upholstered couches and chairs and antique wooden tables. Hundreds of leather bound books, all classics in ancient, indecipherable German script, filled floor to ceiling shelves; and stained glass shades tented the giant light bulbs of tall, steel-shanked lamps. The top floor contained bedrooms.

Tomaso and I were both twenty-three years old and too inexperienced to know then how monumentally naïve we were. We were to learn that we shared a common, redeeming trait, however: intelligence, his classically honed, mine raw but alert. We would also find that we didn't really want to be in the army, but choice was not an option. The volunteer army did not yet exist. At that time one either served or spent time in jail. Heading for Canada wasn't part of our youthful world view. Serving our country in the military was required and, depending on one's upbringing, one viewed it either as an obligation or an honor.

What initially motivated Tomaso I was not immediately sure. I accepted the requirement of military service as a paragraph in the contract of being an American citizen and a man. I believe I vaguely sensed an obligation to give some small part of myself to our country, perhaps even to the world. This concept was not incisively etched in my mind, but its vague presence helped me justify Intelligence work, and enhanced its emotional magnetism. It all had to do with an ambiguous idea I had acquired from my mottled southwestern education, something about democracy and humanity being living concepts of importance. Worth defending, I believe the phrase goes.

—

Seventeen years after World War II, German buildings still bore visible scars. The Germans' wounds were mostly invisible.

I remembered being a seven year old boy in 1945 back home in Tulsa, watching the woman across the street bang out of her front door and onto the lawn, yelling.

"It's over! The war's over!"

If so, why was I required to be here? Intelligence school had attempted to teach me that my presence was needed. My perception is that I simply held the situation in awe. After all, I was just the son of a semi-literate Oklahoma stone contractor, fresh from the heartland, abruptly established officially as a member of the clean up detail after the world's largest armed struggle, and more: commissioned as an officer and, theoretically, a gentleman to defend in a particularly furtive manner our victory. Against what, I was not precisely articulate. Communism remained the relevant political issue of the time. It was not yet as concretely tangible as terrorism may seem today, but as it had been magnified by the media antics of Senator Joseph

McCarthy and others, it nonetheless effectively commanded one's attention.

I was functioning with limited intellectual resources. Certainly I lacked any political or ethical education to help me grasp why I had to interrupt my life at this early age to be a soldier, let alone an officer. My father was a third generation Ozark mountain hillbilly who, although he had not even completed his backwoods high school because he caught scarlet fever his senior year, owned a construction company in Tulsa. His father had been an Ozark Mountain miller and the owner of a combination grocery store, filling station, and post office that served the hundred or so farmers of his village. His rare trips to a town of any size had been to buy items he immediately needed to ply his trade and could not wait to be delivered from the Sears and Roebuck Catalog. When I prepared to climb the steps to the commercial jet carrying me across the Atlantic, my father had embarrassedly offered me good luck.

"Bag a bad guy for me, son. Then get back here and help me run the store."

"Sure, Dad. I'll work on it."

"That's the stuff. Write to me now and then."

"Of course."

My rudimentary Oklahoma education had left me with only the roughest sense of anything, some bare bones stuff from Fitzgerald, Hemingway, Faulkner [fumblingly), Wolfe, the drugged Beats, a disorganized mishmash of ancient English poets and storytellers whose names mostly I could not even remember, a smattering of social psychology, a scant knowledge of history, and four years of military indoctrination. Truthfully, my entire college education had left me with little more than a blur of impressions. I could not have told you what metaphors and similes were or how many members constituted the Senate. I passed my requisite English writing exam defending the simple tenants of fundamentalist Christianity, not because of belief but because I did not know how with any competency to argue an opposing view.

Tomaso could provide no viable answer to my unvoiced inquiries of life; his mind was too stuffed with the world's literature. As he had dreamed of studying the world's writers, I had milked cows, raced quarter horses, and shot running jackrabbits in the back of the head with a single-shell .22 rifle. While I perceived our situation as little more than a *Catch 22* of being an American, he was still obsessively ambling through a philosophical garden, entranced by the beauty and magic of the written word.

"You like to read, lieutenant?" Tomaso asked me before our first class.

"You mean literature?"

"Yes."

"I like stories, people doing things that hurt or feel good. Adventures, I guess."

"What kind?"

"I just want them to tilt me up on my toes or slap me down on my back."

"Well, that's a lot of what it's all about."

He was being kind to me. My only real glimmer of what writing might be about I had gleaned from my wife, Robbie, an English Literature major with a keenly nuanced mind, whose mouth tenderly trembled when she quoted an obscure sixteenth century poet, or kissed me, her tongue timidly slipping between my lips. As Tomaso and I, among our small circle of professional friends, found our footing and professional relationship, as we advanced from novices to accomplished agents, he and she, sharing literature, would eventually become not lovers, but soul mates.

Advanced language training under Herr Brandt introduced us to our first subtle understanding of German Intelligence jargon – to shadings that would mark us eventually as professionals, both to our more experienced colleagues and our indigenous recruits. Brandt taught orally, as had the Army Language School; but, drawing directly from his military experience and European education, he pushed us deeper into German. His questions required inner exploration for answers to pass his test of adequacy; he demanded we be able to express why we were thinking something, not just what. Apparently my affinity for the idiom of Intelligence was more than acceptable to him, for one day after a series of questions directed solely to me, he halted at one point, a faint smile on his lips, and said:

"Sie sind ein tiefer Denker, mein Herr."

Following class, upstairs under the eves of the attic rooms we shared, Tomaso first revealed a personal thought and we really began to get to know each other.

"I believe Brandt's idea about your being a deep thinker is not exactly correct."

"You don't agree I'm a tiefer Denker?" I laughed.

"It's not that. I don't mean you're not intelligent. But I believe deep thinking is more a sign of patience than anything else. The deep thinkers I've read haven't been as perceptive and fast as they have been thorough. They took the time to sift through obscure bits of information and opinions until they reached a conclusion of their own – one that was valid to them. I think that's what Brandt meant."

A broad, tooth baring smile spread over his expansive face. His thick, black hair swirled about his ears, a shock of it fell over his forehead, and he tossed his head back while talking in unrestrained enthusiasm. I was soon to find he was like this whenever he felt he had discovered a truth.

"Would you like a beer?" I asked.

"That's a good idea," he agreed.

"All us tiefer Denkers eventually come up with one," I answered.

This led us out onto the cobbled streets, where autumn

leaves were already floating, fat with color. We young innocents, in training to defend our country, found a Bierstube and,
over mugs of liquid bronze and plates of dense sausages, continued exploring one another's ill formed thoughts. We talked
of three things: women, our still unproven young president,
and our singular position in his new America. Like most youth,
we identified with him; we commiserated with the failure
attributed to him by the aborted Bay of Pigs invasion of Cuba
and with his first head-to-head encounter in Vienna with the
wily, tough Soviet leader, Nikita Kruschchev. To an indefinable
degree we believed in his Camelot and hoped change for the
better would ensue.

I introduced to Tomaso the subject of Robbie, my soft,
cerebral wife, who remained still in the states. He questioned
me about her and, upon hearing she wanted to become an English university professor, declared how much he looked forward
to meeting her when she finally joined me. He remarked that
Kennedy might prove to be as tough as he needed to be. We
jointly agreed we too might eventually prove adequate to our
task of acquiring meaningful Intelligence about Eastern European countries. The beer was cold and rich, the sausages tasty,
the conversation inspiring. We ended the day anticipating that
our coming three years would not prove to be as wasted as
we had previously thought they might. A trim, young German
Frauelein caught our eye and, at my invitation, joined us.
Eventually, I went off with her as Tomaso walked back alone.

"May I show you my town?" she had asked.

"Natürlich," I had answered, naturally.

At the end of our German course, the army offered Tomaso
and me posts in Berlin, Frankfurt, Hamburg, or Munich. Berlin
was tempting. One hundred ten miles inside East Germany,
the city was divided by a concrete wall the Soviets and East
Germans had erected that symbolized the political situation
much as suicide missions and roadside bombs do today. How

much simpler and neater it was than hijacked airliners destroying near allegorical skyscrapers, or fanatically crazed martyrs exploding themselves and others into bits. Berlin still conveyed the mood of heroism associated with World War II, that of avenging Americans fulfilling their destiny to save mankind from evil. To be confronting Communism within this contentious island would surely prove our mettle. What would it be like to live three years in such an assailable fortress surrounded by a clearly visible enemy?

Had I known the Arthurian legend, as I'm sure Tomaso did, I might have envisioned Berlin as the place to seek my holy grail. Did I instead choose Munich to safeguard Robbie and our new child? I believe that was my rationalization. Was it valid? Did I personally really want a safer place for myself? I don't know. Tomaso knew, however. For art, truth, and beauty, he too chose the picturesque old Bavarian city. We soon found ourselves there, headquartered again under the eves of a German building that our bombs had spared: a long, brick, three story barrack inside a small military camp called a Kaserne. I could not help but remember Marlene Dietrich's opening line from the famous song Lili Marlene: *"Vor der Kaserne/vor dem grossen Tor/stand eine Laterne/und steht sie noch davor."* Before the barracks/before the great gate/stood a lantern/and still stands she there."

———

The army assigned us to a cover unit named something similar to The 33rd Field Supply Unit. I believe our actual assignments reflected the differences in our educations. I was put into the East German Positive Intelligence section. Tomaso was placed in the elite Counter Intelligence unit. The appropriateness stems from the judgment that my Oklahoma education suited me well for work that was clearly defined. It was like an OU Football team assignment where the object was simply to go head on head with the opposition and beat them up. Alfredo was better suited, by his more refined education, to deal with the intricate subtleties of creating double agents. The assignments also reflected Intelligence Corps disregard for rank, subordinated to the more serious criteria of actual individual abilities. We soon were hard at work.

While Tad, as I had learned to call him, and I acclimatized ourselves the first year to our new environment, unknown to us an East German lathe operator named Werner was busy planning and executing a night escape, swimming across a canal from East to West Berlin; and an East German female engineer, whose name I never knew, was preparing a trip to an East/West Technical Fair in Switzerland. These two events would eventually impact us to produce the most telling aspects of our brief Intelligence careers. But, for that first year, more common things commanded our attention. Tad found a German girlfriend, a tutor of English to well-to-do Germans' children, and I too detected the presence of the Bavarian women. With their beautifully athletic legs, high, full breasts, and energetic enthusiasm for life, they were a temptation I found hard to resist. The clandestine job made it all too easy for a young man of limited ethical or moral constraints to stray.

Imagine. You spend most of your days carrying official documentation identifying you by another name, possibly another nationality. Accompanying this, you have memorized well-crafted background facts of your alter personality, a cover story in depth of the new person you have become. No one you meet will ever be able to find out who you really are. Anything you do is done by a non existent person. You are meeting and interacting with other people far removed from your local military life in a wide variety of situations throughout Western Europe. Your part requires concentration. Real adversaries from the ubiquitous other side are playing a similar part. Sometimes you are armed. So are they. As in a

Broadway play, if you miss an entrance or muff your lines the consequences can be serious. A low key pressure, created by the constant awareness of your surroundings, by the continuous counter surveillance measures to maintain your security, bears upon you. Most of the time you work alone. When your job is done for the day, you are alone. You become lonely. You are young and healthy and your testosterone level is typical of your age. No one is watching over your shoulder. Decades of Intelligence literature are not far off the mark; women are always around. You have money and an expense account. You are trained in deception; it is your trade. Women become the natural day-to-day reward.

Tad's and my political and human aspirations were real enough for our time, but writing about them now I feel almost as naïve as I was then. It seems akin to revisiting Graham Greene's *The Quiet American*. Both put down on paper today are unconvincing. Our times have become too strident. The non-striated expansion of religiously fanatic terrorists leaves little room for protective, sensitive hope. Life today appears to hang by too fine a thread.

We talked about life, Tad and I.

"Why are you here?" I eventually asked him.

"When I finished graduate school, like you I didn't have any choice. I didn't have enough money to work on my doctorate. I figured I'd do an Army hitch and finish it later on the GI Bill."

His was a far more precisely defined life goal than anything I had ever contemplated. Honestly, I had little in mind for my own future. I was simply caught up discovering life as I saw it around me. The scenery of that time remains sharp in my mind, but it doesn't feel the same today, for I bear the weight of the years through my body. It was not so then. I could fly. I was as light as a thought, and I was supercharged with uncontrollable energy for the totality of living. I ran on unbearably powerful batteries. I was a natural-born eating, drinking, lusting machine. My acquisitive father had taught me little of life more significant than satisfying my needs from whatever was available. For the taking, he implied. An aloof, sickly mother had added nothing meaningful to my unformed philosophy of life. Tad once told me I was Nietzschean, which was inaccurate as I possessed no concept of *over coming* myself. Like a shark, open-mouthed, always moving, I was not evil, but life-engorged, strong, fast, and supple. It was not so much that I sensed any danger to defend myself against, as I perceived a tangible world to be devoured. Tad and I talked about John Kennedy. He had struck a chord in both of us. The idea of doing something not just for ourselves, but for our country, had generated a spark. That much at least. If not yet enthusiastic, we were interested.

"He has style," Tad said.

"I hope he means what he says about working for our country," I said. "He helps me believe at least there's hope to do something more in life than just make money."

"I know."

"My Dad hates him."

"Why?"

"He believes that financial pillaging and burning constitute the capitalist model. He's a redneck."

"That's a harsh thing to say about your own father."

"Isn't truth harsh?"

"Complex, not harsh. You should honor your father."

"Is that your Catholicism speaking?"

"Possibly."

"It would be fine if he has real ideals."

"Kennedy?"

"Yes."

The locked radio code room was off to the right just after we climbed the steep stairs from the top floor and entered the steel-caged gate monitored by a guard with a .38 snub nose in a shoulder holster.

"Cerebrus," Tad said the first time we entered.

To the left, our offices stretched a block long on either side of a single, narrow hallway. The memory of my Munich Intelligence mates is surrealistic. There was Barry Carpenter, the tall, clean-shaven corporal, owner of 'Old Blue,' his ancient, well-kept Mercedes Benz convertible. It is possible that Barry was a closet homosexual, although no one then would have dared voice the fact. We were not so enlightened sexually to acknowledge such a thing, let alone devise a formal policy to deal with it. I remember him once leaning against his 'Cabriolet' and proclaiming: "It is a member of a dying breed; and, as such, it is honorable." He wore Ivy League suits with button down shirts, and worked inside as a clerk, rather than outside as an agent like the rest of us, who all carefully wore German suits to blend in with the natives.

Private first class Joe Magioni was a former New Jersey taxi driver. His hair was as black as Tad's, but slicked down. He was as charming as a Rome whore, and had the pilfering knack of a Basque Gypsy. During a trip he and I once took to Frankfurt in an unmarked Army sedan, he was assigned as my driver. Acting as the unit's weekend courier, I was delivering to headquarters a thick-skinned, leather overnight bag filled with Secret documents, secured by a large combination lock, discretely wrapped inside brown paper and hidden in the trunk under a spare tire. Magioni on our drive unilaterally delivered a mesmerizing monologue about booze, baseball, and broads, and by the time we reached Frankfurt he owned my mind. If we had been home I would have helped him sell the Brooklyn Bridge to a newly arrived and ignorant Russian refugee. All he required, though, was that I let him load an electronic keyboard from the Frankfurt Post Exchange into the trunk for the return trip, so that back in Munich he could sell it at three hundred

percent markup to a German rock and roll musician. He sold
whiskey too. He was an honorable black marketer, though, and
didn't deal in drugs.

Steve Horten was a corporal. He was short, wiry, also Ivy
League, and had an infinitely subdued personality. He was an
icily self-controlled fellow who kept you at your distance by
the power of his brain. You simply knew he was smart. He
never asserted himself, and his response either to affronts or
requests were so diplomatically phrased you could never take
offense – even when he refused you something. I am guessing
he was Barry's secret lover, the female half of the couple.

Don Wandering was the Boston patrician. He was far
beyond cool. Middle height, lean, and erect, he established
his presence from a distance with a carefully combed, long,
smooth expanse of straight blond hair maneuvered suavely
over the sides and back of his head into a clean waterfall-like
curve that lay thin and tight to his scalp. He mastered all situations by silently taking your gaze straight on and wordlessly
announcing: "I am immensely handsome, intelligent, well-
educated, well-connected, and gracious to all human beings to
a fault, and you will be wise to treat me with respect." While I,
with my semi-rural upbringing, in a tight situation would have
announced to an adversary that when cornered I was dangerous, Wandering was the kind of fellow you imagined would
in a pinch simply move in close, smile and slide a thin stiletto
into your rib cage, emptying your heart's contents into your
chest cavity while whispering in your ear a compassionately
soothing farewell.

On my first day Captain Portman introduced me to Hans
Bernstein, a German born, naturalized American master sergeant who spoke flawless English. He was distinguished by
a broad, thin-lipped incision of a smile under a pair of bright
blue eyes. After we talked a few minutes, he enthusiastically
told the captain to inform the colonel that my German was

very good. I followed the captain to the colonel's office. This pot bellied, gray haired man, who kept dabbing his watering eyes with a white handkerchief throughout his short greeting to me, told Portman to deliver me to Major Brown. Brown was to be my boss. I was apprehensive. Since this was my first assignment after eighteen month's Intelligence training, I knew that how he and I got along would define my tour of duty. When I arrived at his desk, I braced stock still at attention and saluted. Seated, Brown waved a hand, palm out, casually over his right eyebrow, as if he were flicking a fly off his forehead.

"Tom," Brown said to the captain, "would you tell Bob to bring us two cups of coffee? How do you like it?" he asked me.

"Cream and sugar, sir."

"Sit down. Make yourself comfortable."

He was a big man, about six foot two, two hundred twenty pounds, a football player type with a broad nose that looked like it had been repositioned several times. His hair was as brown as his name and lay straight on either side of a ragged part. He had an avalanche of a smile that he barely kept under control. His hands were as hairy as bear paws. He tilted his wooden chair back behind a plain wooden desk, the black barred window behind him reminding me of the cage we were in under the eves of the building.

"What's your first name?"

"Cal," sir.

"Fine. I'm Matt. We don't use ranks or last names here. Get used to it. It's the Army, but it's not. We've got a job to do, and it hasn't got anything to do with any kind of pecking order. I'm your boss and you'll take orders from me and try to do your job right, but you'll call me Matt. Understand?"

"Yes, sir."

"Sir's not necessary."

"No, sir…"

"...Ah!" Brown said, accepting the coffee from a quiet guy who disappeared before Cal could form a take on him...

"...I've got it," I said.

"...Matt." Brown said, emphasizing my meaning.

"...Matt," I echoed.

We got down to work. He assigned me two agents: German-Italian, man-and-wife, long distance truckers named Partone, who delivered supplies to West Berlin through East Germany twice a week. Their handler was Master Sergeant Paul Kemper, a congenial, down-to-earth fellow from Detroit who spoke German with vastly more vocabulary than I possessed, but with a total disregard for grammar. He took me to his office and pulled out a dossier six inches thick.

"Read this," he said.

For the next two days that was all I did. Matt gave me an office of my own next to his with an open door. I was the only other officer in his unit, and he said he wanted me to have access to him so I could learn fast. His smile turned out to be permanent, and he was every bit the fair, even-tempered officer he first appeared to be. He was to make the next three years a bearable experience. When I had finished the Partone's dossier, Paul gave me my first practical lesson. He took me down to the motor pool and taught me how to work the quick change license plates on the tiny civilian VW sedans we drove. That evening he navigated while I drove the VW to my first agent meeting. Hitler's little bug wasn't fancy, but for reliability it was hard to beat. We roared along at a nifty seventy miles per hour through a thick forested, two-lane road.

"Turn right up here," Paul said, indicating a short field leading to a copse.

I guided the VW fifty meters before Paul said, "Left here." I swung the wheel, and cozied the VW behind the huddle of trees.

"That's good. Stop."

Changing plates was easy. They were held in place by a screw-type device with a spring that let us remove the old ones and put new ones on in the dark. I put the old ones under the hood and reversed back to the small highway.

"What if somebody saw us do that?" I asked.

"Then we'd be stupid, wouldn't we?" he answered.

I understood mine had been a stupid question, and decided to keep my mouth shut. Ten minutes later Kemper pointed to a small house just off the highway with a high-pitched roof, and a tractor and trailer parked out back. I pulled off, inched along a short driveway, and stopped the VW. We walked to the kitchen door, where a round, jolly German woman with frizzy hair opened it and invited us in. This was Frau Partone. In a moment her husband, Mario, joined us. He was a beamy, redheaded fellow with hands almost the size of footballs. The Partones were as gracious as hotel waiters. They served us Kaffee and Kuchen as Paul got down to debriefing them about their last trip to Berlin. He pulled East German Army order-of-battle portfolios from his briefcase. Frau Partone had driven the last trip, so she pointed out several unit arm patches in one book, and then from another identified some small arms weapons she had seen. We spent over an hour with them before packing up to head back to the Kaserne.

"Why do they do this for us?" I asked as we returned down the highway. "Is it for the money?"

"Of course. We've promised to help them get a special West German trucking franchise after another year's work for us."

For a month or more I didn't do anything but help Paul debrief the Partones. One evening as we were ready to leave the Kaserne, he said: "I'm going home." He turned on his heel, and I was on my own. From this point on, the Partones were mine alone to manage. I got to know their two young daughters; they and Frau Partone added five pounds to me with their homemade Bavarian pastry.

Several weeks later Brown assigned me another agent, a young married woman in a Munich suburb. She was a strikingly beautiful blonde I wanted immediately. My God was she lovely. She liked me too, I know, but her husband never let us have one minute alone. My heart was in my throat whenever we met. She possessed an animal magnetism I was hard put to deny. Her professional value to us was that as secretary to her boss, a scientist, she prepared reports about trips he made to East German technical conventions, which she copied for me. I met her periodically, always at her home, to pick them up.

Tad and I didn't actually see a lot of one other in the office the first several months. His Counter Intelligence unit was at the end of the main hallway, literally a half block away. Need-to-know being the Lord's Prayer of Intelligence, visits between departments were not encouraged. In the meantime, though, the other East German team members, Larry, Steve, and Don, and I had gotten acquainted. Tad finally joined us one day for lunch, and we drove to a nearby Greek café. It was a rough hewn, open door place in the middle of a large dirt parking lot. Instead of menus, the cooks took us into the kitchen and pulled the tops off the pans and skillets on the stove to choose our meals. The food was exquisite. From this time on, we all became thicker than thieves: my team-mates and I and the owners of the cafe. The Greeks loved Americans and took us in like family. Our first New Years Eve they invited us in to party with them. We all got high on Ouzo and they taught us how to break our glasses after each drink in the open fireplace.

The middle of March, Matt told me Robbie would be arriving soon. I picked her and our daughter up at the airport on a warm April Bavarian morning. Once tiny Hilary, who had been born while I was still with Robbie in the states completing my basic Intelligence training, was now a chubby half year old, well on her way to becoming a stubborn, self-defined personality. Buried under all the minutiae of real operations, I had by now practiced most of the skills that eighteen months of stateside and indigenous experience had packed into my brain cells. It all left little room for fatherhood or loving a wife. I was not the same man Robbie had known when he left her months before. She didn't seem to notice. My professionally acquired ability to deceive apparently was not easily discerned. At my request Matt requisitioned for us one of the civilian German apartments that the unit maintained in Schwabing, the student quarter near the English Garden, Munich's largest and most beautiful park. This was good fortune. We would not have to live in the American housing near the Kaserne, but would be living on the economy among Germans in Munich's equivalent of New York's Greenwich Village.

As soon as we had settled into the apartment, I arranged with Robbie a Saturday night home cooked dinner for Tad. I decided to make it a real affair, and invited Barry, Steve, and Don too. They all got on well. Barry and Steve shared recipes with Robbie, Don brought her a small white rose bouquet as a housewarming gift, and entertained us with his cool while we all drank several bottles of Champagne. Robbie had worked up a wine-soaked Beef Bourgignon the day before.

Late in the evening, shortly before the party broke up, I stepped out on the balcony and looked over the brook that ran nearby on the edge of the English Garden. Robbie and Tad were wrapped up inside a conversation ranging from Boethius to Kerouac. Steve and Barry were whispering on the sofa. Don sat alone in the corner listening to classical music, occasionally watching Tad and Robbie define the world through literature. Hilary slept peacefully in the back bedroom. My mother and my father were six thousand miles and light years away. As I listened to the crackling stream, I wondered, had I really escaped Oklahoma? Was I finally a man? I had at least accomplished the escape. I wasn't so sure about the manhood.

Matt greeted me more seriously Monday morning. He was not unfriendly, but he seemed abrupt and distracted, in a hurry, under pressure, I thought.

"Your wife happy with the set up?"

"She's fine."

"You ready to take on another agent?"

"Of course."

"You're going to like this one."

This was lean understatement. Matt gave me the dossier on the senior reporter at Vienna's major daily newspaper. "Come back to me when you've got this down," he said. The dossier was fascinating. Army Intelligence had recruited the journalist, Konrad Bachman, as World War II ended. Since, he had reported to us on a variety of subjects to which he was privy. Because Austria maintained political neutrality, it was a mixing pot for Intelligence agents. The official myth was all you had to do was sit in any of the hundreds of Viennese cafes eating pastry, and you would hear enough secrets to start a war. The city was full of well dressed, but indistinguishable, people from every country of Europe, and several farther afield. Barry once said that one out of every three was likely in the business. He might have meant it. It was alleged he kept statistics on such things for our unit. Vienna was definitely very Harry Lime like. I always wondered, as I sat in every café, which one was the third man? Then I remembered. I was.

In Germany, the authorities supported us. In Vienna, they allegedly hunted all of us. As we tried to dig secrets from one another without each other knowing it was happening, politically the Viennese pretended to want to catch us. On a higher level it was, I suspect, just a gentlemanly ruse. We each and all had our country's money to spend, the Viennese music played from every street corner café while the restaurants, nightclubs, and high-class prostitutes prospered. Business was good for everyone.

"You've got to play this seriously," Matt stressed before my first trip. "If the Austrians catch on to you, we'll have a diplomatic incident on our hands. Understand?"

"I'll be careful."

"Do that."

The trips could not have been more romantically dramatic. Once a month I boarded the Orient Express in Munich as it passed through on its way from Paris to Istanbul. As the train cut through the Austrian mountains, breathtaking views assaulted my senses. My Vienna cover story was that I was a former Englishman who'd lived in America a number of years, and become a naturalized citizen. I was a free-lance writer for small papers back home. If anyone ever checked, I had membership in several American journalistic clubs and associations. Headquarters planted a few stories under my name in obscure little journals. It was a fluid, ambiguous story, hard to disprove, and as I met fellow travelers in the compartments of the famous train, I found it wore well. I learned how to play my part so that it became more me than the real me. On my first trip, I shared my compartment with a very ladylike young Viennese woman who had just gotten married. We got along famously. Her loyalty to her new mate was complete. I was to be a friend, nothing more. It turned out well. We really did become friends. She invited me to her house and introduced me to her mother. They served tea and Viennese pastry, and we chatted.

In Vienna, Konrad and I always met in excellent restaurants, where he informed me which authorities from East Germany, Czechoslovakia, and other East Block nations would be visiting Austria in the coming weeks. I didn't press him for how he got his information. I doubt he would have told me, anymore than I would have given him my real name. That was part of the unvoiced bargain between us. Surely, the various countries' press relations people communicated with him in some prescribed fashion. I had no need for the details. Before and after meeting him, as part of my cover story I always spent an evening in the city, visiting cabarets and clubs, before returning to Munich. Writers I presumed like bars and clubs. And their women. My real purpose was to see if I could ferret out any tail that might be on me. And to scour for new contacts. Matt eventually gave me the names of other potential Vienna-based sources to check out. I became a regular and the city became a routine. Konrad was different from my other agents. Like Tad, Konrad was a well educated man, and, as an Austrian of some social stature, he was elegant, sensitive, and sophisticated. I don't remember details of our meetings now, but I remember how richly enjoyable they were. It was heady stuff for an Oklahoma country boy in his early twenties. I particularly wanted to tell Robbie about Konrad, but this remained impossible. Matt had convinced me about the importance of strict secrecy. The consequences of a loose lip were too real. Successful Intelligence work on the ground, he explained, largely results from a controlled mouth, and personal safety results from playing the role carefully. So, I developed in earnest the necessary caution as I plied my trade and honed my skills.

———

The trades craft of my job included reading photocopies of intercepted mail. One day I happened onto a letter from an East German woman to her son, who had one night swum a canal to the West. He had moved to a Munich suburb, where he now worked as a lathe operator. The interesting part of his letter was about a friend of his, Guenther, who had just joined the East German Army. When Matt saw this, he told me I had a winner on my hands.

"Your swimmer," he said, "is either very brave or very stupid, or both. In any case, he'll make a good agent. You'll want him to get to the army kid."

For three months I investigated my target, Werner Lumpke, and, under Matt's careful guidance, wrote a recruitment plan that headquarters approved. One Saturday night I introduced myself to him at a strip joint he frequented, bought him a few drinks, and soon we were buddies. He had never known an American. I was entirely outside his normal circle. This was a fascinating new experience for him. Werner was a dirty, stringy-haired blond young man who, I learned, leaned more toward the stupid than the brave, but when I finally told him what I wanted and how much I would pay him, he embraced the idea of putting his life on the line returning to East Berlin. Over the next several months I taught him a lot that would, hopefully, keep him alive – for awhile, at least.

I arranged an alternate mailing address for him miles from his real home, and created a false identity and cover story that East German authorities could check out through one of their Western agents. For the first time I started watching people very closely on the Munich streets, wondering who might be there observing Werner and me. I taught him how to do secret writing with blood and water, and how to identify East German and Soviet Army equipment, as far as we knew it. His task was to help us know more. Although he wasn't swift, Werner was motivated and he worked hard. It took almost a year to prepare him for his first mission. Then, as Sherlock Holmes used to say, the game was afoot. In the background, Robbie and Hilary barely existed. Tad was just somewhere out on the edge of perception.

Headquarters gave me the final OK. Sixty days later Werner and I flew separately to West Berlin. His job was to take the *U-Bahn* subway from West to East Berlin, meet his soldier buddy, recruit him, train him how to write secret letters inside real letters, and return safely to West Berlin. My job was to wait it out and debrief him when he got back. If he got back.

The first trip went without a hitch. The next year Werner visited East Berlin twice and his buddy sent him three letters with secret writing that spelled out officers' names, ranks, and duties, equipment, training, and logistical details he was able to report about his company. The operation had a weakness, though. Headquarters decided our trips to Berlin were too dangerous. They levied a requirement that we figure out how to train another permanent East German agent to visit East Berlin and actually meet the soldier. They said that would make the operation safer for the soldier. Theoretically, it was a simple step to add another physical cutout in the training communication. However, finding that other agent in East Berlin would take time. Headquarters told us to wait, they'd come up with someone, and to sit tight.

"I've got something to talk to you about," smooth Don said a couple of months later. Matt was on leave. Tad was down at the end of the hall in the Counter Intelligence section. I was in Matt's office, covering for him.

"What's up?" I asked.

"Let's go to the Greeks' for lunch."

"Sure."

I'd not spent a lot of time with Don, although Robbie, Tad, and he had become closer. Boston had packed him with enough education to be conversationally literate about literature, so Robbie and Tad had brought him occasionally into their investigation of the world's artistic product. I'd not been part of this, so he was still somewhat a stranger to me as we stepped into the Greek kitchen and selected our meals. The waiter brought us a bottle of Ouzo and one of retsina wine. We sat outside at a rough wood-planked table. We did a shot or two of Ouzo, which set the mood. I ran my finger through my cowlick, attempting to bring it under control. Don's sleek mane lay keenly against his smooth head, not a hair out of place.

"Before Matt left on vacation he asked me to talk to you."

"What about?

"About your soldier."

"He told you about him?"

"We're going to work together."

"You and the soldier?"

"Yes. . . No…Yes and no."

"You're not making a lot of sense."

"Listen."

"I've worked hard on this operation," I protested. "I don't want it compromised."

"Headquarters still doesn't like the operation the way it is."

"Why don't they tell me?"

"They did. I'm reminding you."

"Why you?"

"Because I can help."

"You'll just complicate it."

"Not true. It just appears more complicated. It's true though that if your soldier meets another East German agent, your guy over here will be safer. And so will you, by the way."

"They think I'm in danger?"

"You're running an East German Army agent through a former East German citizen. Don't you think if the East Germans found out about it they wouldn't like to nail you? You think they don't have people over here?"

"Go on."

"You're going to introduce me to Lumpke. We'll tell him I'm taking over."

"No!"

"You'll still be in control…"

". . . How can I do that…?"

". . .And I'll write the contact reports to Headquarters. You read copies, keep a detached perspective, and watch how things progress all along the line."

"What am I looking for?"

"Mistakes."

"Suddenly I'm just quality control?"

"More. An objective look at your over-all situation will help you make better judgments. Look, I guess I have to put on the line. You're learning to love the work too much. You need to love it less and respect it more. Learn how to give it respect and the work will love you; and it will set you free. It will help you get your personal life together."

What we were now discussing was not entirely clear to me, but I believe I was starting to get an idea. I'd heard something of Don and Robbie meeting without Tad now and then. That he might be replacing me on two planes filtered through my thinking. I think it did, anyway. All I could do though was look him in the eye and listen, try to make sense out of what he was saying from a pure business sense.

"I've been added to provide you room to reassess your situation," Don said.

"My situation?"

"Your priorities are off. It's affecting both sides of you. Your work and your life."

What was this Boston Brahman saying to me? This sleek man, who I knew conducted himself with utmost discretion when he and Tad and Robbie met together. His discretion when alone, I dared not judge. He could have been speaking Russian. Greek. Sanskrit. I heard the words, they were familiar, but I couldn't allow myself to understand them.

"By over controlling one," he said, "you are under controlling the other. And the other is more important."

"Why should I allow you into...my situation, as you call it?"

"It's no longer your choice."

"Why not?"

"Can't you see other forces are at work here? You've created the situation that puts the choices in others' hands. That's no way to run your operation...or your life."

"And if I don't want to allow you into…my situation?"

"There's a Zen concept called emptying your cup."

"Jesus! Is this what they teach you guys at Harvard?"

"It means opening your mind to change, to options. If you are too close to anything, you fail. If you are too far away, you fail. The alternative in Zen is called extending your Ki."

"What the hell is that?"

"Your intuition. Call it your gut. Change your situation by letting the change happen without battling in your mind. Besides, the change is an order, not from me, but from upstairs. From Headquarters. You understand?"

I sucked on one of the sixty non-filtered Camels I smoked a day and thought about this. *Empty my cup. Extend my Ki.* Were they positioning me to create the operation's strategy? Is that what Don was saying? As to the unspoken by him about Robbie, it was best left that way. I appreciated the subtlety of his candor. He was a gentleman. We drank some more Ouzo and muddled through some operational details. What options remained to me? I had to accept the idea. A couple of days later when Matt returned, he called me into his office. Don was there. Curiously, so was Tad.

"You know DiMarisi," Matt said.

"Yes."

"He's got a Swiss agent who knows a woman in East Germany. The Swiss is a technical type. So's the East German. It gives them reason to meet at technical fairs, over there and here. One's scheduled for a couple of months from now in Zurich. The East German is coming out to it. DiMarisi's going to recruit his Swiss agent to train her East German colleague to be your East German soldier's contact in East Berlin. DiMarisi will actually recruit the East German in Zurich too, when she comes over. If she accepts recruitment, then he'll reveal that his Swiss agent works for us and is to train her. Got it? You train Tad. Tad trains his Swiss agent and recruits the

East German. The Swiss agent trains the East German, who becomes your soldier's physical contact. You pass local control of Lumpke to Don. You step back and become the case manager. Werner Lumpke just becomes a communication point while your responsibility increases."

"Don told me about it."

"You understand why we want all parts of the operation separated?"

"Yes."

"No problem?"

"It seems complex."

"It's supposed to seem complex. It's not."

Matt leaned back in his chair. Tad smiled. Don gazed down on his fingernails, a contemplating Buddha. The sun gleaming through the window bars stenciled thin shadows across his face. The office still looked like a cell to me.

———

While the mission developed, the colonel organized a Christmas party to which we were all ordered to report in full dress uniform. I had never bought one, and I had no intention of breaking my civilian cover now by showing up in the Kaserne in uniform. So, I simply didn't attend. No one said a word. If the colonel noticed, he kept his peace. Maybe Matt explained the importance of the mission and my need for total anonymity. Again, I don't know. But the incident gave me an indication of how casual U.S. Intelligence practices could be. It showed me how careful I needed to be to avoid compromise by my own superiors.

Tad and I couldn't help becoming more engrossed in things. It was not hard to sit here in Munich, the site of one of Hitler's major organizing coups, and settle deeply into our roles. The job separated us from everybody whose daily bread was earned believing honesty was important, that telling the truth mattered, that believing what people told you necessarily reflected reality – all dangerous conceits in our occupation. In the meantime, the Patrone's had started pushing for the concession we had promised them. Matt told me to tell them we would start the wheels rolling, to be patient. Meanwhile, I gave them extra requirements to fill. We'd gotten new directives about how the East German border guards inspected vehicles. I asked the Patrones to note precisely each step they were obligated to fulfill for the Volkspolizei, the Vopos. Plus, I increased their pay an additional fifty percent a month. That quieted them down, and their concession demands temporarily slipped into the background.

Once, I bumped by chance into the scientist's secretary on a Munich street, and we had a coffee together. With her husband absent, she became an excitable woman, gripping my hand spontaneously during conversation, sliding close to me. It was all I could do not to respond. She was irresistible. She was disappointed when I left, I could tell, and I reported the incident to Matt.

"I'll assign someone else to handle her," he said when we talked a few days later. "Besides, the soldier deal's going to take most of your time. And the Patrones won't last long now that they're after the concession. You'll be busy handling the details of that one too. Forget her. You did well staying out of her knickers. It's hard sometimes. Believe me, I know. Give me her dossier. By the way, Tad got the East German agent. Come in tomorrow, and you and he and Don and I will work out details. Tell me, how do you like the work now? Think you might want to do it longer than your present tour? I could get you an extension, you know. Another three years over here and you'll go back to the states to teach a course at the Intelligence school. You'll be a captain by then. Maybe a major."

The thought of becoming a professional had never entered my mind, although admittedly the thrill of the work was climaxing. Crossing foreign borders as someone else, with the full faith and credit of a nation behind you, is addictive, even if the nation is pledged to disavow you under embarrassing circumstances.

"I'll think about it," I answered. Matt smiled.

"Good stuff, huh?"

"Good stuff," I agreed.

I'd gotten thick with one of the strippers from the joint where I'd recruited Werner. Helga was a large-boned, well-muscled woman who worked herself nightly out of a leather outfit with brass studs, swinging a black whip about, cracking it on the stage as she unveiled her body. She joined me one evening at the bar for a drink. We talked, and that indefinable spark occurred. We met weekly somewhere to visit the zoo, to see a movie, to walk along the Isar River. Sex eventually arrived, and we really liked each other's company. She wasn't a dominatrix at all, but a hometown girl, plain, two years from a Bavarian farm, uneducated but sweet, and Munich street smart. I liked the farmland smell of her and how her long brown hair felt when it covered my sweating body after we had made love.

———

Below the wispy marble skin of Robbie's ankles, her veins flowed beautifully blue. Despite my fear, I felt a unique pride about this lovely woman. Secretly stealing an admiring glance during an evening Munich Opera performance, I watched her graciously slip her feet from beneath her long, silk skirt. Her ankles were sensitively braided over by the finely tapered leather straps of the French shoes she favored, those that so handsomely complemented her beautiful legs. Why was it I feared Robbie? For that is what dominated my feelings for her. I knew why. My fear centered simply for me in my belief that her intelligence was so superior to mine, that I did not deserve her, could never hope to keep her love for a lifetime. She could read meanings into literature I could never see as I rode surface stories, like on a galloping horse, oblivious to the subtleties of the hidden gems writers scattered throughout their brilliantly elusive productions.

I felt as if I were unable to trust my own good taste in having desired and won her love. As I savored her ankles, intrusively incongruous visions of past summers of sweating laborers and stone masons covered with rock dust and cement invaded my mind and tormented me with my workingman's background and its consequence: my intellectually inadequate education. The roughness of my mind's capacity to perceive nuance, embarrassed me. I didn't think of it clearly that way at the time. Only later reflection provides the insight. There is an intriguing psychological phenomenon: *"Approach/Avoidance Syndrome."* It is when you have found, and may actually have within your grasp, exactly what you want, but you are prohibitively afraid to embrace it, to draw and hold it fervently to your heart. That was what I felt at the time about Robbie.

An historical event evaporated the paralysis of my personal frailty. As soon as the curtain fell on the opera's final act, a man stepped quickly onstage and held up both hands before the audience could get into full applause. Everyone stopped clapping, and the man said simply in German that President Kennedy had been assassinated. I'll never forget the phrase. "Ist zum Opfer gefallen," *has fallen to sacrifice.* I remember a deep sense of loss. The forces of mediocrity had assassinated Camelot's King. Little reason remained for what I was doing. It was now just business as usual that someone was required to do.

Shortly thereafter, the Vienna reporter Konrad told me he couldn't work for us any more. He'd written some prominent pieces on the growing involvement of America in Vietnam that had brought him to the attention of the paper's editorial board. They'd promoted him to Executive Editor.

"It's too dangerous. If they found out, I'd be fired. You understand? Ask your people for me. Tell them. Let them know."

"Yes, I will."

"Bitte."

Please. So polite, the Viennese. I couldn't tell if he was demanding or begging. When I wrote my report and received Headquarters' permission to drop Konrad, I invited him to a farewell night in a Vienna club following his final debriefing. We had the Saturday night of Saturday nights. During the evening, we met two Russian women, a divorced mother and her daughter, and I spent eighteen dollars on them for wine, getting their names, their Vienna address, and their phone number. When I reported this to Matt, he praised me and said not to worry about Konrad.

"Just between you and me, his publisher's our man too. We'll let him deal with Konrad. We've things to work out with the Patrones about the concession, remember? Are they still pushing?"

"They've been quiet lately."

"Good. Let me know if they ask again."

"I will."

Barry, the gentle gay, murmured aside one day something about Don and Robbie. I was deaf. The extra money, false identities, broken laws, intricate schemes, the exhilaration of planning and living lies, potential or imagined dangers, the allure of the game: everything had accumulated, like heroin in the blood, and numbed my common sense. Tad was too discrete to raise the subject. Besides, he was busy training his Swiss agent to train the East German agent. He and I hadn't time for domestic issues. We talked about the mission, though, outside at the Greeks' place one day. It was decidedly cathartic, particularly after a half dozen Ouzos in the fresh Spring air. Out of a minute's dark silence, after we had provided the answer to every detail we were able to conjure about the coming Berlin trip, another question flowed from my own mouth, one not consciously on my mind.

"What has happened to us here, Tad?"

He didn't look at me at first. Just kept his eyes on his Ouzo glass, as if he were attempting to understand what I was asking. Then, he seemed to get it, looked up at me, smiling, and responded in a very quiet voice.

"They kidnapped our innocence."

"Do we have to pay a ransom to get it back?"

"I'm afraid we've already paid it."

"Do we get it back?"

"I don't believe so."

"I can't remember ever having had it."

"Neither can I."

"It's not been three years since we met."

"No."

"I feel older."

"Perhaps it's wisdom."

"I don't feel wiser."

Tad imperceptibly acknowledged this, indicated he'd heard it by an already jaded intensity of gaze directly into my eyes.

"I've made a great mistake," I said.

"Don't castigate yourself."

"You understand? I've hurt Robbie."

"It's not entirely your fault. Too much happened to us too fast."

"I need to find the humor in it."

"We"ll have to make it up."

"Create humor ourselves?"

"Not create humor."

"I don't understand."

"Atone for our mistakes."

"How?"

"By ourselves."

I could smell the Alps. The crispness of the air from their peaks carried to us with ease. I heard Tad's words but I was unable to understand them. It was years later before they made any sense to me. I sipped my Ouzo, thinking only that I had to carry on a few more months until my Army discharge. Definitely, I decided then, I would not stay in the service.

———

Shortly thereafter, Robbie got a job as the secretary to the executive director of the American funded Russian language radio station beamed into the Soviet Union. I went to a party with her there once and met some of the Soviets. Their nature struck me as being a mystic, Asiatic take off of emotionally volatile Latinos; they were fervent, loquacious, passionate. I considered that the Soviet agent handling the East German soldier would be like that too. Only obliquely at the time was I becoming aware of the stateside protests about our escalation in Vietnam. That's how narrowly engaged I was. I wasn't even entirely sure where Vietnam was located. My little world was just East Germany and Munich, and getting out of the cage.

It was almost summer as Don and I prepared to execute the mission in West Berlin. He and I were to take a military courier flight while Werner flew commercial. Don would dispatch him from West Berlin to East Berlin while I stayed in the background, in the Hilton actually, waiting to do whatever was necessary to pick up the loose ends. Tad would remain in Munich. He had completed his part. The new East German agent wouldn't meet with the East German soldier until Werner had introduced the concept of the change to him. Magione and Horton were to come along as surveillance security for the operation.

Shortly before I left Munich, stripper Helga and I lunched on the banks of the Isar River near the Institute where they played Beethoven's Ninth every New Year's Eve.

"We must stop this," she said.

"What?" I asked.

"Meeting."

"Why?"

"You are someone educated," she said. "You have some sort of important position. I am a country girl who strips off her clothes for a living. There is no future in this for you. And it would not be fair of me to try to make one for myself."

I tried to protest. She was too wise.

"Go and be who you really are," she said, leaving me with a gentle kiss on the lips. There was a sadness as she walked away, but I didn't try to stop her. She made too much sense for me to protest. All that remained was the task of finding out who I really was. A few days later, Tad and I were walking down Leopoldstrasse, Schwabing's main boulevard, when, without warning, he stopped stock still and looked up. The sun was shining through a temporary break in the clouds. Raising his head to the sky, he screamed:

"Aaaaarrrrggghhh!"

"Good God, Tad, what's wrong?"

Tad swilled a breath; his eyes glazed as if he'd been shot. They opened and he smiled.

"I can't quite put my finger on it."

The team for the mission blossomed into bureaucratic excess. Steve Horton and Joe Magioni came on separate planes, and rented other small German cars to tail Don and Werner throughout Berlin as they crisscrossed the city in a tiny VW. They spent well over a hour making sure they were not followed. This was not enough. Afterward, they all disembarked their cars and, for another hour, Joe and Steve counter surveilled them on foot. As Werner turned over his army buddy to an East German contact, we wanted maximum assurance we were accomplishing the job undetected by the Vopos, the Volks Polizei, *The People's Police*; and The Stasi, The Staats Sicherheit Abteilung, *The National Security Department.*

Everything went well in Berlin. Don dispatched Werner while I waited in the Hilton bar. Several hours later, he left a prearranged phone message indicating Werner had arrived safely back in West Berlin, and they would return separately to Munich next day. I was to follow later. Magione and Horton were already on their way out. That night, a formidable blonde German woman seated at the far end of the Hilton bar with two men, was left by them late in the evening after brief hugs, alone. We spent the evening dancing in the roof lounge, and the night in my room. We never bothered to exchange phone numbers. It was an understanding that required no words. No trust. No commitment. Next morning, I put her in a taxi and she rode off to work.

———

The pain hit my left side while I was walking through the Tiergarten, Berlin's zoo. I knew what it was. My lung had collapsed once during college, and it had happened again. I couldn't go to a military facility or a private hospital because of my false documents. I stayed in my room, kept off my feet, and ate lightly. Although it was hard to breath, the pain subsided. Next day I flew back to Munich. Matt put me in the base hospital immediately, where a young doctor who'd never treated a spontaneous pneumothorax before was assigned the task of opening me up and patching me back together. After I got out of the hospital, Robbie nursed me a month back to health, often with dinner at the outside café near our apartment. One evening, after we'd drunk coffee and talked for an hour with the old, bearded, retired German professor she'd lately discovered there, she pretended to discuss my job. As we talked, Hilary entertained the professor at the next table, her tiny fingers wrapping around his thumb.

"Don tells me you and he have been working together."

"He told you about that?"

"Nothing specific."

"We're not supposed to talk about it."

"He gave me no details at all."

"Where'd you see him?"

"We talk…sometimes…about books."

"… Yes…we do something together…sometimes."

"He likes you."

"Really?"

"Really."

That's as close as we ever got to discussing anything personal regarding Don and her, and me. It wasn't something I knew how to talk about. All I could do was pretend it didn't exist. Robbie sensed it was useless to pursue and didn't push any further. When the Patrone's started demanding their promised concession, Headquarters ordered me to drop them without prejudice, which I discovered meant they didn't get their concession, but could work for us again sometime, if they wanted to, if we wanted them to. Headquarters disallowed the eighteen dollars I had spent on the Russian women in Vienna, suggesting I was just having a good time. They soon took me off the East German case, explaining they were developing a better job for me. They suggested I just lay back for awhile, and they'd return to me. I decided to bide time. It was now on my side. My tour was nearing its end.

On my twenty-seventh birthday I went out in the evening and got drunk. Late at night, riding down a Schwabing backstreet on an old BMW motorcycle I'd bought a few months before, I jumped a curb. Somehow I kept the bike upright, and as I guided it back to the street a toothless old hag stepped up to me, put her face in mine, and asked if I was lonely. I wondered whether she was asking out of kindness, her own loneliness, or professionally. I got the cycle back in gear and rode away. The last I saw of her she was shuffling off through the night singing to herself. The next morning the Colonel called me into his office with Matt and Captain Portman. They all looked very serious.

"Where were you last night?" Matt demanded.

"Why?"

"We'll ask the questions, if you don't mind," the colonel said.

"It was my birthday," I said. "I had a bite to eat and a drink at a place."

"That all?" Portman demanded.

I considered explaining about the bike mishap and the old lady, but caught myself. That couldn't be it. Better to keep my mouth shut.

"Yes, sir."

Abruptly, they all laughed, and Portman produced a box, which he handed to the colonel, who put out his hand to me.

"Congratulations."

The box held a shiny silver new pair of captain's bars I'd never wear. Along with them came a pay raise. A few months later, my tour finally ended, and at my request the Army discharged me in Europe. It was Honorable, of course, and they gave me a Letter of Commendation and a Letter of Recommendation. Robbie announced she was going to return with Hilary to the United States to pursue her Ph.D., and a divorce. I attempted to dissuade her.

"What about…"

" It's best for us, you know."

" Robbie . . ."

"I've already got the tickets."

"We should talk…"

"My folks will put me up…"

"I want to stay in Europe awhile . . ."

"Don's staying too. He's going to sell mutual funds to soldiers."

My mental state didn't encourage further discussion. Matt, Barry, Steve, Sergeant Kemper, and Magione remained on duty. If my decision to leave the service and remain in Europe bothered Matt, he kept it to himself. The day he gave me my discharge papers an American guy in another European suit stepped up to me in the Kaserne parking lot and asked for a cigarette light. As I obliged, he told me he was from Big Brother. That was what we called the CIA. He wondered if I would like to talk to them about a new job. I said no. I found work with the sales office of an American manufacturing firm in Brussels. Six weeks later, someone passed the word to me that my entire unit had been shipped to Vietnam. Six months later, I heard, most of them were dead. Maybe all of them. Not Tad. He'd beaten me out of the army by three months, and ever since had been living in Rome.

———

After a year in Brussels, I moved to New York City. I went home first to try and put my marriage back together. Robbie tried too. She even returned to New York with me, and we looked for an apartment together. We actually found a one bedroom rent control with brick walls, just off Central Park on Park Avenue. It even had a back yard, mostly mud, but with an effort we could have made grass grow. The skyscrapers and the concrete didn't attract her as they did me. Within a week she let me know she'd made her final decision.

"I'm going back to school, Cal."

"Can't we…?"

"We're not a real match."

"I'll work on it. Why not go to Columbia?"

"I've got a scholarship in Ohio."

"Robbie . . ."

"You be well. It'll all work out."

She left. I vaguely sensed I was losing something I'd never find again. I didn't know how to save it, though. It was beyond me. All I could do was watch her slip off into my past. Tad eventually moved to New York too. I found a job with a large advertising agency, and he got one as the assistant to the president of an essential oils company. A year later, one night over Scotch at The Four Seasons bar, he finally let the cat out of the bag, or, as he liked to put it, freed the truth from the well.

"You remember your East German soldier?" he asked.

"Sure."

"One of my team mates still active called me recently. He brought me up to date."

"What did he say?"

"That was a setup. The East German woman I recruited to replace him and meet the soldier in East Berlin?"

"Yes?"

"Apparently, she was already on our payroll, but upstairs had found out she'd been doubled back on us. She was feeding us corrupt information. The Russians were running her through East Germany. Headquarters put her onto your game to expose her relationship with my Swiss agent to her handlers."

"Why'd they want to do that?"

"To confirm her bone fides. It strengthened her reputation with Soviet Intelligence. When I recruited her, cutting you out of the operation, it signaled they could safely use her to recruit my Swiss Agent. Which she later did, or her handlers thought she did. And I was able to double the Swiss lady back against them."

"What happened to my soldier? Guenther?"

"They doubled him back against us too. We played along with it awhile. We discounted everything he told us, of course. My mate tells me he was eventually considered expendable, by both sides. Finally, he just disappeared."

"The poor bastard. What about me? Why'd they pull me off the operation?"

"To protect you. Werner was no mental giant. He had no ideological underpinnings. He could have lead the Soviets to you. Although you only had a few months to go before you got out, they wanted to make sure you stayed clean."

"Who cared? I wasn't important."

"No? The Army, even Big Brother cared. If Werner'd compromised you, which he well might have in your last couple of months, they wouldn't have felt secure bringing you back to duty. And if a political emergency made that attractive, they wanted...they want...to be able to reactivate you. They've spent a lot of money on you. On us. They like to insure their investment."

"They might recall us?" I asked.

"We're squeaky clean. We might be valuable again, some day."

"Was Werner doubled?"

"He was taken out of the loop. They did something else with him."

"What?"

"That little morsel of information, we're not cleared to savor."

"Into the Black Forest."

"Well put. I'll make you one of the literati yet."

"While you were active, how'd you know where everyone's real loyalties lay?"

"I didn't. It was always just a guessing game. Headquarters analyzed the data produced, made the final judgments, and directed me accordingly. I just followed orders. What else could I do? What else did you ever do?"

"We were checkmated from the beginning, weren't we?"

"Intelligence is not based on a deep affinity for metaphysical virtue."

"Your problem has always been that you're over educated."

"Probably, would you like another Scotch?"

"That's a good idea."

"All us over educateds eventually come up with one."

———

I suspect the former Army Intelligence colonel, who was personnel director at the New York City advertising agency I had signed up with, hired me out of military loyalty rather than any corporate executive potential I might have possessed. I wanted to ask him, but a couple of months after I started work, his building super called in police, who found him on the floor in his midtown apartment, garroted to death. Today, I still can't walk down a street without watching my back.

Tad and I kept close for a while in New York, but he eventually married a very tall, blonde lady and moved back to Europe somewhere, to be a librarian. I've always wondered if that was not just a cover story for another operation. Anyhow, we lost touch, and never reestablished contact. Robbie finished her Ph.D, then met and married another college professor. Hilary eventually married too, although she doesn't talk to me. Doesn't even let me know where she lives. I hear I'm grandfather to two wiry young boys. For thirty-five years, I was a private marketing consultant. In 2001 after the towers went down, I lost my entire airline-related client base, so I decided to retire. I never remarried, just didn't ever feel I would be able to pull it off. Rather, I learned how to live with my inadequacies, what others might call my afflictions.

I theorize that Intelligence got to me too early, before I'd developed a center to myself, constructed a set of rules to live by, regular standards, like other people. On the other hand, sometimes I speculate what might I have achieved had I stayed on the job: taken over Matt's position, or accepted Big Brother's offer in the parking lot of the Kaserne? Conceivably, might I not even have become a man of some estimable destiny?

As for Tad, although he and I spent such a short time together, he left an impression on me I'm unable to cast off. It's not anything specific, just the memory of a gentle man so genuine I can't forget him. I'd like to see him again. If he still lives, I wonder if someone could get a message to him for me?

If they could, I'd say, tell him: *Tad, contact me. We may have been obliged to start our lives with lies, but we don't have to end them that way. We fulfilled our contract. The job has passed on to others now.*

Four decades later 9/11, of course, changed everything. I just try not to think about it.

The Crazy Man

The milk is sour. I only bought it yesterday, but it is definitely sour. I pour it into the kitchen sink, drop the carton to the floor, stamp it flat as an anemic pancake, and toss it into the waste basket. There is a hole in the wastebasket through which the last ounce of leftover milk gurgles onto the floor. Dropping to my knees, I sop it up and a straggly string from the rag I am using wiggles off and sticks to the floor, consummating its relationship with some previously positioned, rancid marmalade of the long defined past. I bend again to my knees and scrape it all up with a case knife which, in the process, breaks. I poke the two pieces of the knife into the wastebasket and open the fridge to get another carton of milk. The refrigerator light flashes and burns out, leaving the insides entirely dark.

The next carton I retrieve is chocolate milk. I want a bowl of cereal. I do not like chocolate milk on my cereal, so I return it to the fridge and close the door. Almost. The hinges stick and the door will not close completely. I push and hear a grating, push harder, and the upper hinge cracks, leaving the door hanging from the bottom hinge only. The upper portion falls to the cabinet top where it chips the porcelain of the sink. Pulling the fridge from the wall in order to face it against the cabinet, and thereby temporarily hold the door shut, I pull a muscle in my back. As I wait for the pain to subside, somehow the fridge's electric cord short circuits, flashing sparks which scatter into the wastebasket and ignite the paper nestled therein. As

I attempt to draw water from the tap with which to quench the flames, the faucet handle breaks loose and water squirts into my eyes, temporarily blinding me. Unable to see, I step accidentally on the tail of the cat, which has unseen slipped into the kitchen, drawn I must assume by the smell of the sour milk. It screams, frightening me. I jump again, hit my head on the low hanging lamp that my wife has told me endless times to raise, and I fall to the floor.

The flames leap from the wastebasket to the curtains, which being light cotton catch immediately and ignite the wallpaper which I only last night repaired with fresh, and apparently highly flammable, glue. It is a scant five seconds before the wood framing of the wall is ablaze. The cat scratches my leg and I scream, attracting the dog, who grabs the cat over eagerly in its jaws and breaks its neck. My three year old daughter enters, sees the dying cat, and breaks into wilder screams, attracting my son dragging his panda bear behind him. The bear's leg catches in the wastebasket and the boy immediately bolts from the flaming room, pulling behind him into the dining room both basket and flames, spreading yet farther the fire.

We all get out of the burning house in time to save ourselves, but outside I remember…I have left $25,000 cash in the cookie jar. A postman restrains me from entering the house, but I break his arm to get away from him, and he sues me successfully in civil court for $100,000 and, eventually, I am convicted in criminal court for assault and battery. My wife divorces me, and the judge, due to my violent nature he says, refuses to grant me visiting privileges with my children. My Facebook Friends start passing around nasty notes about me on the Internet before the whole world; seems they have a grudge against me for some reason back in highschool, and Monday morning my boss tells me he's read them and is firing me in a general downsizing of his small business as a large multinational corporation starts knocking him out of the market by price fixing. I am three days short of retirement funding. Remorseful, I buy a .357 magnum, shoot him squarely between his eyes, for which I am – rightly so – convicted and sentenced to twenty years, parole possible at seven with good behavior. However, as fate will have it, after two years the prison is destroyed by an earthquake, and in the hubbub I get away to hide in the giant national forest nearby. For twenty years I live off nuts and berries until I am an old man, then return to civilization disguised by a long, gray beard and a bushy head of hair. I am determined this time to make a go of it.

However, as I am crossing the street one morning, a terrorist kidnapping a school bus sideswipes me, careening into a lamp, knocking the driver unconscious, whereupon the bus overturns, trapping the children inside. Just as I get the door open, freeing the little tykes, a passing elephant recently escaped from the city zoo when a street gang busts the gates down, tramples upon and crushes one of my legs. My new crutches collapse on me the first day and a splinter of it catapults into the air, entering the eye of a passing grandmother out on a stroll through the park. In anguish, she beats me into submission with her pink umbrella. Retreating from her onslaught, I pray for deliverance. Heaven opens up, the entire scene is drenched in a torrential rain, which turns to hail, causing the temperature to drop to twenty-five below zero accompanied by gale like winds, bringing it all down to a wind chill factor of fifty below. Public transportation and communication are halted by the   elements, all business terminates, the Governor calls out the National Guard, and I, according to the judge having frightened the elephant, am cited this time for cruelty to animals. The jury decides I am criminally insane and puts me away in one of those places where every one is far, far over the edge. I am aghast at first, horror stuck, panic stricken, petrified. I am determined to escape.

Except...soon I notice that the fridge works and the milk is always sweet. There are no small children, no terrorists, no street gangs, no estranged wives or vicious old ladies. The place is totally peaceful. We talk a lot of nonsense all day, sleep long nights, eat well, have no work to do and don't have to pay taxes. I have yet to note a single rampaging elephant on the place. Matches are forbidden, it's all in a valley and therefore has no lightning bolts, the temperature is mild, providing moderate weather making us all frisky as goats. They let us range freely over twenty acres of land. There is a dark, tall, stone wall to keep us from escaping. But why should we want to? The other day they gave me a Ballolamy or Bollotomy, something like that, and I have developed amnesia. I can't remember my name, where I am, where I came from, or how this story even started. Since it's being written on an old computer I found that is broken and won't let me back up, I guess I must simply just watch where all this leads, creativity, in my case, being totally a positive experience, which fully enhances my already bucolic days.

They've put me in a private room where for some technical reason I cannot fathom, the wiring in the computer now causes it to obliterate every word as I write, so that not even the last word behind me is available for reference. I'm sleeping a lot between writings and can imagine the sense of the thing must be slightly obtuse by now. It doesn't however seem to me it would be fortuitous, or courageous, not to complete the work, it having got this far. You know, I've heard say that a million monkeys with a million computers would finally create the Bible, maybe even the Koran. And with this technology at my beck and call who knows what achievement I may attain?

I'm guessing *God* must be helping me, or I would certainly no longer be here mesmerizing myself with these words, one by one, to the point that the entire known universe has for me become the blank space after the last word, waiting for the next word, the sound after the last sound waiting for the next sound, the void after the last thought waiting for the next thought – the *in between* of it all as it mysteriously unfolds.

I've just discovered another person inside my head and we talk together. He asks, isn't everything similarly so for every one if we get right down to it? Isn't this existence, this being here at all, a dreamlike attempt to capture life as it drives on its independent way? Isn't the sour milk the norm rather than the exception? The burnt house, the upset wife, the accidents, the pain, the gangs, the mayhem, the frustration, the anger, the fear? How much of it truly makes any sense? Is it as we thought it would be when we, as children, first heard it was headed toward some darkly predicted death out there? After an intermediately unpredictable future? Is it not entirely different from where we imagined it would be? Have not all our ideas of where we thought we would be, and what we thought we would become, have they not altered as the years have progressed, digressed, regressed? Whatever? Is it not so? my friend asks.

And I ask, have I not been blessed? Have I not been rewarded to be here where my new friend and I are so happy? I wonder is it not possible that everyone else is missing the joy? Do others ever fear to fetch a carton of milk from the fridge? Is it a strain for them to look into their child's eye? Was their job and marrying their wife, their husband, the best they could do? Or was there better possible? And did they try? Have they attained their enlightenment?

Although it appears that so many variations inhabit life, and despite all the anticipation and hope we attach to them, I believe there are really so few conclusions we may expect to discover. My new friend says: how much touching, tasting, seeing, smelling, hearing, thinking, feeling, loving, hating, sensing, and simply being – all ostensibly, to naught. I suspect he may be right. And then, I could be wrong. He could be

wrong. I'll have to think about it some more. It needs careful examination. But not now. No. Tomorrow. That's what tomorrow is for. There's where the answer lies. That's when I'll do it. I'll do it tomorrow. For, tomorrow…is another day…
    …I think.

Long Walk To The Showers

Dylan continued to read *The Wall Street Journal* two years before he understood what was really going on. The Maserati and Bentley ads tipped him off. And those for exotic rum drinks, precious jewels, and distant island vacation retreats, where corporate presidents avoided the issue of his lost income. Sitting on the curb, his tennis shoes soaking up the morning fog from the gutter, Dylan wonders where it went, precisely. The income; not the fog. He knows where the fog goes. He'd had his own business, was doing pretty good...before the bottom fell out...again.

"Hey, buddy, ya got a cigarette?"

Who is this? It's hard to tell; Dylan has been drinking lately. He didn't the first year, but one day somebody slipped him a bottle to share. It helps him pass the time. He doesn't see too clearly anymore. It doesn't make any difference. He hasn't got a cigarette.

"No, I don't have a cigarette."

"You sure?"

"Yeah."

"Got an extra buck?"

"No."

"I hit ya on the head with this bat, I'll find out."

Dylan lifts his head. The guy's got a two foot piece of wood in his hand.

"You'd be doing me a favor, pal. Go on. Hit me. Hard."

When Dylan drops his chin to his chest and sits still as a stump, the guy lets the stick gradually slide to his side.

"You all right?" he asks Dylan.

"I'm being honored at Lincoln Center next week, you know? Go on. Hit me!"

Seeing he's getting nothing out of this situation, the guy hobbles off down the street. Dylan fumbles in his dungarees, finds a few quarters, and searches his memory for the nearest Starbucks. He'd been running a nice little business, been an ad man in the city with his his own little shop. Did brochures for small companies, local radio and cable TV commercials, billboards sometimes, Web Pages, that kind of stuff. It wasn't big time, but . . .

Coffee. Jones Street. That's where it is. About a block away. He'll get a nice French Roast with some cream and sugar.

It's mostly deserted this early in the morning. People will start hitting the streets about six or seven though – as the sun heats up and the fog burns off. The Vietnamese will be opening their restaurants. A few early morning hookers will be trying for an early score. Addicts hurting for the next jack in the box up their arm to set the world right will be there too.

He remembers when he was a sergeant in the army. That was a long time ago. He's got an appointment at the VA hospital this week to check his blood pressure. They told him to go easy on coffee. Yeah, what should he get instead: a latte with Courvoisier on the side? A flute of Dom Perignon? He opens the door to Starbucks.

"What'll it be, Pops?"

She's a tiny thing, with high perky breasts. Can't be over eighteen. Minimum wage, but with tips she gets by. Probably still lives at home. Her skirt is half a foot over her knees, her white cotton socks hang on her ankles, black flats are a little scruffy, but with a red ribbon in her dark hair and blue eyeliner, she makes Dylan's morning come alive. He remembers when he too had a daughter like her.

Did they have recessions then? He can't remember.

"French Roast," he says. "And leave room for cream."

"How about a cinnamon roll?"

"Got any cheap used ones from yesterday?"

'No, sorry.'

"Nothing else, then."

"Go on, take one. It's on me."

How about that? She's nice. Maybe she'll grow up to be a real human being. He pays and sits down by the window. Sips the coffee. Damn! It's hot. Where was he last night? Must of slept somewhere. Couldn't find his boat, that's for sure. It's still there on the docks at Pier 39. Or was that last year? No, it's still there. He just must have got lost last night. Oh yeah. Barney had a joint and a bottle and he'd back slud with old Barney. Got to get his act together. Got to. After all, he's college educated. He had the whole nine yards, laid out like the road to heaven. What happened? His doctor at the VA Hospital wants him to visit the Mental Health Clinic next week. Doesn't think anything's wrong with him. Just wants to check for depression, you know.

"I'm not depressed, Doc. I just need a job."

"Thing's will get better. Trust me. Go on in. Talk to them."

"I had my own business. I was living in a nice neighborhood. Went to Rotary, you know?"

"I know."

"What happened?"

"These things occur. Finance is complicated. The pros are working on it. The government. The big corporation presidents. The economists. It'll all turn around. You just have to hang in there."

"How long you been a doctor?"

'I graduated two years ago."

"You like it?"

"Yes."

"You like helping us Vets?"

'It's a good deal. We've got the latest technology here."

"What do you think about the President's health plan?"

"The country needs something new. We don't see it here because you guys get the best. And we test new ideas on . . ."

He pauses.

"On us?"

"I didn't mean that."

"It doesn't make a lot of difference, Doc, when you've lost your job, wife, and kids."

"That's why I want you to go to the mental health clinic."

"If they find something wrong, will they give me a tranquillizer?"

"They'll give you what's right for you…if you need anything."

"I need something, that's for sure."

"So, you'll go?"

"Yeah, I'll go."

Dylan takes the street car to Pier 39 and walks down the dock to his boat. The tide is flooding and the current is bouncing his boat like a basketball. He clambers down into it and turns on the radio. *NPR* is in the middle of a news analysis.

"This is Sally Somebody and you're listening to Clean Air. We're talking with Andy Macomber, deputy executive director of the conservative non-profit think tank, *Forging Forward*. Mr. Macomber, what's the latest thinking on the economy?"

"Well, Sally, it's still early in the game. We've got to wait it out. It'll turn around. It always does."

"Yes, well, but congress voted down unemployment insurance for a million of the fourteen million unemployed. What effect will that have?"

"Do the math, Sally. It's not a big deal. It's less than 7.142 percent. That's statistically insignificant in the over all scheme. You have to average these things out.

"What about the other thirteen million people?"

"They'll find something. It's a great country. Great people. Great spirit. Resilient citizens. The vibrant underpinnings to the financial network of corporations will integrate their resources and a year or two from now thing's will be buzzing. We'll have forgotten all about this."

"But the people without jobs and income?"

"There are food banks, Sally. Wonderful places. The American people are filling in. They're volunteering. The churches are helping. We'll all take care of one another."

"I visited a food bank recently, Mr. Macomber. There are just Beans, rice, fruit juice, and some pretzels, not much in the way of meat and veggies unless you're in the front of the line."

"Sally, hard times build character. The American people will work it out. Thanks for having me here. I really hate to run, but I have a committee meeting now. Ask me back again. I always like joining you and the American people like this. Where else … huh? I ask you, where else?"

It's time for Sally to read a non-commercial promotion.

"Clean Air is brought to you by Devron Oil, bringing you the power of people thinking deep thoughts about people. America's secret weapon. And by people just like you."

Dylan tries to remember when he last showered. Last week? Yesterday? He looks in his laundry basket. It's full of dirty jeans and t-shirts and underwear and socks. No, that's laundry. That's not an indication of his last shower. He looks at his under arms. They don't *look* dirty. He can't smell anything, but when he takes off his shirt, he notices a dark ring on the inside of the collar. Maybe I ought clean up, he thinks. Tomorrow. I'll do it tomorrow. The shower's are a block away at the end of the Pier by the Marina Office. It's a long way. Not now. Tomorrow.

His cell phone rings. He turns the radio down and checks the screen. It's an 800 prefix. Probably a credit card bill collector. Ignore it. They can leave a voice mail if they're serious. He turns the radio back up. Sally's still on the job.

"My guest now is Hippity Hop, the newest Pop Power on the scene. Hippity has been here in New York now for a week, playing at the Super Duper Theatre. His new CD is called Making Out Downtown. Hippity is the stage name of Tommy Bundlestiff of Port Orford, Oregon. Tommy, when did you leave Port Orford to become Hippity?"

"About two years ago, Sally. I was pumping gas at the Devron station and got an inspiration to sing and took the bus to New York and started singing on the streets of the West Village. A song promoter heard me, made a demo, and it's been downhill every since. You know, as a member of the new generation of Hippers and Hoppers we can take the essence of music down to its bottom line and the thing about this kind of music is it salves the soul of poor people and helps them get on with life, you know?"

"Will you give us a sample from your CD. I particularly like your song: *Getting Rich In America*."

"I like that one too. Sure. Here goes."

Tommy swings into it with a high tenor voice that sounds like a cat who just got his tail stepped on. Dylan tunes him out, but leaves the radio on out of loneliness.

"That was wow, that was, I mean, wow, Hippity!"

"Thanks Sally. You're a sweetheart."

The background radio is a narcotic that diverts Dylan's mind from his reality. He sops his soup up with a piece of bread.

"Local underwriting is brought to you by the University of San Francisco. offering an MBA for striving kids who want to make it in a big way. The time is ten thirty. The Dow is down. Bonds are up. The dollar's down. Prices are up. Now, Hipety, give me another song. You choose this one."

"OK, Sally. I call this *Outdoing Everybody Else*."

"You can win the hottest game
Like others all 'round town;

Beat 'em out, with a triple crown.
It's easy as fallin "off "a log.
It may seem gross, but it's really not,
It's how we do it as we' all get bought...Off.

"Oh, Hippity. That's so cool."
"Well thanks, Sally. I try to touch a nerve, when I can."
You stay right here, Hippity. We'll be right back after a station break."
Dylan jumps up and turns the radio off.
The latest San Francisco paper lies on the starboard bunk.
Dylan picked it up yesterday, but hasn't had time to read it yet.
He scans the stories.

Two percent of Americans own ninety percent of all assets. The bottom fifty percent don't own much more than their toothbrushes. And those in the middle are joining the toothbrush class. The Government seeks half a trillion dollars for new jobs program. Economic turnaround imminent. Thirty million under poverty line. One in three kids doesn't finish high school. One out of four can't read a book. Fifty million Americans are floating on Marijuana to cope with reality. An ad says a local society restaurant charges *two hundred bucks a plate for dinner not including the wine, coffee, dessert, and cognac. Will mail special dishes to you while you're on vacation. Sells its elegant chili in red wine at supermarkets for twenty bucks a tin. Provides a gallon to take home for a hundred dollars.*

Who wants to read that kind of stuff? Nobody. Not the *The New Yorker* readers, not the *Rolling Stone* fans, not *Esquire* junior gentlemen looking for the new styles, not *PC World* geeks, nobody.

Dylan throws the paper down, picks up a bar of soap and a towel and shampoo, and climbs out onto the dock. What the hell, he figures, I may as well clean up right now. He looks down the dock. It's a long way to the showers. Dylan lowers his head and steps out.

9/11 was when he lost his first client base. Small business manufacturers for the airline industry. Actually, he'd lost his clients in the mid 80's too when he'd been a stock broker and the Silicon Valley had imploded. This last time was the 2008 mortgage scam. Wonder what it'll be next time? Don't see Senators lose their pensions. And they have health care no matter what...forever.

Fog's coming in again. Must be a low pressure cell developing somewhere. Dylan can't see five feet in front of himself, so he leans on the wood railing and moves slowly. The showers are out there somewhere, if he just keeps moving. There's got to be a shower at the end of the dock. Just put one foot in front of the other and don't stop, don't give up. He remembers the buck seventy five for coffee was his last cash until Social Security comes in a week. Maybe the Doc can loan him a tenner to get some more rice. After the shower. He'll be more presentable then. Make a better impression.

The deep moan of a tanker's foghorn guides him toward the showers. He hopes, anyho. He's lost his grip on the wood rail, but inches slowly on.

He's heard General Motors has a new small car. Plus a big one with over 500 horse power. How'd they get those out so fast? They were bankrupt just a few months ago. That Corporate Bailout money sure works fast for corporations.

The concrete under his feet is really slippery. He falls down. He's not drunk. Sober as a judge. Just worn out.

"Where you going, Dylan?"

It's Doctor Klein from the Chris Craft, the old German philosophy professor from Berkeley. Has a nice farm in Napa, but lives on his boat to stay in touch with the city. Likes the theatre and symphony and ballet.

"I'm going to take a shower," Dylan says.

"Keeping a clean machine, huh?"

"Yes."

"Pull your head up."

"Yes. Up."

"I got to go. See you around."

"Around. Yeah."

Dylan remembers the annual tax on the boat coming due. Wonders, how's he going to cover that? He'll have to, or they'll take the boat. Cut back on food, I guess. Eat Less beans and rice.

He heard lately on *NPR* that *some* frogs somewhere are becoming hermaphrodites. Jeezuz, what's *that* all about? And where *are* the showers? It's taking so long. Maybe down this walkway. Get the gate open. It's slippery. Be careful. It's rolling; the tide is high now; it's really bucking the dock.

All of a sudden, Dylan loses it completely.

Oh, Damn! I slipped, Damn. In the bay! Wouldn't you know? Cold as hell. Kick! Hold my breath. Kick harder! It's very cold. I feel sleepy. Think I'll just keep my eyes closed while I kick. Won't need a shower now. Hey, that's good. I saved myself a long trip. I won't have to go all the way. I didn't want to. It was such a long way. Now it's all OK. It's really good. Easier this way. More efficient. Probably wouldn't have been any hot water, anyhow. I think I'll take just a little breath.

The hand on his collar pulls him up just as the water starts to enter his lungs.

Dr. Klein drags him out of the bay.

"Jeez, Doc. Huhwhaaahhk! What brings you back?"

"I had a feeling, you know? Thought I'd forgotten something. Then there you were, so I hauled you out. How's it going?"

"Better."

"I'll walk with you a way."

"That's nice. Look, the fog's lifting."

"It always does, sooner or later. Keep the faith."

With that mysterious piece of advice, the Doc takes off. And the sun shines through the fog and the water of the bay reflects off the universe with a glint of hope.

Dylan eventually finds the showers, strips off his clothes, and lets the water flow over his shoulders and down his back for a long time. It's very warm, very soothing. As he watches the water pour down the drain, he thinks some more.

I'm not sure how I made it, but I did. The shower water's so warm. Man. Hang in there awhile longer. Yeah. One way or another.

Who knows?

Maybe the Physicists are working on an answer. Or the Astronomers or maybe some graduate Biology student some where working on his PhD will come up with something.

Or, say: maybe those hermaphroditic frogs are onto the answer. Maybe they'll figure it all out.

God knows, somebody needs to.

I Can't HearThe Drums Anymore

From far below the washbasin, my arms grope upward toward the water flowing out of the spigot. My mother stands beside me.

"Why do you wash your hands so often?"

I am only three; how can I possibly know? I simply want my hands to be clean. I stretch farther to reach the water. I suppose it eventually cleans my hands, but I don't remember. The next I do remember is sitting before the coffee table in the living room, looking at the family album. It is a cheap dime store album, bound in cardboard. The edges are frayed and the pictures are held in place by corner tabs. Many have come loose and the pictures cringe in the fold of the album.

One particularly catches my eye. There I am, the center-piece of the photo, still no more than four, if that old, held forcibly by my father's muscled arms, the fingers of one hand gripping my jaw so hard it is bending my face into the bone structure. Tears are flowing from my eyes like lava. I cannot see her, but I know it is my mother taking the photograph. I cannot remember what happened to cause the event, what childish error I must have committed, but their vengeance appears to have been wrathful. For the rest of my youth, I feared always, especially when returning from fishing trips when I would lay my head on his lap as he drove us home in the Chevy pickup, that my father was going to murder me.

For the rest of my life, I feared that my mother would deceive me. They had conspired against me at this early age and I felt I could never forgive them. My desire was to have had their love while they lived, of course, but that did not permit me to condone my forgiving them now that they had violated my childish trust. Twenty-four years later, when the phone call came, my father was on the line telling me my mother had died. She had placed a plastic bag over her head and neatly tied it closed around her neck with a red ribbon, and then had pulled the covers up. I did not feel pain or remorse, but a dull blankness, a deadening of my senses. I flew home and confronted the preacher who was to read the service.

"Don't make it long," I said. "She was not a believer of anything, I think. Keep it short, will you?"

"God forgives all, my son..."

"Please, keep it short."

"Tell me about her..."

"Short, do you understand? She lived, she died, she's dead. Put her away and let us get on with our lives."

"Son..."

"Short."

I turned and walked away.

From somewhere, I heard the drums.

Thum thum.

What does one think of inside a plastic bag with the covers over one's face as the air grows dull and thick and one's lungs suck heavy for oxygen? How does one not pull the bag back off, but simply lie there knowing one is dying, and do nothing?

Years later, thinking of her death, I tried it. I pulled a plastic bag over my head, not intent to die, but to experience what she experienced. The air becomes something other than air. It becomes poison and it insists that one find fresh, real air. It commands the hands to find air. It demands they do it. I did. I could take it no more and jerked the bag from my head. She did not. She lay still. She left me.

I never knew her. I never remember her ever touching me, holding me, her kiss, the taste of her mouth, the smell of her body, nothing. She was never there, but in body to be seen. Who can she have been? She was not a beautiful woman, although not unhandsome. I remember she was tall, long-legged, dark haired, with a large nose, a full, sensuous mouth, substantial breasts, and dull, dark eyes, which were as deeply withdrawn as were her thoughts, inwardly-perforating, outwardly observing me as though she did not trust me.

I wonder if she trusted anyone? Did everyone, when she looked at them, see the same thing? Did they all sense she did not trust them? Or was I alone in this? My sister never spoke of this, nor my father. We did not speak of such things when I was a boy, or as a young man, or even when I was older – when finally I became what I supposed was a man.

"Do you think they are together now?" my sister curiously asked after our father died years later, his body eaten away to a wisp of himself by the invasive cancer.

"I don't know about such things," I answered.

He had been a mountain man, a mason, a hewer of stone, as had been his father, and his father. He had in his life also become a hewer of men, and a ravager of life. He and my mother were country people, she the daughter of a quarter breed Cherokee Indian woman and a misplaced Scots/Irish/Englishman, who was the sheriff of a tiny Oklahoma plains town.

All that is a long way from this Hollywood cafe. I do not consciously remember her as I sit outside sipping coffee and observing the dark ringlets of massed hair on the head of the beautiful women at lunch today. How do such beautiful women come into being? How far away they always seem to me. I see them with my eyes and I recognize that the short distance from my table to theirs is a lifetime – even as we exchange simple lunchtime pleasantries. Perhaps they would be closer if we did not speak. They have all seemed so far away, all these beautiful women. So distant. So unreal. But for them, though, I would never have remembered the drums.

Thum thum.

When did I first hear them? I can't remember precisely, but I sense when it might have been. I think it was even before I was born, when the Cherokee came to Oklahoma on the Trail of Tears, one of the six civilized Indian tribes driven to reservations by my Anglo Saxon ancestors.

Thum thum.

My memory bows before the mountain stars toward the level plains and a template of meaning impresses a design upon my mind. Faint, ghostlike beats tumble into my thoughts. By night they sounded, the drums, on trails first distant then close, low on the plains, carried by men without women. They sounded on the ground while the men's feet bit the earth as they marched their broken march. They came to be together now that they were beaten by my white ancestors, without women, to huddle, to smoke the pipe, to tell stories to one another. They poured from many directions, as does the news of a printed journal, and over many hills to meet on plateaus where the high far mountain winds screamed down over the ridges and into the valleys like enraged serpents, and then abruptly glided to stillness on the level plains to cool their meeting place, the cooled air then warmed at night by campfires of gathered mesquite and oak.

One, or another, would start. A yarn, a tale of muscled men, a fiction, a narrative, a chronicle, a revelation, and they would imagine themselves in their minds into other men. Each man came alone, without his women and children, without his sister, without his mother; and each man spoke for himself alone. Man did not go to man and say, "join with me in my thoughts."

That is not the way of mountain men or plainsmen.

Such men stand alone.

Existence is a vital struggle to such men: singular, consisting primarily of being one with oneself and knowing that one's oneness is the essence of being. Male alliances are forged, but each man in an alliance is keenly aware that he is solely responsible for being where he is and may depart at any time without betraying the alliance. The alliance is fluid. Being alone, a mountain or plainsman knows, is permanent. It is what it means to be a man. One does not huddle to be manly. One is manly alone. One sits before the fire and thinks one's own thoughts, and his most private thoughts he does not share, as the smoke from the fire climbs into the sky.

Mother was smart. She was more. She was keenly intelligent. I remember that much about her. I see this now. I did not see it earlier for my need was to possess her love. That is no longer my need. I need only to forget her, so I may let her go, let her be. Possibly, I do want her love even now, but more, I need to let her go. She has fought her battle. And I have mine to fight.

Father was not so keenly intelligent as she, but he was clever. He suffered fools poorly. Like prophetic fisherman of old, he was patient, and stealthily planned his strategies. He knew that resignation brought all things to fruition: with forebearance, the fish would bite. Imperturbably manning one's line a long, silent time would snare the trout, as it would also eventually snare the truth.

Raised in the shadow of the Cherokee, he remained only a mountain man, a hillbilly, an uneducated white woodsman who dropped onto the plains to better his lot in life. He was, I like to believe, a contemplative soul, imprisoned in an ignorant mind hiding in a roughened pioneer body. He was driven not by any philosophy but by basic survival needs. Inside him dwelled, I think, a dwarf of potential nuance who could not transcend his large outer roughness. There was certainly something charismatic about him. He charmed people without effort, he gathered them to him. He knew this and used it to become successful in his trade. He sensed his own power, and it freed him to rise above his monumental ignorance. His was a life of pure instinct.

How did he, this ignorant man, join with this intelligent, withdrawn, unfathomable woman? Such are questions beyond my capacity to answer. My stoic Indian ancestors, these men with their drums, the drums so far from my father's comprehension, these Cherokee mythmakers who sat in circles under the stars, these braves without women, telling the tales of their forefathers whose cloth had been deerhide and bearskin, they had been hunters. They had lived discreetly from and on the earth, and the drums intoned their lost simplicity. These were the drums I first must have heard: the simple drums of life transformed into rhythms and chants from simple beats of the heart.

Thum thum.

Thus they guarded their innermost hearts from women. Their tales wove into themselves the mythology of the relationship of men to women. Of husbands to wives, of brothers to sisters, of lovers to lovers, of sons to mothers. They taught themselves the necessity for the keeping of the peace with women through gentle deception. They were the original heretics, who pretended – for women's sake – to acknowledge an eternal spirit, but believed in their hearts that the black earth of the mountains and the plains was the real god. It was what sustained life. It was what could be taken in the hands and felt with the fingers. It did not require subjugating oneself with false humility to any unseen god. It told man to accept himself and all humans as all powerful and all responsible. It made him, he thought, self sufficient and inviolable...untouchable.

And so he sat by the fires at night and thought, and beat his drums.

She did not touch me with her hands, but she taught me small things. She taught me how to fry lemon rinds in sugar to make candy. I remember that much about her. Did she remember that as the air grew stale inside her plastic bag? We would peel the rinds off and cut them into tiny slivers. Then we would dip them in sugar and fry them in a butter-filled skillet until they were crisp. They crystallized and their bitter sweetness was astounding to the tongue. When I think of them, however, I cannot truly discern what is memory and what may be imagining on my part. Did she teach me how to cook these sweet and bitter lemon rinds; or have I invented it to create one tangible, intimate memory with her to last me a lifetime?

After her funeral I go into her bedroom. Upon the dresser is a book. I pick it up and read its title: *"One Hundred Ways to Play Solitaire."*

I lay it back down upon the dresser and look at the pillow covers of the bed. What am I to do with this? What am I supposed to think? What am I supposed to feel? I step into the bathroom. Again I wash my hands. Silently, the water flows. I listen intently for an answer.

Where are the drums?

I can't hear the drums anymore.

Seriously, Prometheus

There are those destroyed by unfairness and those who are not.

–Michael Ondaatze
The English Patient

"**O**h! Pardon me."

"No; excuse me."

She spoke first; I had only reflected her thought. It was to be typical of our relationship. We had literally bumped into one another at a street corner. It was one of those oblique events that mark the more common aspects of life: rain pelting one and all, bodies scurrying, attempting vainly to rush between the drops, when suddenly there we were eye-to-eye, inches apart, one of those immediate in-your-face sort of things. We had of necessity either to kiss or to speak.

"It's my fault," she insisted.

"Not at all," I protested.

Thunder clapped and she dropped a hand on my arm in reflexive anxiety, drawing instantly from me a protective squeeze of her wrist, which lasted only a second before the gravity of the situation dawned and she drew back. A women of an indeterminate age, she was possibly young, conceivably mature. If the previous, she was well worn; if the latter, well preserved. Impassively her eyes took me in and she appeared to be truly disturbed by the violent weather.

The nearby revolving door of the waterfront restaurant emerged peripherally in my vision like a flickering shadow, beckoning me unrealistically toward it, and I found my arm had lifted itself and guided her unresistingly inside where we caught our breath. It was as if I had rescued her from a menacing dragon and now quietly awaited her favor, the unacknowledged knight serving the purest of ladies. Remembrance of college freshman English class hinted at the chivalry of my move: recollection of the lectures about King Arthur's men of the round table, the honorable sirs and their vulnerable ladies, chaste and innocent. This image in my mind replayed like a video tape, justifying my abrupt reaction, and – with this legitimization to believe in – I spoke up.

"You're cold. Let me buy you a drink. It'll warm you up."

"Oh, I couldn't," she began.

She gathered her composure around her as I was to do my eventual suspicions, blanket like, and protected by this she froze, silently waiting, it seemed, for something. Then we both shuffled a moment, glancing about us at the other people, who were either drinking or eating or serving those who were.

"I insist," I said.

Deep within, she weighed, measured.

"I do feel better inside here" she said, nodding at the tables, "for the moment."

The Victorianism of it struck me as absurd, but somehow poignant. She was not beautiful, and the instant chemistry a man occasionally feels for a woman in a chance meeting was not there, Nevertheless, the situation so suddenly thrust upon us called for resolution. She seemed to sense it also and hesitated a moment longer, discerning the degree of safety in the place before consenting. When finally satisfied, she looked me straight in the eyes as if to say, I trust you.

"Wouldn't you like a coffee while the rain continues?" I said. "Give it a chance to slack off before you're on your way again?"

What a contrast my eventual suspicions became, compared to that first unfettered moment. I made myself believe that my collaboration with her was devoid of any expectations whatsoever – other than the money, of course. But its true importance developed as she mentally transported me half-way 'round the world. I could trace most clearly the eroding pathway taken, step-by-step, street-by-street, touch-by-touch. Finally, I simply tried not to feel like the fool. That she had been deceiving me I first only suspected; so, instead, I hid my mistrust, allowing it to fester as does flesh intruded upon by a thorn just below the surface of the skin.

"Coffee would be nice. French roast, if they have it," she said, brushing the torturing raindrops from her sleeve, her eyes diverted toward the glistening window pane so near.

"I'm sure they do."

"I learned to love it in France."

"Me too," I answered.

Her head turned back to me.

"Such a civilized country."

I ordered two cups and real cream, not half and half, plus raisin cinnamon rolls and a pat of butter. They didn't have any croissants or I'd have asked for them. They would have enhanced the mood. Our passion developed slowly – took weeks indeed to form, providing us really with time to get a feel for one another. She was a darkly diminutive personality, not given to emotional extremes, but also not unfeeling, not coldly mechanical as so many professional women can be. Oddly, she struck me from the beginning as possessing nothing in her character more strikingly present than the trait I had always sought in the agents I had handled years before: that of discretion.

"Do you live here?" I asked as we waited for our coffee.

"Sometime," she said.

"You're traveling through, then?"

"Not exactly. . ."

She held a taut tongue, not revealing any personal demons, let alone releasing them. I suppose I should have recognized the source early on, but as salesmen are the easiest sold, so are deceivers the easiest deceived. When you've believed in nothing most of your life, you wish desperately to believe in something; or someone. I had learned that the young are too inexperienced to profess any answers other than obtuse guesses, and most of the old too worn out to have any answers at all, She had caught me at the point in my life where I was becoming fully aware of my alienation and the revelation that its source was simply the distant starting line where my personal race toward death had begun. It was simply my own nature that I was discovering.

"Thank you for thinking of the coffee," she said.

"I need a cup too," I reassured her.

"You're American, of course."

"Yes. Aren't you? You have no accent."

"I've lived here off and on a long time."

"Where were you born?"

"I'm not sure. My parents moved about. My passport indicates my birth in Tahiti, but my parents are of mixed Middle Eastern origin. I don't know exactly how they got to the South Pacific other than by boat. Apparently they migrated to the Black Sea, passed through the Bosporus, and eventually sailed from the Mediterranean. I've spent time there too, and in Africa and Asia. Most recently I've been in…"

We both backed temporarily into separate quiet spaces, anticipating her puzzling disclosure.

"…Somalia…Pakistan…Afghanistan"

"Really. What do you do?"

"I'm a free lance journalist."

"Sounds intriguing."

"It's a tenuous existence, at best."

I've insinuated she was a diminutive personality. That rings of condescension; it was more that she was formed up of subtle stuff, of firmly conceived opinions deftly expressed, or haltingly, as circumstances dictated. She possessed a distinctly nuanced personal style: her perfume, her clothing, her delicately exposed feelings about allegiances and what she called honorable responsibility. She was definitively dark, with midnight hair and eyebrows, mahogany skin below ebony eyes, oaken cheeks, lips of deeply burnished golden teak.

"But not boring, surely."

"Sometimes it's…tedious."

Physically, she was unremarkable except that upon closer inspection she was unusually built. No more than five feet four, she was strong rather than large breasted; I mean her breasts were highly positioned and distinctly separated. I mention them solely as a point of departure, since a woman's breasts are so different from a man's chest. Hair may be long or short in either sex, but breasts are distinctly feminine. I don't mention hers to distinguish us politically, but to help define her, like I might describe a dull versus a sharp knife…or mind.

"Tedious? Really?"

"Documenting the follies of humanity is not an inspirational exercise."

Her mind was neither dull nor sharp – rather, it was meticulous, functioning synchronously with her discretion. It picked and chose cautiously from among the various options available to it, expressing them dryly when at all. More often she thought silently and expressed her views only when specifically queried about a particular point. Her responses evaded depth.

"You hold your cards close."

"Cards?"

"You choose your words carefully."

She produced the first of what infrequently passed as a smile. She insinuated it by crinkling her eyes, barely suggesting a turned up corner of her mouth. I would have missed it had I not been studying her face intensely. Her eyes pouted as lips usually do; they were a drowsy presence almost, the harbingers of her sexuality more than any other feature. That and her hands, especially her fingers whose texture was not anything soft as velvet, but rather more like the gentle, assertive touch of wide wale corduroy, insistent and strong, but more restrained than, say, wool.

"It's because I don't know you," she explained.

"Are my questions intrusive?"

"Questions don't intrude. Rather the motives behind them."

"You question my motives?"

"No! Please forgive me. I meant only in general; one needs to be careful in life."

An elusive intelligence flowed from her dark chocolate eyes, a slow, thorough leakage of deeply placed common sense, unencumbered by any outward signs of fanaticism, religious or otherwise. She projected a vaguely remote image of an eternal mother symbol, the very bedrock of humanity, and it was this more than anything that caused me to begin trusting her. Certainly it was this fertility of hers which tempted my confidence, forced my assumption that she might be a womb of ideas constantly in the process of birthing. How else to explain my ability not only to fall under her spell, but to permit her finally to recruit me.

I appraised her appearance. Black boots, black slacks, black blouse, black leather jacket, black scarf, black beret. Everything about her added up to studied city chique rather than the frame of mind that her costume more truly projected. But how was I to know that? How could I possibly have suspected the truth?

"It's still pouring down," I said.

"It's likely an ocean storm blown in. They're commanding and can be lengthy. I love it later on when the refreshing afterglow of muted sunshine and the foreign aroma of damp streets leave only soaked shoes and drying hair."

An absurd phrase came to mind to describe our talk: city earthy. Country talk among the skyscrapers.

"And what do you do?" she asked.

Her caution had made me wary too. I hesitated before answering.

"I fund new businesses."

"A capitalist."

"To me it's more a craft."

"Permitted, however, only by capital."

"Yes, I suppose so."

"Do you like it?"

"It's challenging."

Her gentle interrogations gradually persuaded me to conceive of her as being not unfamiliar with my former occupation. I might evasively hover for you, dropping a hint or so to let you gradually ascertain it, but there's no reason not to say it straight out. As a young man I'd been an undercover Intelligence officer, at a low level, serving the national powers that be. As a mature man now, it was clear to see that the most difficult part of my former job had been the realization that none other than those of us who did such work could ever understand what it is really all about. The simple describing of it renders it either flat or preposterous; there seems to be no middle ground. Putting it into words is like describing a drug related experience: it brands one as somehow no longer a part of the human race, but rather an aberration. It certainly is not at all like being a consumer or a digital code in a data bank, one of the sheep of the flock.

"You have a military air about you," she said when we had gotten to know one another.

"Really?"

"It's your attitude. How you carry yourself internally."

"What a novel perspective."

"Not really. I simply mean you're confidentially poised."

Was she referring to confidence or confidential? Was she guessing or intuitive? Or conveying the double meaning? Was she subtly criticizing me? After all, we professionals are somewhat like elegant prostitutes, reflections of the murkier deeds of mankind, those chosen by either fate or design – who can say which? – to be the tools of others possessing political power and financial lust. This is what paints a black edge on all we do and say. It is this, perhaps, that she perceived.

"I'm demonstrative when required," I said.

"And constrained when not. A strategy?"

"A tactic, perhaps."

Her hands were tiny, the veins rising out of taut skin like worms just below the surface, alive, pulsating, traveling. Her nails were short and buffed, but unpolished. The effect was of nature assisted to achieve an unstudied beauty based on function.

Within a week we had met again; and thereafter twice weekly, bantering endlessly about shallow things until, inevitably, we ended an evening by spending the night together. After making love the first time, we began to talk in earnest, gradually lifting veils from our secret selves.

"What was it like to be in the military?"

"Everything was planned. There was little spontaneity."

"Spontaneity produces ideas; planning defines goals," she said.

Reflection showed me that when revealing herself, she was actually drawing me out. She started dealing ever so minutely with facts. Surreptitiously she side slipped from insinuations to solid details. A bed is an excellent tool of interrogation, cover for deeper intrigues.

"I love to visit new places unknown and view unusual sites undetected," she said. "To learn new things."

A cover story is easy to spot when you've lived such deceptions yourself. I can't begin to describe the thrill I felt recognizing we were kindred souls. Our banal exchanges were necessary, of course, to allow us gradually to disclose our lack of innocence, both of us being too far removed from that state of grace any longer even to pretend we could remember it. If misery loves company, the alienated love to share their disaffection, their loneliness some might say. There is still remaining in the mind of those of us who have been pushed to the extreme bank of existence by our experiences, an elusive harbor where we can tether our moral skiffs and bob a few moments together, regaining a semblance of sanity in a world we perceive to have gone entirely awry.

We grew closer.

"Darling," she said one day, "there's something I want you to do with me, a sort of sport actually."

"A sport?"

"Like hunting is a sport. It is hunting, in a fashion."

She put her arms around my neck and drew me nearer her face. Her breath smelled like warm, sweetened milk. I embraced her, not from need of physical touch but of emotional exoneration.

When engaged in clandestine work, I had never been able to justify it sufficiently to overcome my sense of guilt. When you, however, plumb such depths of combined loneliness with another, there is a leaving of the body which occurs in both, an intertwining of souls on some immeasurable level where the judgmental mind dissolves. You are aware of being in your body, you know that the planet exists, that day-to-day reality is there, the universe even, but you finally understand that they are – for all practical purposes – no longer tangible, that true tangibility resides elsewhere.

By the time she offered me her proposition, we were already of one mind. We needed only articulate it to put our hands on it and gauge its texture.

"What exactly are we hunting?" I asked.

"My present employer wants information about the oil refinery's tanker dock across the Bay. Surely in your work you know something about this, or may find out from others."

My stomach muscles contracted. There it was, out in the open as delicate as a butterfly alighting on a flower. There would be no need from this point on to circumnavigate the subject.

"That will be costly," I said.

"My employers are not miserly."

"You and I will need to collaborate closely."

"I know! Won't it be fun?"

She was like a school girl being invited to her first prom.

"But, I must assure them we can deliver," she added.

So, like most women, she wanted security. As we guided our relationship less ambiguously toward a mutual conclusion, she demanded it. The process was singular for she was conducting the vetting now – rather than I. She had assumed my former role; and I was doing the following. I had led many others down this path, but this was the first time I had ever been guided down it. It was as natural as falling in love, and felt infinitely safer. After all, I too needed security. When I actually realized she was recruiting me into her scheme I embraced it. I understood for the first time the fascination it had held for my agents. It felt like all my life experience had prepared me to play this ultimate role of the actual person who takes the bit in his teeth and runs the race's course, consequences be damned, and wins for the enemy his golden chalice.

My stomach calmed, but my heart fluttered like the wings of a butterfly, launching itself this time from a flower.

"There will be consequences if we fail," she said.

"And if we succeed," I said.

"You demand a quid pro quo from my employers?"

"I also have employers."

"I thought you worked alone."

"No one works alone."

"I wonder what your motive is?"

"Not ideology, I assure you."

"Nothing left to explore now but philosophy," she said, with another of her rare smiles.

If not our personal, at least at this point our professional understanding deepened. It was so welcome to realize we could actually talk together openly, without self conscious embarrassment, about things other than seduction or consuming, or sports, music, nature, of fitting in, being right or wrong; or of god. For the first time in my life I felt good in my own skin. She permitted me to reveal externally what I believed internally, neutralized my hypocrisy. She reciprocated and we discovered such close agreement with one another that the experience reversed the most common and violent physical climax possible: she ejaculated truths she felt, while I crested upon the waves of her mental discharges, riding them like an ocean surfer. Then I felt the swells of her mind lift me, buoying me to contentment. That it remained an anxious peace mattered not at all. Nothing is perfect.

"The crux of the matter is that we will have acted upon the world," she said one day, "not that we will substantially influence it. Or even know for certain that our actions are correct."

I held her close. She smelled of dank musk and pungent cinnamon, subtle nutmeg and fertilized earth, and the faint, salty scent of the sea.

I would have killed for her then, was actually planning to, I see in retrospect. My commitment was already complete, as pure as unfounded faith. She didn't know this, however, and I was obligated to present objections to test her resolve. This was the addictive part of our emerging conspiracy.

"What more can you tell me?" I asked.

"When we supply the dock dimensions precisely, a tanker will enter the bay, tie up there, and proceed to unload its crude oil. A focused blast will obliterate the refinery and the entire community behind it, eliminating symbolically a vital portion of the flotsam and jetsam that the American economic system is incapable of redeeming."

"Does that mean the blast will be atom ...."

"Don't even say the word," she interrupted. "What is the quid pro quo your people demand?"

It was here I recognized how entrapped I had allowed myself to become. If I'd had adequate presence of mind, I'm sure I could have improvised an answer, but something, my basic honesty, perhaps...or was it simple naivete?...compelled me to blurt out the truth.

"I don't have any people. There is no quid pro quo."

"I don't understand."

"I don't have anything...don't have funds...live off a subsistence trust of my family."

"You've been lying to me?"

"Yes."

She inhaled deeply and held her breath a long time, as if meditating.

"It possesses a beautiful symmetry," she said.

"I couldn't tell the truth. I knew I'd lose you."

"It's exquisite."

"Our meeting seemed so charmed."

"Dear, you don't have to explain. It's all right."

She took me in her arms and held me with all the primal force of a mother. All I could do was accept her charity, absorb the depth of her compassion. It was better than before. Being accepted by her when I had nothing exceeded the charade I'd been living under. Beyond any comprehension, I now just let it happen. I was totally under her influence. My trust was complete, and cringing in her arms I reveled in it. It was like being reborn.

"What will you tell your people?" I asked.

"I'll inform them of the truth. They'll understand."

"You're so certain."

"You must understand the breadth of our commitment."

They cared for me. They cared for all of us. That was the point. I did understand. It was easy to believe. It became my reality.

"Do you mean we can continue, despite my admission?"

"Of course, my darling. Nothing has changed.

"Will we be far away when the explosion occurs?" I asked.

"In another hemisphere, below the equator."

"Together."

"What else?"

"Do you have any qualms?" I asked.

"Darling, we really want to help people like you. Nine of ten people on the earth believe that an invisible intelligence existed before even the universe, then created that universe and them, and now watches over and guides each and every one, waiting to receive them in a hidden paradise when they die. We know it's really left up to people like us. People supporting governments and terrorists are obviously unbalanced psychologically. Through organized or guerrilla war they systematically kill one another. Their leaders either become, or cater to, the wealthiest in society, or to the most piously dogmatic charmers claiming personal anointment by their invisible creator. Do you really believe what we are doing is not as commendable as the acts of these pretenders? Should I really have qualms about us compared to them?"

"Do you believe what we are planning makes us any better?"

"Darling, you're missing the point. These people justify their militancy with Gods and Devils. I don't mind them believing in gods and devils. What I mind is their highly profitable addiction to war in the name of God. There are concrete alternatives to war in every instance that every conscientious

elected leader and ethical business professional is obligated
to faithfully attempt before switching off the safety of one's
national defense weapons. They are not making that effort.
They are denying it"

"They'll accuse us of treasonous insanity."

"Insanity? Let me tell you about insanity: The wealthy,
civilized minority are insane on money, on their imagined
future profits; The people are insane on hope and their imagined future release from legally indentured servitude to the
wealthy. Those claiming to be representatives of God are
insane on invoking His name in their successful pursuit of
money and political relevance – far more than their proclaimed
wish to acquire a comfortable home in Paradise."

"But without them, don't you think people might
be worse?"

"Oh, come now; you know what Nietzche's philosophical
soul mate said."

"Who…?

"Joseph Conrad; he said we don't need supernatural
sources to justify our own evil. His exact words were: "Men
alone are quite capable of every wickedness."

"And you suggest also of every goodness?"

"Why not the reciprocal?"

"Even if the means are radical?"

"Dear, so called radicals have forged every great advance
of history. It was mariners willing to sail to the edge of the
ocean, testing the premise the world was flat, who determined
it is really round. Our work will awaken millions from the
myth of their mental prisons. From their depressing sense of
sin. What a diabolical philosophical concept enslaves them.
They're victims of scoundrels. We will free them to think for
themselves. And when enough of them awaken, they will face
their responsibility and change the world."

"The outcome isn't certain."

"Is it presently?"

"No."

"Then how can we possibly be faulted for trying?"

"What of the damage we may do to...thousands."

With the assurance of a poker player, she took measure of my doubts and cast them out with the creativity of her logic.

"Do you remember the story of Prometheus?" she asked.

"Wasn't he the fellow who...? No, I don't recall."

"Prometheus stole the secret of fire from Zeus. We're doing the same thing. We're stealing the secret of ultimate power from those who are using it to manipulate the world. We're turning their own weapon back upon them."

"But we're not sanctioned to do so."

"Aren't we? Darling, five million children under the age of five starve annually; they have for decades. They'll sanction our action for us. Do those now sanctioned to wield force use it to save them? Do they use their profits to save anyone but themselves? Do they deserve our respect? Must we require it from them?"

I had no answer.

"They are immune to the suffering caused by their actions, oblivious to the fact their avarice ejects people from their homes while they sip champagne and spoon caviar over gourmet crackers. While investing their bonuses in defense stock, do they dwell on the thousands of veterans who go jobless and homeless? These are not rational human beings, darling. They are running the world by fear. They are endangering life on the planet with greed. They require an awakening. We must bring it to them...in order to civilize them."

"I..."

She placed her forefinger upon my lips. They trembled. I felt the minute space between the epidermis of her finger and that of my lips; I actually sensed the infinitely small breadth of nothingness as if it were that total lack of anything which existed just before the fulmination of the universe from innate energy. And everything loomed up clearly before me. I understood the energy's source preceding all existence and how it infused humans here now. Transcending that primordial state, I passed through millennia so clearly that I actually grasped the importance to the present of what she was saying.

"We have to do something," she said. "We can no longer allow those in charge to to guide the earth in the direction it is headed. They have no rights above ours. We bear an obligation to intervene. How can we possibly allow them to continue to use us to enrich themselves by endangering all life, including our own?"

"Won't we be stepping outside our place?" I asked.

"Our place? What place? What do you mean?"

"How may we presume to override them? After all, on all sides, they are the acknowledged..."

I groped for accurate words. There were none sufficiently precise or elegant to describe my meaning. I was left with only the most banal clichés imaginable.

'They are the establishment, the legal order, the spiritual leaders."

"They are killing us," she said in the quietest tone possible. "Darling, they place our lives at risk with their decisions. Their power is absolute. At every turn they have either criminalized or excommunicated us. We can't get out of bed without breaking some law or being damned to eternal hell by the latest fanatic. We have earned the right to protest their actions to the ultimate extreme."

"But we are nobody, nothing," I murmured.

"Dear, all existence came out of nothing. We have as much right as they to make ultimate decisions."

"But for us to..."

"Listen, darling: whether they are academics, politicians, financiers, publishers, editors, writers, or sectarian zealots of any persuasion, they are deluded by trivia. They are collectively afraid to be either humane or human. Their very use of language has lost all semblance of meaning. They are too myopically paralyzed by convention to attempt greatness; they are irrevocably immersed in, no – consumed by – mediocrity. Someone must do something to return them to life, for they are dead. They no longer exist; they are not even vegetables. Do you understand, dear? God! Tell me you do. You do understand, don't you?"

Her passion was relentless, unwavering, entirely dedicated. The veracity of her plea touched me to the core of my being. I saw it. Everywhere parasites thoughtlessly enslaving others, either directly or by omission. Her logic was impeccable. She had pierced my heart. Finally, I understood.

"Yes!" I exclaimed.

But this did not yet satisfy her. She needed irrefutable confirmation of the depth of my comprehension. She demanded a final test of my cognitive capacity.

"Every effect has a cause," she explained with utmost patience. "Every action is only a reaction to another's action. Do you doubt that their actions against terrorists are simply reactions to the terrorists' actions?"

"Of course not."

"Then does it not follow reason that, in their minds the actions of the terrorists are just reactions to previous actions of theirs?"

This I felt was beyond my depth. I looked to her for some signal. Not a hair moved on her head. Not an iota of shift occurred in her whole body. She had become nothing but pure mind, and she pushed me beyond my mental limit. I listened to the turmoil of my own mind, feebly scratching like a fingernail on a blackboard, for an answer. Her logic was true. But, it did not deal with the moral issue…she interrupted me before I could raise the question.

"Do you doubt that their strategies against terrorists would alter if they were required by law to conduct them on a purely non-profit basis? Solely for the good of the country, of the world, of humanity?"

This question stunned me to attention. The quantity of dollar profits lost would be staggering. The flash was like when one finally intuits the meaning of a Zen Koan.

"No," I answered.

"You have no doubt?"

"None whatsoever."

She threw her arms around me, literally jerking me to her breast; it was like being guillotined. Together, we wept until our bodies ached with the truth, until our pact was complete. Sanctified. Holy. Nevertheless, I made a final, skeptical attempt to dissuade her.

"Zeus sent an Eagle to pluck out Prometheus's eyes, didn't he?"

"Yes," she said.

"Might they not do that to us?"

"They'll never even know we did it. And the poor, the helpless, when they see what we have done for them, they will protect us because our cause is just. You do believe our cause is just, don't you?"

"Are you still testing me?"

"I'm testing us, my dear."

She had me precisely where she wanted me. She understood that I sought love. No, more than that! She understood that I desperately needed it! That I could not live without it! She embraced my weakness. I could now let go. I had no further need to pretend I was strong. I released my weakness to the world. Now I was free.

Once she comprehended this, she convinced me that everything we did served the ultimate cause. It provided justification for anything, including the violent, random death of anyone, innocents especially. That some of the powerless and the poor had to die to save the others was their salvation. The inevitability of their martyrdom rekindled our sexuality, welding our minds and our bodies into a single, fused, soulless act. Thereafter, we were beyond reproach. Blameless.

I went at the work with the fervor of faith. I reported to her that The Banshaw Lady out of Singapore was due at the docks on the 18th of January at 3:13AM; The Little Kiev from Moravia on the 21st at 4:46PM, The Catalina and The Paragon Cascade, both Panamanian, on the 22nd at 6:17AM and 7:39PM respectively. She rewarded me with passion unadorned by the slightest hint of emotional involvement, but so intense that I was mindlessly swept along.

Finally, she made her move.

"She how they cluster?" she observed. "Every twenty-one days, four tankers at a time arrive simultaneously. Two unload while the two others anchor out nearby. If we guide our single ship among them, its blast will take them with it as it clears the refinery from the map. The next cluster is in a week. We must sail a boat to the dock for our final observations immediately. Let us go tomorrow."

It was this abrupt enthusiasm that piqued my suspicion, raised the question, finally convinced me that something was still wrong. It took deep concentration, but finally I understood she was truly deceptive. She had to be cheating on me with her own handler. Why else would she so precipitously demand we act now if not influenced by his passionate insistence? Hadn't our emotional attachment evolved beyond love? Hadn't it become an altruistic function? After all, humanity was large enough to take care of itself once we had planted the seed, turned the key, provided the design. Having subjugated ourselves to the greater good of all, which had spawned a shared optimism that approached perfection, our duty was clear. But I nonetheless now turned on a dime and felt her betrayal with the certainty of truth. It dug into my bowels.

"Here's a kiss for you," she said next day, pressing her lips to mine as we slipped my boat from its mooring and headed across the bay to the tanker dock. I was no longer under any illusion about her loving me. This became my advantage. My years of professionalism gave me the edge. That is what counted. And I had so effectively drawn my private blanket of suspicion about me and considered what action I should take, that I no longer felt I was the fool. From the vortex of our affair I had found my center. All I needed now do was let things take their course. My passivity would save me.

"Think of the youth we will save from their own immaturity," she reflected.

"Darling, is there anything more," I asked, "that I need to know? Some possibly forgotten detail?"

I'm not positive why I urged her at this specific point. Did I hope she would still express the sincerity of her love? Preserve the sanctity of our sex? Did I want her to disprove my fresh doubt? Was I still hoping against hope that I was wrong? She appeared exhausted that morning. I surely was. I wondered had she ever really known what love is? Were her unspoken demons so deep she was unaware of them?

She answered me by calmly adjusting her head slightly to the side, gazing askance through my eyes into an impermeable space of her own. The fog lightly skimming the water's surface embraced us grayly as the light wind behind nudged us toward the tanker dock. She stood behind me, one hand on the safety rigging as I manned the wheel. The tankers loomed before us. I was certain we were undetected. It was then I turned to her and softly posed the question.

"Darling, have you fallen in love with someone else?"

She was so intent on our task it took her a moment to understand what I was asking. When she grasped my meaning, she just stood there on the aft deck and looked at me as she had that first day outside the restaurant in the rain, with the purest eyes imaginable. Then, without any indication whatsoever of what she was about, she dropped off the deck into the bay and was gone, lost beneath the silent wake. Stunned does not begin to describe what I felt. I brought the boat smartly about and returned to the tiny expanding wavelets which signaled where she had entered the water. She had simply disappeared, without a parting sound. I don't know how I kept myself together. I believe I instantly imagined that she had never existed. That I had conjured it all.

Her body was never found. The tankers, active to this day, remain unscathed by our intrigue, unloading their black liquid gold. I remain a mass of internal confusion. I am at a loss to think or speak. The experience of her was like a comma, it was so ordinary. She appeared, we met, we made love, she discovered my past, invited me to her task, heard my doubt, and vanished. Was I the cause? Had I no valid reason to doubt her? Or had she used me to forward some ambition of her own and I prevented her success? Had there ever even been a potential recipient of our labors? Had her real trade been a deeper personal deception I would never comprehend? Had she been the one who really needed inviolable love? Could she have made up the entire scheme simply to add flavor to the banality of our relationship, to spice our alliance against a cold world, to camouflage her mental fragility? I never knew. Her secrets remained her own to the end.

"Don't ever change," she had whispered to me one midnight.

This was long before I fell to her charms, long before I did change, long before she uncovered my past and infatuated my imagination, long before she ever thought of asking me to spy, long before she invaded my mind, long before we abandoned fantasy for action, long before she added to her argument that the mountains of the Mideast used to be the satrapies of ancient Athens, and still today women must live behind robes and veils from which they must be liberated; long before I posed to her my final question of her love.

Naturally, I reassessed what had happened, what our relationship had been. Had I actually so fallen under her spell that I considered treason to my country? Had my need driven me to such a decision? Can love have been so infectiously contagious? If so, weren't there mitigating circumstances? I had only barely skirted the disaster of my life; what could I have been thinking to have even considered her proposition? And the big question: had her death redeemed me? Was I now innocent? Or, conversely, was my new found guilt the indication I had reached adult maturity? Yes, I believe I was redeemed by the experience. Thinking is not doing. It is only thinking, after all. All I had done was think with her. Surely that was all, and I was left as sound as a two penny nail.

But if it had all been my fault, if I was wrong, if she was the healthy one, and I – the words catch in my throat; I am mute. I don't know what to say. I don't know what to do. I am at my wit's end. I know only our affair should have had a better ending. It deserved a crescendo, at least. Or a coda. Certainly, it deserved more than the first fast sudden raindrops and the final faint expanding circles of the shallow salt laden bay.

Memoir of an Aging Lothario

Truly, it started in all innocence. Studying the photograph of me as young boy, would you ever have suspected that within but a few brief years I would be well on my way to a career of seduction? Never. Mine was the appearance of a young man possessing flawless virtue. And indeed, I ever meant harm to neither young nor old maids. Inflicting pain was antithetical to my entire intent. Pleasure was my only goal: for them and me. Ah, so lightly led astray, so easily tempted by life's hedonistic byways. And the conclusion, the inevitable result, one may see in today's photograph of me as an aged man, my life of dissolution painted on my face as if by a master artist! Oscar Wilde's Portrait of Dorian Gray comes to mind.

One may only imagine the fine career I might have had, the kindly visage you might see today upon my face, had I trod a purer path. But life, oh trust me, is not so forgiving. However, I have learned from it and, with any luck, may pass on to future generations of young men the lessons they need to prevent them from committing the same mistakes I so blithely accumulated in formidable abundance. It is my hope that from my misdeeds I may provide valuable insight to hundreds, nay thousands, of young men, who today view the beginning of their lives with the same beatific expression I once possessed before my fall. If I am able to accomplish this, perhaps I may yet acquire personal redemption.

I wish to make plain that I savored every moment. What, I ask, can be more pleasurable for a man than to spend an evening and night with a beautiful lady? How much I enjoyed the first few moments after meeting a new woman. Playing the perfect gentleman was itself of utmost satisfaction. Remaining slightly aloof, revealing not the least indication of potential carnal interest, making sure I did not allow a single glance of mine to be detectable as I subtly inspected the smooth curve of a woman's breast, noting, if she were astute enough to have worn a moderately delicate blouse, that faint line where the curve intersected the base of her nipple, and determining if the tip prevailed softly or had already tautly risen to an erectness indicating nascent passion. I loved piercing deeply her eyes to see if they turned away or held firmly their gaze, accepting my own, while her mouth spoke of the most inane subjects, as if we were not already communicating our true desires. What a delightful game it is, this mutual enticement between man and woman.

My strategy was to seek leanness, for fat puts me off entirely. Only a taut body, with teeming muscles under soft skin, excites me to action. Never once did I bed a gargantuan lady, one unable to restrain her epicurean appetites, one with flabby rolls of corpulence rolling over upon themselves. No, my ladies were always lean, often actually tiny, and beautifully formed, pliant, resilient, delivering endless love when eventually they let down their guards and allowed themselves. I thrilled at imagining, when one struck a brief pose that allowed me to intuit her body, the look of her twin breasts naked beneath her clothes, and the smooth roundness of her belly flowing to the low meeting of her upper thighs, at which point of triangulation her sweet muff crouched secretly, awaiting eventual pleasure. A perfect body is able to make up for a far less than perfect face. After all, when lights dim, it is the sense of touch that guides us all – that and, with a woman, the scent of her body, of the deep clandestine chemical magnet that is the secret of her allure.

I adored the first close glance of a woman's wrist, the underside where the tiny blue veins glide gently, just barely beneath sheer skin, the warm blood coursing through her body, sharing the hypnotic power it acquires from the nether parts of her anatomy. And the first touch of her wrist with my fingers, my ability to feel the pulsing message of her artery and gauge the courage of her heart. Occasionally, the situation permitting the right atmospheric conditions, I could even at this early stage actually smell the musk of her secret parts. No amount of purchased French perfume, however impressive, could disguise the essential scent of a woman's sex, early aroused.

It would electrify my mind. I was able to conceal my growing ardor only with the most stringent conscious mental effort. This borderline, where of necessity I had to constrain myself, created an underlying tension that began to emerge between us, and that would eventually lead us to the intimacy we both unconsciously sought. I cherished that first signal when the woman turned her head away in a veiled attempt to convey disinterest, but which in fact indicated that she too was becoming aware of the implicit level of communication operating just below the surface of our chaste acquaintanceship. How sweet our first mutual steps of deception as we pretended only to be casually leading to tea and innocent conversation. At times such as this I would initially envision what the ultimate goal of climax might be like: how deep, how abandoned, how exquisitely accomplished for us both, that instant when all pretense completely disappeared and we coalesced the transcendent melding of our physical bodies into a single emotional explosion and release. That twin final fine ripening of desire. The consummation. The little death, as the French so aptly put it.

Before attaining the ultimate crux of the matter, I must perforce deal with the perspective of those men drawn not to women, but preferring their own sex, and also to all dutiful women who may wish to inspect my observations, seeking a device to defend themselves against the unprincipled onslaughts of other male predators. Ladies, I advise, note particularly the inner emotional needs of men that I reveal. It is understanding these that will armor you, for attempting to block their physical demands will ill serve you in your defensive quest. You will hold them off only when you know their minds, for we men know that your physical needs are only mirrors of our own. As for you men of the gentler persuasion, I have no patience with you at all. You have no concept of what you miss as you abandon your masculinity in pursuit of other males. I bear you no ill will but, unless you eventually sense the insecurity of the choice you claim to have made, I have nothing to teach you. My predispositions toward the gay sex revealed, I am now able to revisit her white panties, those of the first woman whose secrecy insinuated itself to me.

I am lying on my back under a table in the kitchen of my mother's home, my home, and I am less than four years old. I know this because for years my parents told me we left this home for another just before I turned five. I am looking up the dress of the new babysitter my mother is interviewing. Her thighs provoke me: the soft skin rising up to the cotton edge of her plain underwear. Elastic slightly pinches her skin at the apex of her legs, causing the mildest indentation of the flesh, and there, there in the triangle, rises the gentle concealed mount of Venus. I am ignorant of its hidden meaning, of course. I am yet innocent of physical desire. But mentally, I am filled with intellectual lust for the masked intent of this mystery. I yearn for the 'X' to complete the rebus of the conjoining of her thighs to the delicate hillock I see. I pine for the touch of its magic. Without knowing why, I crave to rise under the table, hidden from my mother, to glide my lips from her ankle to the shadowy conundrum that has captured my young imagination, to kiss her there upon her tenderness.

"What are you doing!?"

My mother interrupts my reverie with the subtle bluntness of a hammer. This woman has caught me, this woman who never touches or speaks to me, but remains ever aloof and as cold and distant as an eclipse of the moon. I am able to make no connection between her essential non-presence and the ineffable existence of the feminine mystique I have just discovered. Her attack upon my senses is untenable. I am destroyed by the severity of her insensitive assault.

"Nothing, Mama."

I back out from under the table and jump up to meet her passionless gaze. Her frigidity pierces me to the core of my being.

"Go to the back yard and play. Your father will be home soon."

Without answering, I run from the room, bang out the back door, and fall helplessly into the sandbox. The hard, dry grains invade my short pants, itching my waist and sliding down into my own underwear as I stand. They are gritty, irritating, intimidating. The displeasure is palpable.

The preceding memories seem to have become connected in my mind. I believe I have associated the grit of the sand with the beautiful mystery I had perceived. Through the age of eighteen I am next obsessed by their breasts. Seemingly a handsome boy, I date dozens of the local girls, and always I am able to slip my hand beneath their blouses and caress their muted breasts. They are timidly welcoming in their acquiescence of my invasion of their privacy. Although I know still the deeper mystery exists between their thighs, I am reluctant to explore further. Then, as I approach full manhood, my interest reemerges. I wish to know. The opportunity arises with organic simplicity. Having discovered alcohol, and living where it is forbidden by law, it is – of course – readily available from those black marketeers known as bootleggers. The institution is so well organized that illegal nightclubs on the edge of town, hidden in nondescript houses and maintained by ample graft paid to the police, make it available even to teenagers such as myself. A friend introduces me to a young girl bearing maturity beyond her years and, together with him and his lady friend, we go one evening to such a club. Surely we will kiss sometime; likely I shall know her breasts and, while dancing, will press my body to hers, down there – where the mystery remains.

Her precocity rapidly exceeds my expectations. Upon being seated, she asks for a drink. Rather, she places her order with inordinate assurance.

"Please," she requests, "fill my glass with gin almost to the top. And put a splash of lemonade on top."

I comply. When I have received my own bourbon and water, she clinks her glass to mine and drains it in a single draught.

"Again," she sweetly asks.

Within twenty minutes she has placed her hand in my pants pocket and is unabashedly introducing me to the fundamentals of human sex. I must forewarn you not to read on with prurient interest as your motive; I am fully aware that serious matters such as terrorist bombers and manipulative politicians consume public attention. But, I am describing the magnet that has kept the human race evolving for millions of years. Do not misjudge my motives. I only add to the breadth of knowledge we have of our destiny. I fit our carnal nature into the wider perspective of the historical development of humanity.

Within forty minutes the young lady suggests I tell our friends that she has suddenly taken sick and I need to drive her home. I pass this intelligence to my companion, who loans me his car, and she and I depart the club. Soon, at her home, she introduces me to the overt particulars of the mystery of woman's hidden mount of pleasure. I am an instant convert. She convinces me that kisses and breasts are but minor joys, the merest preludes to the ultimate gratification attainable by the human body. I lie in her arms, spent, smothered by the perfume of her body, content as I have never been before. Nothing I have ever experienced is as pleasurable. No religion, no knowledge, no anticipation, has ever so exceeded its promise as this. Henceforth, I am a changed man. I have not been saved, but transformed. It is a profound permutation. Some deep part of me is resolutely altered. She has whetted the most intrinsic edge of my personal psyche. I have become a felicitous inciter of pleasure, a sharpened blade of joyful love, a piercing foil of excitability, an incipient deliverer of ecstasy. Only one experience remained unfulfilled in order to consummate my aptitude for pure seduction, to provide the germinating seed for my unbridled desire to eventually defile the purity of unsuspecting female chastity wherever I might find it. It rapidly arrived.

She begged I help her to the bathroom, pleading real sickness. Filled still with the fullness of our experience, I would have carried her a thousand miles to assist her in her affliction. In the bathroom, she dropped to her knees before the toilet and disgorged herself of the gin. Then she looked up at me, kneeling by her side, my hand upon her shoulder, and with the most vituperative expression I ever in my life encountered, spat at me.

"Get out! I have gotten from you what I want. Go! Leave me! You make me sick! I never want to see you again. Out! Now!"

Her attack upon my senses was demonic. She destroyed me with the severity of her insensitive assault. Perhaps for good. She created in me a cerebral wreckage I was able never in my long life to repair. And it, I fear, unless I can confess my sins to the full, may be the death of me. However, I wanted more of that forbidden pleasure. She had awakened in me a longing I could not suppress. I could not forget the peak of the experience, the deep intimacy that occurred when, after painstakingly driving one another touch by touch to an almost mystic transcendence, we synthesized into an alloyed commingling of being and together imploded into a single temporary culmination of oneness. And it is this singular experience that masked the pain I felt deeply within myself of her rejection; that indeed drove me forth consciously forever in my relentless quest for women. I beg you understand that if the inner pain was the true motivator of my propensity to despoil innocence, it was the desire to bring unbearable gladness to every woman that consciously drove me on, day by day, month by month, year by year, to the present time. For I admit it. The irresistible magnetism of a woman's own carnal hunger remains my finest wish, even as I write, to this moment of this very day.

It would be impossible to describe every encounter. I do not wish to boast, but the numbers are substantial. I started at eighteen, I am today seventy-two. The math is simple. Assume fifty-four years, figuring an average of one new woman every third day, configure the calculations with whatever factor of conservatism you wish, and the sum remains considerable. But it was the variety that counted, not the numbers. Each fetching creature was a delight beyond the last. Every single lady as she became a woman opened up new aspects of me to myself as she revealed herself. I learned so much I can never explain. It is this self-knowledge that is so dangerous, which drugs the young man of virtue deeper into vice. It is not the physical that corrupts, but the self-awareness that is awakened in one that builds the addiction. It is the self-seeking selfishness to know one's own corrupted self better that builds the enslavement to the endless craving.

The ultimate object of my fathomless lust to sexually conquer was a woman of unsurpassable beauty and refinement who lived not in Hollywood, where her body resided, but in my fertile imagination, fueled by her many diverse renderings of feminine roles wherein she epitomized the crown of cosmopolitan chastity. Ohhhhh, just thought of her still takes my breath away! She was the ultimate thoroughbred of her kind, the presumably unattainable intent of my sexual obsession. I had to have her, to violate her well guarded virginity, in order to fully realize my innate potential. Her name was Alienor Liadhan. She was not the vibrant blonde you might envision. Not at all. Her virtue was of profounder mettle, exemplified by the sable nest of hair whose ebony hue concealed the flaxen genesis of her impeccable purity. In appearance on the silver screen, it was her ability to visibly assume the role of the virtuously resistant woman, while secretly harboring the soul of a harlot, that had earned for her inexpressible fame. She among all the countless stars of tinsel town had mastered the ability to mix desirability with inaccessibility. She was the penultimate mystery woman all men seek, and will die for. When eventually raising her downcast eyes to you, with but the merest lift of her lids, her coal black pupils could destroy a man in a single glance. Hollywood's most virulent heroes had one-by-one fallen to her power. Studio moguls trembled in her presence. All men perceived her unfaltering aura of purity as the archetype of the faultless female. She was mother, sister, daughter, cousin, and saint, rolled into one idealized creature of transcendence, that indefinable woman in which all men wish simultaneously to commingle their sense of honor with the uncontrolled release of the passion stored deep within – that which I remind you has kept the human race evolving for ten million years.

At heart, according to jealous underground movie gossipers, she was suspected of being a blowsy, sluttish woman. How else, they opined, could she pull off her charade? No one could be as pure as she seemed. She must be a deeply fallen woman to know how to pretend to such perfection with such sensitive and masterful aplomb. Although her Oscars filled the mantelpiece above the roaring fireplace of her ocean front Malibu estate, attesting to the degree of perfect sublimity she brought to her international image, at bottom, they were certain, she must be as depraved as they knew themselves to be. If not, how could they continue to live? How otherwise could men stand to be near her, inhaling the inflamingly intoxicating scent of her body?

It was simple. I had to have her. How ever could I call myself an accomplished debaucher, if in my lifetime I were unable to infiltrate the clandestine passage to her inner self, to her essential soul? To breach her immaculate defenses and tap her erotic longing? To get to the animal in her? To bed her in the full glory of my dominance, reducing her to shriveling passivity? Ahhhh, I shudder still, recollecting the first moment I envisioned my quest for her.

How was I, a non-member of the film community, to attain her attention in order to ply my charms? That was my premier obstacle. I needed a plan. This required deep consideration. Daily I deliberated on the options available to me. I might write a letter, to be sure. But it would only mingle with the thousands of fan mail she received. Something far cleverer was required. I needed an introduction from a credible source. That was the answer, of course. Whom did I know who could bring me before her scrutiny? For such must be my strategy. Before I could penetrate her moral armor, I must place myself in her presence, so that she might immerse herself in her own amusement, so that she might define the degree of danger I presented to her. She must initially view me as the object of her moral conquest before I could finesse the situation and attack the righteous works of her high minded ethical fortress.

Few men recognize the subtleties one must entertain to accomplish a superlative seduction. This is why so many of them lead paltry lives of pitiful inadequacy, succumbing repeatedly to the beguilement of elegantly conniving women who, deflecting their true natures, make of them but whimpering husbands, slaves to their own emasculated rapture. The secret to my success was always to keep in mind the insidious aggressiveness of women as they feign innocence, intent on parrying each male assault upon their virtue with an effective ploy. How devious females may be, my young apprentices. My long-range design may be to save you the fate that I have come to, but forget not that to avoid it, you must first engage your enemy. You must, as the Buddhists well understand, absorb evil to be able in the end to overcome it. That is what debauchery is really about. By vanquishing the superficial rectitude of the virgin queens, you play a cosmic role: you perpetuate the species. It is only when you overdo it, as I have done, that you fail in your duty and descend to the deeps of degradation. It is a fine balancing act that is called for. So, read on. Your welfare is the root object at this point in my licentiously libertine life. Underlying your welfare, I admit, I do desire my eventual personal redemption; however, I realize it may be too late for me.

Fate, that inevitable intruder into the affairs of life, upstaged the scene at this point. For a change, he did so in an entirely fortuitous fashion in the form of Jay Pennington Prombrake, attorney at law, renowned throughout the Hollywood Hills as legal advisor to the stars. Mr. Prombrake had been researching the facts of a class action suit regarding the public's right to criticize artists in the media. As part of his work, he was conducting a nationwide telephone poll of randomly chosen people, and – wonder of wonders – my name appeared on his list. During his questioning of my movie going habits, he happened to let drop a comment regarding a recent Mullholland Drive tennis party he had attended, where it occurred, via a drawing of tennis balls on which the names of all attendees were neatly etched, that he had shared a brief doubles partnership on the nets with Alienor Liadhan. I immediately recognized my good fortune and cooperated with Mr. Prombrake to the extent that we within a brief span established an unusually intimate first time rapport with one another. It seems that Mr. Prombrake, though obviously still a neophyte in seduction, was himself developing a fair degree of success with aging actresses seeking financial security in their waning years. Of course, our discussions were held on the highest possible plain. No open references made to our mutual avocation or, as he liked to call it, our divertissement. However, on a far more sagacious level, as I obliquely remarked on my admiration for his tennis partner's acting talent, the gentleman picked up on my drift, and at the end of our conversation he suggested a means whereby he might be able to effect an introduction of myself to Ms. Liadhan. I restrained my enthusiasm, of course, and answered, almost reluctantly, that such an event would be quite acceptable so long as it did not intrude on Ms. Liadhan's sense of privacy.

"Oh, no!" he exclaimed, clearly intent on establishing the depth of the social credibility he had already established with the actress.

"She would invite my advice on such a matter," he explained. "She is avidly interested in the heartfelt opinions of her fans, so long as they arrive from, shall I say, tasteful sources?"

"Beyond question," I commented.

"She is cautious of dealing with common rabble, you understand."

"As she must be," I exhorted.

"We understand one another, then?' he concluded.

"Perfectly," I acknowledged.

"Well, then, I shall see what I can do."

With that, our first conversation ended. I was ecstatic. How had such fortune betaken itself to me? I admit that the potential prospect of so easily attaining personal access to Alienor [privately, I had already begun to think of her by her first name] infused me with a new vigor. An overwhelming sense of confidence insinuated itself into my psyche. I felt a virtually uncompromising and ultra modern appreciation, indeed an increased aptitude, rising in my breast regarding what I already considered my relatively advanced capacity to deflower unde-flowerables. Now, I nearly trembled from the newly acquired spunk of my developing métier. I was so sensitized, I had to drink a cup of herb tea to calm my nerves. A week later, Mr. Prombrake called again.

"Sir," he began, "if your proclivity has not altered, I believe I've found the opening for your initial gambit with Ms. Liadhan. Where you may be able privately to express your profound admiration for her talent, shall we say?"

"Indeed?" I gently swallowed, with a touch of humility in my voice.

"Yes. There is another private party being arranged for a large gathering at the estate of one of Ms. Liadhan's leading men. He has suggested that if each guest can bring a suitable public movie fan, one of superlative taste and refinement, that the mix of artist and public will be a uniquely original inno-vation of the Hollywood scene. I have already suggested that I have one candidate in mind – without yet mentioning your name, of course, until you agree."

I held my breath. At this stage, I had to assure the good lawyer that I would not betray his trust in my discretion. Although I was unsure whether he intuited my true motive, I deemed it vital I orally impart to him that my real interest lay purely in increasing Ms. Liadhan's sensibilities for her public. We rambled on about the subject for a half hour until Mr. Prombrake assured me he was content that my intentions bore the proper degree of respect and artistic ardor. I had done it. I had established in him the conviction that I would in no way endanger his social or professional position within the elite Hollywood hierarchy. We were now becoming more than intimates. We had, unspoken but understood, become gentle co-conspirators.

Do not make the mistake that such details of intrigues can be overdone. No. Such intricacies are the necessity in the game in which we deal, particularly in Los Angeles, where the world of illusion attains its peak of perfection. Play-acting on multiple levels is de rigueur, as the French and certain delicate film directors say. Establishing a credible fallback position, a place of plausible deniability as the Intelligence community calls it, where one may disavow with impunity any charges leveled against one if, by chance, his motives are eventually suspected: this is fundamental to the seducer's craft. Being able to walk away clean from a botched job is the key to being able to continue one's life work. Safeguarding one's career is important in any discipline, but nowhere more than in my chosen field.

Let us however not get lost in theory. For now, the solid die was cast. I had to plot my moves carefully. If I were to be placed socially into a party where perhaps dozens of other alleged fans had access to my seducee, I must, when the chance came to speak with her, excel in charm. I must stand out as exceptional. She must find me not only beyond reproach, but irresistibly enticing. I must make of myself, within the limitations of my role, as formidable a star as she was in hers. I must cross over, as the music world puts it, from one genre to another. I must slip from being perceived as her fan to being accepted as her anointed insider of the scene – a task I took to be the most challenging I had ever faced in my long struggle for peer supremacy. I must, as the cognoscenti of the creative music world would say, get down.

Since this seduction preceded the advent of the Internet, its research required that I physically visit my sources of information. To know Alienor, contrasted to knowing Ms. Liadhan, to know the real person behind the public image, I had to uncover sufficient detail of her inner life. A shallow attack would find me wanting. A depth of preparation would gain me the advantage. I proceeded to the Writers' Guild where hundreds of original scripts were kept from famous past films. Selecting each script Alienor had read, in order to delve into her part of it, I began to glean the delicate nuances of, at least, her persona, which I knew would lead to her self. I spent hours reading not only the scripts, but, at the Directors' Guild, found many of their notes, some of which mentioned her personal creative quirks and ticks, with substantive notations on how to finesse her many moods to achieve artistic mastery over her considerable talent.

Scouring the film journals, I catalogued every article ever written about her. I also researched the professional and personal histories, as well as the artistic preferences, of her leading men. This was necessary because it provided the initial clues to her opinions regarding the male of the species and, as I was to discover, to the occasional females in her private life. This latter was most instructive. Who knew that dalliances with women may have formed an essential facet of her character? When finished with my work, I knew the facts, although to reveal my knowledge here would be to violate the trust I sought from her. Even at this late date, I refuse to do that. Her seduction, after all, was not the stuff of superficiality. It was the final step in my discovery of my self.   Understanding her was not to expose her, but to comprehend myself. And, although I was fundamentally selfish in intent, nonetheless an innate spark of disguised goodness in me wanted to safeguard her from the world. You will, if astute, have surmised that I have created Alienor Liadhan as a nom de deception, that it guarded, and guards to this day, the real identity of the woman. It will be, I hope, perceived by you as a saving grace of mine, a token scintilla of human essence that may someday acquire my atonement for the several heinous transgressions I have in my lifetime visited upon unsuspecting female souls.

It was my conclusion that the key to her soul lay in her love of separation from others. When with others, or when acting, she was on stage, pretending to the world to be the vivacious creature all desired. But when alone, she became her true self. At the time I did not understand that this is the secret to every person, that we are really only our selves when alone with our thoughts, our dreams, and our fears. That it is solely when alone we are able, through the power of our own will, to become one with our distinct and unique self. Few during life are able to reach this stage. Clearly, she had. And she utilized it to the fullest extent to nourish her image in order to control as much of her professional life as possible. And to shelter her fragile quintessence.

I had concluded that the pathway to her most treasured secret, the expedient to her carnal downfall, was imbedded within, but rose to the surface of her mind when she stood alone on the shores of the Pacific Ocean. It was when she, for as long as a quarter hour, her feet buried to her ankles in shifting sand, silently viewed the endlessly throbbing mystery of the sea. This enthralled me, for I am a self-taught ocean sailor. I too know the power of the deep green depths covering three quarters of the globe. If I could enter this mental space with her, I would discover, indeed she would reveal to me, precisely what I required in order to overcome her final line of conscious moral defense: to permit me to steal her heart from her mind.

After hours of preparation, I was ready. I awaited only the final message from Prombrake as to date, place, and time of the party. As if decreed by fate, it arrived when I felt I had discerned the trajectory to the nucleus of her being. It were as though some greater power had guided my step. Jay [we had become less formal at this point] called early on a Saturday night, just as I had completed the singularly simple pre-dinner job of misappropriating the virtue of a particularly flavorless but youthful blonde television starlet then on the rise in the New York soap opera trade. I had not really wanted her, but figured I should maintain practice, since my research time had kept me nearly celibate for a week. As she lay insensate, following the consuming zenith of our exertions, drained of any further desire due to the stringently forceful thrust of my loins, I was able to focus totally on his words.

"The party is on," he opened.

He might as well of said, the trap is set, so presumptuous had I become.

"How gratifying," I responded.

"Yes, we'll meet in Malibu for a weekend of sailing, swimming, and sashaying to the tunes of a half dozen currently mainstream local bands. It's at a beachfront villa owned by no less than the top English character film actor of the world. I'd mention his name, but he wishes to remain anonymous. He's got a reputation as a reformed alcoholic and current beach-comber unencumbered by any pretensions to social graces, and doesn't wish to tarnish his rogue image by hosting an entirely pristine affair. At heart, he's an inveterate party maven who thrives in the midst of drinking, dubious dialogue, dramatic doings, and degenerately posh adult tomfoolery. It's the perfect atmosphere for your launch into movie society and a flawless environment for your making the acquaintance of the lady in question."

I spent a week at home in rapt meditation preparing myself for the party. On its arrival, I plumed myself into the finest silk dinner jacket and cummerbund, ensconced inside an Egyptian pima cotton shirt of impeccable stitching. Upon arrival at the Malibu villa, the English host perceived my natural affability and, with a word from Jay, guided me to the room of my inevitable conquest.

She stood by the baby grand piano. I paused and contemplated my approach to her. She was intently listening to a Chopin piece executed by a dull looking homosexual pianist intently butchering Chopin. Hovering over him was a delicate flower of a man, with faded blond locks, tangerine colored eyes, and an ivory cigarette holder in which smoldered an expensive imported Turkish cigarette. Elbowing the male flower in her eagerness to close her eyes in on the player's fingers gliding upon the keys, a fat Russian émigré in a peasant skirt, sniffed asthmatically, and occasionally giggled under her breath. Across the room a high class French prostitute, her profession apparent only to such a practiced eye as mine, smiled at me as I entered the scene. I ignored her. My attention focused pristinely upon my prey. Gradually, I drew near her, my eyes now solely on the pianist in subdued curiosity. I hoped this would divert Alianor's mind from any thought I might be interested in her. Finally beside her, I allowed but a fractions of a second's eye contact with her, an acknowledged courtesy, then brought my gaze back to the Chopin slaughterer. I waited quietly for a few minutes before preparing to speak. Alienor finessed me with the aplomb of a Cobra.

"He's horrid, isn't he?"

I was taken aback by her directness and accuracy, but quickly recovered.

"Quite. Are you fond of Chopin, when properly played?"

"I prefer Grieg."

"I agree; why do you like him?"

"He's more precise."

"Point on."

"Chopin gets carried away with uncontrolled passion. Grieg controls his passion. I prefer controlled passion."

"Why," I asked.

"It creates a loftier passion."

I pondered her comment. She was indeed the penultimate challenge.

"Would you hold me a scotch?" she asked.

"With pleasure. Any special brand?"

"A good single malt would be nice."

"I'll be right back."

I turned away from her and searched out a single malt scotch. True to her word, she was still there when I returned.

The piano player had quit torturing Chopin and had fallen to the charms of the flowery man. Magically, the corpulent Russian émigré had disappeared. By the bookshelves surrounding the fireplace, the French prostitute was infatuating a very rich looking grey haired old man with bamboo thin legs. Seated alone now at the piano, Alienor was gently picking out, one note at a time, Twinkle Twinkle Little Star.

"Do you play?" I asked.

"I only play at playing," she answered.

As I am reporting this to you now long after the event itself, I wish to alleviate myself of any responsibility for the accuracy of the vaguely remembered dialogue that ensued between us. My purpose here is to provide the gist of our first conversation, not pretend to precision. As you will eventually discover, the moment did not proceed as I had intended or expected.

"One cannot expect to excel in all things," I said. "And your proficiency in another area demanding excellence has been unquestionably established."

"I didn't catch your name."

I introduced myself, asking she use my first name, Alexander.

"Do you accept Alex in informal situations like this?"

"Of course."

"You are referring, Alex, to my acting career, I assume?"

"Naturally."

"If we are to attain any depth of communication, I propose we ignore that subject."

"As you wish."

"Do you"…She eyed me speculatively…"know Nietzsche's premise?"

"Only in the most casual way."

"He insists human motivation is solely centered on the will to power. Would you agree?"

"I've not given it any thought."

"Do so."

"Well…the will to power? Did he mean we all want above all things to be personally powerful?"

"He did. That we in all instances are unconsciously obsessed by it."

"Are you?"

"That is not the point. The point is whether it is the most common trait of homo sapiens."

"I see."

"Do you?"

I was taken aback. She seemed to be challenging me.

"Yes…I believe I do. You're not attempting to attribute the trait directly upon us."

"Not consciously, no."

"But unconsciously?"

"According to Nietzsche, yes."

"Even between women and men?"

"Especially."

"Are you referring to…" I hesitated…" the perennial art of "…again I held back.

"Seduction, sir Alex?"

There. It was out in the open. She had invaded Pandora's box. I fear I may have blushed. She smiled, it seemed, at my discomfort. My seductive art seemed to be slipping from my grasp. I'm afraid I overreacted.

"The last thing on my mind!"

"Really? Then why continue the conversation?"

The devilish temptress. She was incorrigibly provocative. Unlike so many women who brazenly wield the rapier of silence in conversation, she employed the bludgeon of artillery. This had been a warning shot over my bow. Either I attempt to seduce her, she had implied, or she would lose interest. The ploy of credible denial was no longer available to me. I had to retract or forfeit this skirmish.

"Last but not least, I assure you. I was seeking subtlety in the...art of pursuit."

"Admirable, but tenuous in this situation."

"This...situation?"

"Sex, sir. Sex."

Never, ever, had I been so competently finessed. I groped for a response. None came forth. Our eyes met and I sensed she was calmly requesting I dare to dominate her. It was impossible. She had disarmed me completely. The neck of her silken blouse parted every so slightly, as if guided by an unseen hand, and revealed the enchantment of her breasts. They were perfect orbs of molten flesh. I melted. If a member could secretly quiver, mine now did, in abject fear. My God, what to do? How to regain the ascendancy? The ascendancy? How to maintain equilibrium was the question.

She saved me with a single word.

"Yes."

"Yes?"

"Yes. I would like to consider making love with you," she murmured, "sir Alex; however, it will depend not upon animal magnetism alone. I demand you overpower me with your mind."

From this point on, words were not the issue. With her breasts and the scent of her secret treasure, with every movement of her body, she sensuously commanded me to subconsciously proceed, while with her questions and her provocations she forced me to consciously plumb the depth of my brain to stay even with her intellectual prowess. In the end, it was useless. She conquered me. I was as hopeless as Napoleon at Waterloo. True, I was able to maintain the mental pace she demanded. Calling on every scrap of knowledge I had ever gleaned from formal education, I parried each and every thrust of her mind to her satisfaction, and finally, true – I thought – to form, I bedded her and we explored the physical depths of our passion to the pinnacle of perfection. But, the denouement was hers alone. She controlled the finale. The conclusion, under her total rule, denied me the victory. I won the battle of seduction but lost the war.

You may have guessed the consequence; however, I must end this. I hear her now. She approaches from her bedroom. I dare not tarry. My every moment in life is now devoted to assuring I do not lose further face. It is an endless struggle. The consummate challenge. An eternal encounter with her interminable will.

"Darling," she calls. "Mother has arrived. I hear her car. Come. We must join her for shopping. She's anxious to see you again. It's been only a week since we dined with her. Grab your coat. We're late."

"Yes, Allie. I hear."

My innocence is lost. My virtue interminably forfeited. My evil vanquished. My craft utterly compromised. But that is not the problem. The puzzle is that I wholeheartedly embrace her victory. I am pleased she has won. Even the embarrassment of her mother's incessant attentions does not reduce my willing acceptance. For, when Allie occasionally comes to me in the dark of the night and gamely invades my body with her ravenous lust, I realize that by acquiescing to her supremacy I have won. And that, future seducers, is most reprehensible of all. She has purloined my male chauvinism. Seduced my machismo. Destroyed my inherent sexual bigotry.

The truth be known, it was that which I so prized, which drove me on. It was from that deeply iniquitous domicile I was motivated throughout my career. There should be an out from this indignity. I cannot find it. It eludes me. Defaulting to her viewpoint wounds me no end. I am crestfallen, humiliated, dishonored.

"Darling!" she calls.

Oh, the shame. I am lost.

"I hear you, Dear. I'm coming."

Formerly a U.S. Army Intelligence Captain, marketing consultant, and video producer, Howell was also for years an addicted sea wanderer who lived and wrote on an ocean cruiser sailboat berthed in San Francisco and La Paz, Baja, Mexico. Recently returned to the United States, he landed on Monterey Peninsula. There he is busy editing and publishing several novels, short stories, plays, and film scripts. He writes and distributes an email and video commentary called, "From My Corner." Reach him from the Contact page of his website: www.howellhurst.com.